J Peruzzini
3571 Pohl Rd
Alden NY 14004

WADE

JENNIFER BLAKE

WADE

MIRA®

MIRA®

ISBN: 0-7394-2828-4

WADE

WADE

1

Chloe Madison first saw the tall American at the Kashi stadium after a public execution. It happened as the throng, most of them Taliban militia officers, was leaving the sports arena.

The program had been a full one—the removal of the right hands of two thieves, the whipping of a woman who had refused the marriage arranged by her father, and finally the hanging from the goalpost of a man who had struck a holy mullah. The few women present were huddled together near the segregated section where they'd been seated while waiting for their men to push their way through the crowd to collect them. Chloe, waiting with her stepsister, heard her stepbrother's harsh call. Sickened by the barbarous spectacle and also by the suspicion that she'd been brought here expressly to see the woman punished, she was off balance as she swung around to locate him.

It was at that moment that the stranger shoved into her. She stumbled, caught her sandal in the hem of the voluminous burqa that covered her from head to foot and fell to one knee.

Immediately the stranger was beside her, grasping her cloth-covered elbow as he spoke in English. "I'm so sorry. Are you hurt? Let me help you up." Then in a lower, almost inaudible rumble, he added, *"Your dad sent me to get you out of this hellhole. Meet me tomorrow in the Ajzukabad bazaar."*

It was a shock to hear her own language spoken after so many years in Hazaristan and amid the babble of Pashtu that was the lingua franca of a country with several different tribes and their dialects. Chloe lifted her eyes and met the man's gaze from behind the small rectangle of crocheted mesh that allowed her to see. It was an act of outright provocation according to all the precepts drummed into her these past few years, but she couldn't help it.

He looked down at her with clear, steady purpose, this American in his jeans, neatly pressed white shirt and engineer's boots. His broad shoulders filled her view. His chiseled, hickory-tan features, clean-shaven so they appeared ridiculously easy to read compared to the bearded males around her, were set in lines of determination. Shadowing the mint-tea-brown of his hooded eyes was an unnerving concern.

Seconds ticked past, stretching endlessly. The last time Chloe had been this close to a male person not of her stepfather's family, the last time she'd known casual male contact of any kind, was as a California teenager almost twelve years ago. His nearness was overwhelming, his grasp searing in its intimacy. She could catch the almost forgotten scents of American deodorant soap, warm denim and clean male. The combination touched some powerful chord of memory, bringing the flashing images of loud music with a hypnotic beat, dune buggies in unlikely colors, hot sand, cold ice-cream cones, coconut-scented suntan oil and clean ocean breezes. It was a vision from a time when she had been young and free. So young, so incredibly free. Before she could stop them or even guess they would come, tears rose into her eyes.

"Chloe! Imbecile, get up at once."

That command in the harsh, unmistakable voice of her stepbrother struck like a lash across Chloe's nerves. She snatched her exposed foot back under the turquoise blue cloth of her burqa and lowered her gaze. Wrenching from the American's loose grip, she struggled to her feet within the hot, cumbersome folds. The American put out a hand again as if to steady her, but she stepped away from him. Moving swiftly, she rejoined Ahmad and her family. Her stepsister Treena reached to draw her nearer to where she stood with her husband, Ismael. A shiver for the close call rippled along Chloe's nerves. She could have been beaten for the exposure of skin above her ankle, might still be for appearing to encourage male attention.

The American took a hasty stride after her, as if he meant to insist on an answer to his suggestion.

"Be gone, infidel," Ahmad said with a growl in his voice, blocking the way with a hand on the knife in his belt and his turbaned head set at an arrogant angle. "You are not wanted here."

"I was just apologizing to the lady," the American said. "Didn't mean to knock her down."

Ahmad's English was rudimentary since he scorned

to learn the language of a people he considered to be demon-ridden aggressors. Without so much as a glance in Chloe's direction, he answered in his own tongue. "She does not require your apology as she received no injury beyond the filth of your touch. You will not know because you are a foreign dog, but it is forbidden to look upon our women, much less lay hands upon them. Do it again, and your ignorance will not save you."

"Even a cat—or a dog—may look at a queen."

Chloe stifled a gasp at both the American's apparent understanding of Pashtu and the challenge in his reply. Ahmad would not recognize the English saying, but would understand the defiance all too well.

"And a dog may be blinded!" Ahmad began.

"Please," Treena said as she leaned toward Ismael, a slight figure with bowed head, drooping under the weight of her burqa. "The heat, the dust, the...the terrible things seen have been too much... I am unwell. Take me home, I beg you."

Ahmad's sister, pregnant for the fourth time in six years, should not have been present at this ugly spectacle at all. The Taliban government required every able-bodied citizen of Kashi to attend, however, and encouraged those from outlying areas to view the proceedings. It had been Ahmad's pleasure that his family make the drive from Ajzukabad for it today. Since he had become the nominal patriarch after his father, Chloe's stepfather, had been conscripted into the Taliban militia and sent to guard the northern frontier, his wishes must be obeyed in all things.

Ismael nodded at his wife's request, then squared

his shoulders and looked toward his brother-in-law. "Ahmad, brother of my wife's heart..."

"I heard," Ahmad said shortly. "Very well. Chloe must do the chores of my sister for the next week as punishment for her clumsiness. Come." Shouldering his way past the American as if he didn't exist, he led them all toward the exit.

Chloe did not dare look back at her countryman as she followed with Treena behind Ahmad and Ismael. It was Treena who turned her head. Her eyes mirrored both apprehension and satisfaction as she glanced toward Chloe once more. In a voice that was little more than a breath of sound, she said, "He watches."

"I care not," Chloe answered in the same whispery mouthing of air that women had perfected out of necessity in male-dominated Hazaristan. "Though I am grateful for your intervention just now."

"So was my brother, I think. These are troubled times. To take revenge against an American in some dark alley is one thing, but to do so in a public brawl would have been foolish."

Chloe, discovering that her hands were still shaking, closed them on the inside folds of her burqa as she walked. "Just so," she agreed. "But still."

"Yes, my brother has more pride than wisdom, more thought of his rank and consequence than of diplomacy."

"I would not say such a thing," Chloe murmured.

"Which is why I speak this truth in your stead. Ahmad hides behind his importance like a small boy using the shield of his father's legs to make himself brave." Her stepsister's voice held tired resignation.

Then her eyes flashed behind the mesh of her burqa. "Was your American not handsome?"

"I failed to notice."

"Of course you did. He was like the movie stars I saw as a child, I thought. Before the Taliban, before the theaters were closed, before... Well, before."

"It is a matter of indifference to me."

"You lie before Allah, and for what? Your dreams cannot be controlled, and the only time you will ever see this man again is when you sleep."

Was it possible that Treena had overheard and understood? It seemed unlikely. She'd had no formal education, had never studied English. Yet she had lived for years with Chloe and her mother, the woman Treena's father had married after going off to the States following the death of his child bride with Treena's birth. Chloe had even tried to teach her a few words and phrases until the lessons were forbidden.

"If I never see him again, it will be too soon," Chloe said with hard emphasis. "He could have gotten me whipped or even killed."

"True." Treena looked away and was silent.

The cleansing, strengthening anger came then, banishing Chloe's shakes and the chill of horror from around her heart. It felt good, familiar, like the return of an old friend. She had been consumed with rage for so long that she thought she might be lost without that lodestar to point her way.

It had begun when her mother, a professor at UCLA, had told her she was marrying the Hazari lecturer she'd recently met, a man in the States as part

of a special foreign exchange program during the Soviet infiltration of his homeland that coincided with
their occupation of nearby Afghanistan. Chloe had
liked Imam well enough but never expected her
mother to become serious about the quiet, scholarly
Hazari with the gentle smile. The divorce of her parents three years earlier had been a tragedy to her.
She'd never quite given up hope of her mother going
back to her engineer father.

Nothing she said changed her mother's mind. Then,
less than a year after the wedding, the Soviets had
pulled out of Afghanistan and conditions in Hazaristan stabilized. Imam began to talk of going home.
Chloe, barely fourteen at the time, had been appalled
at the idea of leaving the States, couldn't believe that
she was expected to say goodbye to all her friends
and familiar surroundings in California. She'd hated
the idea of living in a country so backward that elec-
tricity and running water were luxuries, New Year's
was celebrated on the first day of spring according to
a weird lunar calendar, and nomads traveled the
mountains and deserts riding horses and living in
tents. That was before she'd even set foot on Hazara
soil or met her new stepsister and stepbrother.

Treena had been nice enough. Ahmad was a different story. He'd met them at the airport, but it was
plain he'd expected to greet his father only. His face
went slack with shock and his eyes filmed with tears
as Chloe and her mother were introduced. Then an
expression that might have been revulsion or even
hatred invaded his face, turning it to stone. Without
a word of greeting, he'd turned and walked away.

Imam called after his son in angry reprimand for the discourtesy. When there was no reply, he started after him, but Chloe's mother put a hand on his arm.

"You didn't tell him?" she asked with a frown of concern.

"I thought it best done face-to-face. Apparently I was wrong."

"Apparently."

Ahmad's father shook his head. "My fault. I've made so many mistakes with him."

"You couldn't have known," Chloe's mother said with quiet sympathy.

"No, but he blames me anyway. I'm sorry if some of that has now been transferred to you."

She pulled his arm against her and put her head on his shoulder. "It doesn't matter. I'll live."

But of course it did matter. And she didn't live.

Ahmad, some seven or eight years older than Chloe and a recent graduate from the university, considered himself a grown man. He made it plain that he had no respect for his father's new wife or her daughter and though he was polite enough in his father's presence, treated them like unwelcome guests in his absence. He seemed to despise women as inferior beings little better than animals. Chloe, in particular, he regarded as spoiled, headstrong and in need of instructions in the proper behavior of a woman. That meant, of course, that she held her head too high, stared men in the eyes too boldly, spoke without proper humility and respect and had an annoying habit of attempting always to walk ahead of men instead of behind them. Correcting her faults and lapses in Hazari manners and customs was a game he enjoyed, as was sneering at her every mistake in learning their language. Knowing that her mother would serve him in order to keep the peace if Chloe refused, he took pleasure in giving orders that effectively turned them both into servants. The few times that Chloe defied him, accidents happened that left her bruised or else destroyed valued possessions, such as a favorite book or cherished ring or pendant given to her by her father.

Her stepfather was not blind to his son's behavior, but seemed powerless to stop it. Guilt restrained him, as if he felt he'd failed his children by remaining so long in the States, allowing them to be brought up by his wife's parents. The only suggestion Imam had to make for Chloe's relief was an arranged marriage that would allow her to exchange the domination of her stepbrother for that of a husband. Only fifteen by that time, she had recoiled in disbelief. The idea of a loveless marriage to a stranger was horrifying, though she could see no possible way that she'd ever meet anyone with whom to build a loving relationship. Her stepfather sighed and shrugged, but did not press her. It was Treena, instead, who married the man that Imam had in mind. This was Ismael, a cousin she'd seen only from a distance at family gatherings before their wedding day.

In desperation, Chloe wrote to her father, begging him to come and get her or send her the money that would allow her to come to him. She sent letter after letter, waiting each time for an answer that never came. All the while, Ahmad did exactly as he pleased, as if exercising some odd moral authority over the

whole family. Life might have been completely unbearable if he had not been away much of the time,
busy on mysterious errands that took him out of the
country.

In the meantime, the country that was supposed to
be so peaceful and progressive after the end of the
Soviet disturbance continued to be plagued by guerrilla warfare. Across the border in Afghanistan, the
Taliban, a name taken from the word Talib, or stu-
dent, agitated for power, forming a militant organization led by orthodox religious teachers, or mullahs.
Youth and dedication to their fundamentalist cause
gave them rabid strength compared to the war-weary
veterans who had fought the Russians to a standstill.
Following their takeover of the government, they began to export their brand of religion-based reform as
the previous invaders had exported communism.

In Hazaristan, the more orthodox Sunni Muslims
adopted the Taliban cause. They created their own
Taliban militia patterned after the Afghan model and
made guerrilla sorties against government forces and
installations. Ahmad was in the thick of it Chloe was
almost certain, though no one ever came right out and
said so. With time, the inconclusive fighting grew
commonplace, so she paid no more attention to it than
to the rumbling of distant thunder.

Then one day she returned home from the bazaar
with her mother to find a bonfire in front of the low
stone house that was their home. On the pyre was
every pair of jeans that she owned, every pair of
shorts, every shirt that revealed her arms. Her rock
posters had been used to start the blaze, and her boom

box, tapes and CDs lay melting in the flames. Her books, her makeup, every single thing she owned that identified her as different in any way from the women around her was destroyed. She'd turned on Ahmad, screaming. He'd knocked her to the ground, then stood over her as he told her exactly what had taken place and how things would be from that day forward.

The Taliban militia, in which he was now a senior officer, had captured Kashi and ousted President Zagros. They'd established strict adherence to ancient Islamic law as put forth in the Qur'an, or "El Noor," the light, along with all the inflexible cultural edits of their Afghan brethren. Men were required to grow beards. The windows of houses must be painted black to prevent women from being glimpsed in passing. Females caught on the street without the covering of a burqa and a male relative to guard and monitor their conduct could be beaten by the police or any male citizen who took exception to their indecent exposure. Women could be punished for talking too loudly, laughing in public, showing the skin of wrist or ankle, wearing cosmetics—the list went on and on. Male heads of household were permitted, even encouraged, to use corporal punishment to keep the females in their charge in order. Conviction for premarital sex or adultery was now punishable by public execution of one or both parties. All schools for girls were ordered closed. Thousands of women had been sent home from their jobs as teachers, lawyers, doctors, nurses and every other occupation, with males appointed in their places.

Chloe had thought nothing could be worse, but

she'd been wrong. Her stepfather had been conscripted into the Taliban army and marched away to guard the northern border. Ahmad had taken over as head of the household, the man solely responsible for guiding and correcting the conduct of Chloe and her mother.

Conditions in the country deteriorated. Food became scarce, imported goods almost nonexistent. Women without male relatives to support them or a way to earn a living began to appear in the streets as beggars. Prostitution was forbidden, but became rampant nonetheless. The government infrastructure began to break down. Crime increased. Rabid dogs roamed the streets. As electric lines were cut and generating facilities damaged, power became available only for government buildings and a few hotels. Traffic lights and street lamps ceased to operate. Life returned to something like the Dark Ages.

And then, less than a year later, her mother had caught sight from her kitchen window of wild dogs attacking a toddler. She'd run screaming from the house to beat off the starving pack with a broom. The policeman who appeared on the scene cared nothing for the injured child, a small girl. Instead he attacked Chloe's mother for leaving her burqa in the house. As he began to beat her with his stick, one or two men of the Taliban appeared, shouting about the foreign witch with her sky-colored eyes who dared defy their laws. Chloe snatched up her own burqa and ran out to help her mother but was caught and held back. A stone was thrown, and then another and another. When it was over, the frenzied group faded away, leaving Chloe alone with her mother's body where it lay crumpled against the house wall.

Chloe felt as if the jaws of a great bear trap had closed upon her. She developed migraine headaches so sickeningly painful that it seemed only cutting off her head could relieve their agony. She spent hours lying in her dim room. Sometimes she slept or gazed dully at the ceiling, but mostly she stared out a small hole scratched in the painted window at the barren landscape of ochre buildings, sun-scorched brown earth, vegetation gray-green with dryness and the encircling mountains blue-hazed with distance and dust. She didn't go out because there was no place to go, seldom joined the others in the common room of the sprawling stone house because she had nothing to say to them. She lost weight, allowed her long hair that could not be cut for fear of reprisal to grow lank and tangled. Sometimes, while she lay awake listening to barking dogs and crowing roosters in the night, she thought of suicide since it seemed the only way out.

It was Treena who saved her, meek Treena with her huge eyes, fade-away voice and constant attention to babies that were nursing, teething, walking or sickening with some childhood complaint. Treena, who concealed the courage of a lioness behind her submissive attitude. She had whispered to Chloe about the Revolutionary Association of the Women of Afghanistan, a group that had banded together originally to help oust the Soviets but were now circumventing the edicts of the Taliban. The RAWA had spread into Hazaristan along with the Taliban incursion. They were in desperate need of teachers to instruct the young girls who were being denied an education. Without knowledge these children would be forever consigned to the role of servants to men. Chloe's mother had been a teacher. Why should she not follow in her footsteps?

How long ago had it been, Chloe wondered, since she'd first heard of these brave women? Five years? Six or more? She couldn't remember. Time had scant meaning when there was little to distinguish one day from another, or one year from the next. It seemed that she'd been teaching her secret classes of girls forever, that her dangerous forays into other women's homes to present an hour or two of classes had been going on since she was a child. The lessons, the smiles of the girls, their hunger for knowledge, the intense friendships with the women who defied the Taliban—these things were what kept her sane. She sometimes thought it was what she was meant to do with her life, that fate had placed her in this place, at this time, where the knowledge she had gained in American schools and then from her mother would be most helpful. She was needed here, had found her true purpose and meaning. What could going away with a stranger offer her that might compare?

The American's presence, his daring in contacting her, had jeopardized her safety. To see him again could put at risk all she had achieved, might even create suspicion that could lead to discovery of her RAWA connection. Her friends, the women who had become like the most loving of sisters, would be in peril since their activity was considered a heinous crime. They could be sentenced to public torture followed by burning at the stake. Punishments had grown steadily more barbaric since the influx of Taliban from defeated Afghanistan.

She could not meet the man. It would be madness to try. The bazaar was a public place where she was never permitted to go alone. Even if Ismael could be persuaded to escort her, it would be foolhardy. No chance of a private conversation with the American existed since he would be as conspicuous in the public market as a black cat on a white doorstep. He could know little of the conditions she faced, much less understand their implications, so his discretion was in doubt.

No, she would not keep this appointment. Absolutely, she would not.

It was later that evening, after they had returned to Ajzukabad and Chloe and Treena were putting the children to bed, that Treena spoke again of the stadium meeting. As she bathed her middle daughter, less than three years old, from a basin of water, she said, "I know the handsome foreign devil had something to say to you earlier. Are you going to tell me what it was or must I guess?"

"Really, Treena, he only apologized."

"And for this you became as still as a statue? Come, now. Such men were most forward in the films I used to see. Was it something improper?"

"Not at all."

"A compliment perhaps? They could be tender as well, these men." Her stepsister's eyes danced with laughter.

"Of course not!" To hide the flush that rose unaccountably to her face at the idea, Chloe picked up Uma, the five-year-old who was the eldest of the three girls, and began to brush her long, soft brown curls.

"He wanted you to meet him?"

Chloe gave her a straight glance. "You did understand him then."

"A little," Treena agreed. "You may as well tell me the rest, yes?"

"It was stupid."

"But interesting enough to keep you silent all the way home. Please, Chloe. It's so exciting that he actually spoke to you."

Treena would not stop until she had every detail, Chloe knew. And what reason was there to keep it from her when nothing would come of it? Paying careful attention to the braid she was making in Uma's hair, she said, "He only told me that he'd been sent by my father."

"For what reason?"

"To...to take me back to the States."

"Oh, Chloe." Distress and sympathy were plain in Treena's face.

"I don't believe it," Chloe answered, her voice grim. "Why would my father send someone now when he never answered my letters?"

"There are many reasons for things."

It was one of the obscure answers so common in this part of the world. They had once driven Chloe crazy, but that was before she'd come to see that they could be an invitation to explore a topic as well as an evasion. "Such as?"

"Perhaps your letters have taken this long to reach your father?"

"My country may be far away, but it's hardly on another planet."

Treena gave her a wan smile over her shoulder as she kissed her daughter, then slipped a clean night-gown over her head. "You thought differently at one time."

"Experience is a useful thing," she replied, since Hazaris weren't the only ones who could be obscure. "I wish I knew if this American really has news of my father. To hear of him, where he is, what he does, would be wonderful."

"But I thought you had hardly seen him since you were a child, even before you left your country. You never speak of him. It has been as if you'd put him from your mind."

"No."

Chloe let that simple denial stand. She'd been her father's tomboy princess. They had built birdhouses and tree houses together, ridden bikes together, gone fishing together and even spent the summer together when she was ten, at a fishing camp beside some lake in Louisiana. Sometimes, when the icy wind blew from the mountains, or when the sky was silver-white with heat and the rain would not fall, she dreamed of those endless summer days beside sparkling water. She longed in her dreams for the Louisiana air that was as warm and soft as silk, for the near-jungle of trees so green that they tinted the world with emerald light, for the lazy amble of passing days that were each a haven of peace and safety. Waking, she felt disoriented, as if she were in the wrong place. And she ached with memories of her dad, and how he had told her she was pretty, repeating it so often that she'd decided to believe it whether it was true or not. How could she ever forget him?

"I'm sorry," Treena said quietly.

Chloe looked away to hide the sheen of moisture in her eyes. "I've wondered if my letters ever reached my father at all. If that was why I never heard from him, because he did not know where to write to me."

Her stepsister made no answer as she knelt, wiping dust from her young daughter's legs and feet, murmuring soft nonsense to keep her still and entertained through the ritual. Something in the stiffness of her back caught at Chloe's attention.

"Treena?"

"All things are possible."

Chloe frowned as she watched Ahmad's sister gently press the child down on a pallet in a corner of the bedroom she shared with Ismael. "Are you saying," she asked with slow control, "that they might have been intercepted?"

Treena glanced at her from the corners of her eyes. "Oh, Chloe, must you always be so exact?"

"Not always." If she wanted answers she would have to play the Eastern game of allusions and suggestions that permitted the speaker to make things known without leaving room for an outright accusation of betrayal. "Might there be a reason why someone would want to prevent this contact?"

"I can think of none."

Nor could Chloe, other than sheer malice. And the

only person she knew who seemed capable of that lived in the same house. "It could have been easy if one had the task of mailing these letters."

"True."

The head of the household naturally handled correspondence, since it was assumed to be a male function. It was infuriating as well as painful to think that Ahmad had taken advantage of that to interfere so drastically. "I could kill him," she whispered.

Treena shook her head. "It may be that he thought it was for the best."

"You must be joking."

"So much anger. You must not let it eat at you like Ahmad, Chloe. To have one in our family so consumed is enough."

She gave a short laugh. "What reason has he to be angry? He always wins."

"Our father left us with our grandparents after our mother died. He abandoned us while he flew away to that far-off magic land called America. Our mother's parents did their best, but they were not young and had stern views on many things. Our grandfather, in particular, had strong dependence on the old ways and ancient laws. He despised modern machines and ideas, and particularly American machines and ideas because they were most modern of all. It was he who sent my brother across the border to be educated by the mullahs in Kabul. When Ahmad returned from Afghanistan, he was changed. All the tenderness was gone from him. He had been forged into a sword of Islam."

"And you?"

"I was younger and a mere girl, so my grand-mother's responsibility. In any case, I was unworthy of schooling. Sometimes, when I look at my brother, I think it was just as well."

The soft voice stopped abruptly, as if Treena could not go on. "Forgive me, sister of the heart," Chloe said quickly. "I didn't mean to speak of things that cause you pain."

"No. Still, I want you to understand. If our father had come home sooner, if he had not replaced our mother with a proud American woman who was more beautiful, more educated, stronger in every way than our dead mother, it might have been all right. If he had not brought home a new daughter in the same image that he obviously loved more than his own children..."

"That isn't true."

"Isn't it? Ahmad saw it as the truth, and that was enough. It became the polish for the sharp blade of his wrath. That and many other things."

"What things?"

"Oh, the intervention of foreigners, foreign government agents in our country and our politics."

"The CIA, you mean." The stories were whispered everywhere of money sent to back one faction or another in the endless war that had decimated the region, but it was almost impossible to separate truth from fiction.

"And the Soviets, the Chinese, the Pakistani, though these hardly matter. It's the Americans that he has turned into demons who seek to control our country or to bomb it into ruins. I only speak in hope you will understand my brother's actions, both past and future.''

"Future?'' Some shade of meaning in the other woman's voice sent a shiver over Chloe in spite of the close room that still held the leftover heat of the day.

"A friend spoke with Ahmad in the *hajra* two evenings ago, the young one known as Zahir.''

"I heard him arrive.'' She had not seen the man, of course. Women were not permitted in this special room while male guests were being entertained.

"Just so. As I passed by the grill, they were talking in low voices. It caught my attention. As I listened, they spoke of money, of a dowry.''

Chloe stared at her. "What are you saying?''

"It cannot have been for Ahmad's sake as he has sworn never to marry, and my Uma is too young yet to be a bride.'' She reached out and touched her daughter's cheek where she sat on Chloe's lap.

"But...you can't mean me. I'm so old!'' Shock left Chloe numb, unable to think clearly. She'd feared this for years, since her stepfather had first broached the subject, but when nothing came of it she had allowed herself to believe it would never happen.

"This is true. But though a younger bride is preferred since she may be more easily trained, you are unusual with your fair skin and coloring. This is an attraction to many men.''

"Ahmad wants to be rid of me.''

"There is the bride-price.''

"Yes. Of course.''

"Do not distress yourself, my dearest Chloe. Any

husband chosen will come to love you, for how could it be otherwise? You are kind and good and will give him intelligent children. They will be fair to look upon as well, for you are beautiful with your eyes as blue as the mountains and yards of hair like shining brown silk.'' She touched her abdomen, barely rounded since she was only four months or so into her pregnancy. ''Your children shall be your consolation.''

Children. Chloe tightened her arms around Uma and brushed her lips across the top of the small head as a slow surge of love moved through her for this child that she'd helped to bring into the world, tended daily and taught so many things already. She hadn't let herself think of children of her own, didn't dare even now. ''I can't,'' she said, her voice aching in her throat. ''I can't do it.''

Treena gazed at her in alarm for a second, then turned to take Uma from her and put her to bed, drawing up the sheet to cover her small legs. ''You cannot refuse. You saw the consequences today.''

''Ahmad made sure of that, didn't he.''

''Just so.''

Treena leaned over the pallet to remove a cloth doll from too near the face of the nine-month-old baby girl who lay sprawled with a thumb in her mouth. Then she put a hand across the small forehead. A gray cast appeared under the darkness of her skin.

''What is it?'' Chloe asked sharply.

''She's hot, so very hot. Oh, I knew she should not be left with the poor, stupid housemaid while we were in Kashi. She only sits with her hands between her knees while my little Anashita crawls everywhere and puts filth in her mouth.''

Chloe breathed a soft imprecation as she knelt beside her stepsister. The servant she spoke of was a widow who had come begging at the back door, offering herself as a servant in return for food and a pallet in a corner of a back room. Ahmad had agreed for the sake of the cheap labor and Treena out of pity, but the widow was barely able to function in her abject misery. Now it had come to this.

In Chloe's mind was the same terror that she'd heard in Treena's voice. She could not stand the thought of losing any one of the little girls. Yet children died so easily here where there were no vaccinations against childhood diseases, few antibiotics to be had at any price, and almost no means available to fight the stomach viruses and infections that were an inevitable part of growing up. Women like her stepsister bore many children because birth control was prohibited, but also in hope that a few would live to adulthood. They bore them in spite of the pain and danger of primitive methods of childbirth or dismal infant mortality rates. Chloe sometimes thought their courage put that of men to shame.

"A doctor," she said. "Ismael must go."

Treena shook her head. "Ahmad will not permit it."

She should have known, would have if she'd stopped to think. With the corrosion of bitterness in her voice, she said, "Pray God the child you carry is a boy. Then he may think it worth a doctor's fee."

"The old women have said it's so." A dismal attempt at a smile quivered the corners of Treena's mouth as she touched her abdomen again.

"We can always say he's the sick one, then, so the girls can have medicine. For now, we must bring down the fever."

They roused the nursemaid and set her to boiling water. In the meantime, they put the child in a cool bath, splashing her again and again. When the water on the stove was sterile, they added salt, sugar and lemon juice and stirred it until it cooled. Then they took turns spooning minute amounts of the liquid between the baby's pink lips. And all the time they worked, they prayed.

In the emergency, the subject of marriage was pushed aside. Treena might have been wrong about what she'd overheard in any case, Chloe thought. Or failing that, the prospective groom might prove uninterested, negotiation of the bride-price could break down or Ahmad might change his mind in disgust. Nothing was really official until she was told it was to happen. She would wait until then to moan about her fate.

2

She couldn't get the man who waited for her at the bazaar out of her mind on the following morning. She pictured him wandering through the stalls with their piles of multicolored spices, wilted vegetables, rugs, silver and hammered brass plates sheltered by wind-blown lengths of embroidered or handwoven cloth. He would stand head and shoulders above most men, so would be conspicuous even without his Western clothes, bare head and beardless face. If he ceased moving and stood back, leaning on some wall as he scanned the women in their burqas for her arrival, he still could not avoid notice. He would be stared at, whispered about, perhaps even harassed by the police.

It was unlikely that he would linger. He would tire before long and stride away, back to his hotel and his life in the States. She gave him an hour at most. In her experience, men had no patience with waiting on women.

She had been right in her decision not to meet him. It was foolish to think of it at all. Yet the regret that weighted her chest seemed to grow heavier with every passing minute.

The early morning was spent with cleaning chores and entertaining little Anashita who was querulous but recovering from her bout of stomach illness. As the sun climbed higher, Chloe gathered her books, lesson plan and carefully hoarded pencil stubs and sheets of scrap paper. Putting them in a cloth sack, she looped this around her neck, then donned her blue burqa. Ahmad had left at daybreak, as he often did, going to Kashi on the business of the Taliban. Treena's husband, Ismael, a quiet young man with the eyes of a poet, a pronounced limp and the slender, perpetually tarnish-grimed hands of a silversmith, would leave soon for the shop where he worked with his brother making jewelry and other items in a trade passed down for generations. First, however, he must do the family marketing. Treena and Chloe would go with him, Treena to advise on the food for a special evening meal ordered by Ahmad who was expecting visitors, Chloe to be dropped off at the home where the secret classes for girls were being conducted at present.

Ismael knew what she did there, of course. He was a special man, a gentle soul who had lost half a foot to infection after a childhood bicycle injury. Sometimes he praised his limp because it meant he was exempt from service with the Taliban militia, and Chloe thought he was only half joking. He did not subscribe to the stringent Islamic views that gave Ahmad such pleasure, and was deeply disturbed over the neglect and destruction of his country's few civilized amenities. The policies of the current government that had brought on trade embargoes in the wake of the Afghan situation were abhorrent to him, but he despised the United States for its sanctions, which deprived the civilian population of food and medicine.

Ismael's disapproval of the restrictions imposed on women came in large part from his mother's experience. A woman barely fifty years of age, she had owned an export business during the previous regime, one inherited from her father. Chic, cosmopolitan and highly organized, she'd made frequent business trips to Europe and the States. Then the Taliban had taken away her business and given it to her father's younger brother. She had fallen into severe depression followed by dependency on the drugs used to alleviate it. Involvement in the RAWA had saved her sanity, as she put it, and it was she who had recruited Treena. Ismael never came right out and approved the RAWA affiliation, but he did not question Chloe's morning visits, ignored her hours spent over schoolbooks while Ahmad was away, and was incurious about the females who came and went, whispering over tea and walnut cakes in the women's quarters. If he knew no details of the activities of his mother, wife and step-sister-in-law, then he could always claim he had thought them busy with nothing more than gossip and female matters.

The class went much as usual. Young girls drifted in one or two at a time, some arriving with their brothers or younger male cousins, one or two escorted by their fathers and accompanied by mothers who drank tea with their hostess while Chloe presided over the classroom. The methods she used depended, in the main, on rote learning since the oral tradition was strong among Hazaris and books and supplies were scarce. While she taught, she kept a copy of the Qur'an at her side. If any person outside the circle of RAWA sympathizers appeared, she could instantly switch to the recitation of holy writ.

Time melted away. It seemed there were never enough hours to teach everything she wanted the girls to know. All too soon, she had to close her book, make her polite and effusive farewells to the woman of the house who was risking so much by permitting the use of her back room, and be ready to meet Ismael and Treena when they came for her once more.

As she joined them in the entrance, her sister-in-law greeted her with eyes that shone behind their mesh covering. ''We saw him, your American from the stadium,'' she said as soon as they had left the house. ''He was there in the bazaar.''

''Not mine,'' Chloe said in instant denial as she reached to help with the string bags filled with grains and melons that her stepsister carried. ''Do you think he saw you?''

''He stared at Ismael for an instant, but gave no sign of recognition. My presence he failed to acknowledge at all.''

Chloe frowned a little as she heard the trace of injury in her stepsister's voice. The feeling of being beneath notice while wearing the burqa could be difficult to endure. She was oddly reluctant to have Treena think that her countryman had intended to compound the effect. "It's considered impolite to stare in my country," she said. "Besides, the man might not wish to risk angering your escort."

"You think he may have recognized us after all?"

"He managed somehow to pick me out of the crowd in Kashi yesterday. Since he could see nothing to go by, he must have zeroed in on Ahmad and Ismael."

"But how would he know them?"

"I've no idea," she answered. It wasn't something she wanted to think about, either, for fear she wouldn't like the answer. "Was he still at the bazaar when you left?"

"Indeed, and looked as if an explosion could not move him."

"He'll go soon, when he is bored with the game."

Treena glanced at her, turning her whole body to see through the burqa opening. "He didn't appear bored. Annoyed, perhaps, but not bored."

"Too bad," Chloe muttered, not entirely for Treena's benefit.

"Are you sure you don't want to discover what he has to say to you?"

"Quite sure." As long as she didn't know, then perhaps she could remain fairly content.

Ismael had been listening as he limped ahead of them. Speaking over his shoulder, he said, "Let us hope he gives up this attempt to speak to you soon, before Ahmad loses patience.''

''You think someone will tell my brother that the American has followed Chloe here?'' his wife asked.

''Of course.''

The idea made the hair lift on the back of Chloe's neck. ''He will be gone by that time.''

''Pray that it is so.''

''Yes.'' In a firm change of subject then, she spoke of the amazing progress of a young pupil who had been unable to recognize her name only two weeks before but was now reading. They continued in that vein until they were home again.

Chloe busied herself for the rest of the day with ironing Ahmad's uniforms, tending the children so Treena could rest, and overseeing preparation for that night's all-male dinner party. In late evening, while Ismael, Ahmad and his friends were eating in the *hajra* and Treena was feeding the children, Chloe had her own scant portion of the lamb, rice and vegetable dish in the kitchen. Afterward, she picked up the bowl of kitchen scraps left on the counter and carried them outside into the walled garden.

The last colors of sunset were fading from the sky, leaving it to the lavender and gray of approaching night. She stopped for a moment to stand staring upward at the inexorable transformation. The day was almost gone. Soon the American would go away as well.

The ache of sadness brought by that idea was surprising. Yet why should it be? She might never again have contact with the life she'd left behind. Some small nostalgia was surely permitted? What mattered was her final decision, not her emotional reaction. This had been made and accepted, and no brief twilight reverie could change it.

Turning her gaze to the stone path again, she moved toward the fig trees at its far end. They were beginning to bear, and could use every bit of mulch she could scrape together to help them through the present stretch of dry weather. Rain fell more often around Ajzukabad than elsewhere in the desertlike country but never enough, and only household wastewater could be spared to help plants survive.

The town was nestled in a high valley formed by the Kashi River. Protected by snow-veined mountain peaks, its climate was subtropical. She grew a variety of other fruits, vegetables and herbs along the walls and in the beds separated by crushed stone walkways, including grapes, melons, apricots, tomatoes, beans, chili peppers, potatoes, turnips, carrots, onion, peas and cabbage in their different seasons. Her efforts added to the family larder and medicine cabinet, as well as providing a welcome excuse for solitude and outdoor exercise.

She emptied the bowl she carried, then she wandered among beds, pinching dead blooms, pulling a weed or two, and inhaling the fragrance of the mint and chamomile, sage and sorrel that rose as her skirts brushed against the sprawling herbs. She was putting off the moment when she must go back inside, she knew, but couldn't bear to trade the peaceful dusk for the strained atmosphere that her stepbrother always brought into the house with his return.

As she neared the mulberry tree that shaded a rough table and chairs in the corner made by the house and the garden wall, she heard the quiet rasp of cloth, saw the shift of movement in the darker shade cast by the tree. She stopped with her heart beating high in her throat.

"Evening."

That deep-voiced greeting in English rasped along her nerves. Instantly she caught the trailing end of the scarf she wore over her hair, drawing it across her face even before she made out the tall shape of the man that emerged from the shadows. "You!"

"Didn't mean to startle you. But you stood me up at the bazaar, and knocking on the front door didn't seem like the best idea under the circumstances."

She barely controlled a shudder at the thought. "If you're discovered here, you could be killed."

"I needed to see you."

"Did it occur to you go back to the States and leave me alone?"

"Not possible," he said with a decisive shake of his head. "I can't leave until we've had our little talk."

She stared at him in the fading light, at the set of his features, the thick dark brows, sculpted facial planes, and chiseled mouth with firmly tucked corners. It was a strong face, even in repose. The emerald glints in the hazel-brown of his eyes only added to the impression. "Do I know you? Did I ever know you back in the States?" she asked finally.

"No, but I've known you, or known about you, for a long time."

"And that's why you're hounding me?" She was becoming used to his colloquial English with its many contractions, she realized. A few of her friends liked to practice her language, but theirs was a textbook-formal style and she'd fallen into a similar habit unconsciously in order to be better understood.

"I told you before that your dad sent me. You could call it a deathbed request if you wanted to be dramatic."

"I don't want it to be anything—" she began, then stopped. "Deathbed? But that would mean..." Her throat constricted to a hard knot while trembling began deep inside her. She clasped one arm around her abdomen and stepped abruptly to the nearby wall, putting her back to its sun-warmed support.

He was silent for so long that she thought he didn't intend to answer. Finally he asked, "You didn't know? You've received no letters in the past six months saying that he had cancer and wasn't going to make it?"

She shook her head, a jerky movement.

"I guess that means you've had no contact with his lawyers, either."

"None," she said in compressed tones. "There

have been no messages at all. Not since I left the States.''

He whispered a soft imprecation. ''No wonder you looked at me yesterday as if I'd dropped out of the sky.''

''I thought my father... I wasn't sure he knew where I was.''

''He had an address, but nothing sent to it was ever answered,'' the American said. ''I verified it for him. And I sent the most recent messages.''

''You.'' The word was flat.

''At his request.''

''And you're positive they came here, to this house?''

''As positive as anyone can be considering the situation these days.''

Ahmad must have intercepted those messages, Chloe realized, just as he'd destroyed her letters years ago. The outrage of it moved through her like a poison. She let it take her, for otherwise she would disgrace herself by crying in front of this American who seemed to have no idea how much he had hurt her.

''So,'' she said with a lift of her chin as she turned her gaze toward the glow of lights behind the high kitchen window. ''I have the news now. You have completed your duty and are free to go. Leave at once, please, before you do something that will get me killed.''

''I hope I have more sense than that.''

''So do I, but I can't depend on it.''

"I promised your dad that I'd get you out of this country and back to the U.S. where it's safe," he returned, his voice deliberate. "That's what I intend to do."

"Impossible."

"Everything is arranged. All you have to do is gather up what you need and come with me. Or come with nothing, for that matter."

"I have no passport." It was a weak objection considering all that she could have said, but the first thing to come to mind.

"You had one when you came here. It's been renewed."

"Travel requires money and I have none."

"Your dad left you everything he owned. He wasn't exactly wealthy, but he didn't have a lot to spend his paycheck on during these past few years, and he had a knack for investments. His estate is worth half a million, give or take."

She faced him again while stunned disbelief moved over her. The amount mentioned was a fortune in Hazaristan where men worked all year long for the equivalent of two thousand dollars and the local currency, the Hazari, was exchanged at nearly five thousand to the dollar. If Ahmad learned of this inheritance, there was no way he would ever let her go.

But he knew already, she realized a second later. Why else would he be suddenly intent on seeing her married. As long as she was single, she remained an American citizen with the right to assume control of

her father's estate and go where she pleased as soon
as she had the means in her hands. Once tied to a
Hazari husband, however, she would become a nonentity expected to put her financial affairs completely
in his keeping. The Qur'an might prohibit a marital
tie between stepchildren, but all Ahmad had to do was
marry her to a Taliban brother-in-arms, one of several
who were under his thumb, and the two could then
divide her inheritance at their leisure.

"I appreciate your effort in coming here to tell me
all this," she said to the man who waited in such
controlled silence beside her. "But I don't believe it's
possible that I can leave with you."

"Come again?" He put his hands on his hipbones
as he stared at her in the darkness.

Her refusal sounded less than certain even in her
own ears, possibly because she'd used the polite fem-
inine form that she'd learned so well. She tried again.
"My life is here now. I have friends and obligations
that I cannot desert."

"Looks to me as if you're up to your neck in something that could earn you a starring role in one of
those productions you saw yesterday."

He referred to her RAWA activities. Voice sharp,
she asked, "How do you know that?"

"Let's say I have my ways."

She preferred not to think what that might mean.
"Then you should understand."

"I'm trying, but it's damn hard to make out why

you'd want to stay in a place where they treat women like dirt.''

"It's not what I want to do but what I must,'' she told him as irritation moved over her for his assumption that she didn't know what was best for her. "I'd have died without this cause, these women who have become a special family. They saved my life. I'm needed here, needed desperately. To teach young girls, to give them the knowledge that will save them from becoming the slaves of men because they know nothing else, is a good and powerful thing. To stand in front of them and tell them what it's like to live in a land where women are free to come and go as they please, wear what they please, say and think what they please is to reveal amazing truths. I have purpose, I have value, I have…''

"A mission?'' he suggested as she stopped.

"If you must call it that.''

"And what good will it do this mission if you're dead?''

She lifted a shoulder. "Perhaps I may inspire others who can take my place.''

"Oh, well, that'll fix everything, won't it?''

She looked away as his sarcasm told her how impossible it was for him to realize the soul-killing effects of the repression she and the women around her faced every day, or how life-giving it was to fight against it. "You are a man. How can you be expected to see.''

"That's not the point.''

"But it is," she insisted, her voice hardening. "You have never worn the burqa that smothers and stifles while it turns you into a faceless heap of cloth. You have never been beaten merely for showing an inch of skin at your wrist. You don't know what it's like to have someone destroy everything you value, to be forced to eat separately from men as if you will contaminate them, to be made invisible by being kept behind walls, to be expected to have no will, no needs, no desires, no dreams. In America, women complain of the glass ceiling that prevents their climb to success. Here, there are ceilings, walls and floors that make a prison of iron, the iron will of men. Who would not wage war against that? And how could I not feel like a coward if I ran away because of a little danger?"

"So you'll turn yourself into a martyr?"

"You demand an explanation, but don't listen when it's given! You only hear a woman when she is saying, 'Yes, yes, you are right. I will do exactly as you command.' Like most men!"

He watched her, his gaze steady on the uncovered portion of her face as if he were trying to read her eyes in the dark. Finally he said, "You don't like us, do you?"

"My feelings are not the issue." She didn't dislike men so much as distrust them, she thought. She'd learned the hard way to walk warily around males of any age. It was excellent programming for covert activities, especially when fear was added to the mix.

"But they are. You're an American, born of American parents on American soil, and no one can take that away from you. You don't belong here. It looks to me as if you're letting something very close to hatred blind you to your own safety."

"You suggest this on the strength of two short encounters? You know nothing about me or of how I've been forced to live for years, almost as long as I lived in the States. The little that you do know of these things is tainted by the fact that you are a man."

"Right," he drawled.

"It matters." The words were stubborn in spite of the realization that she'd just proved his point.

"Of course it does. But that doesn't change the fact that it's crazy for you to stay here when you can go back where you belong."

"Where I belong? I have no mother, no father now. My grandparents, if they are still alive, forgot me long ago. There is no one in the States to care what becomes of me. At least I have something here." Added to that was the fact she'd been away so long she was afraid she'd grown too different to ever fit in again.

"Well, hell, if that's all that's bothering you, I've got more than enough family to go around. The Benedict clan is so big that one more will never be noticed."

"That's your name, Benedict?"

The man beside her took a breath that expanded his chest under the neatly tucked-in black T-shirt that he wore with his jeans and boots. "Yeah. Wade Benedict. Guess I should have introduced myself sooner. But I've known about you for so long, thought about you so much lately one way and another, that it's hard to realize you've never heard of me.''

"You thought of me." Her voice was flat with disbelief.

"Night and day since I gave John Madison my word that I'd bring you home. This isn't a simple operation, you know, locating you, arranging to get you out. It's taken legwork, calling in favors and a lot of computer time. Then we had to assume that you might be held against your will since we could make no direct contact, and because I had a fairly comprehensive briefing on the situation here for women. That made it necessary to organize matters so you could be taken out of here by force if need be.''

She gave a short laugh. "You make it sound like a military campaign.''

"Close to it. What I'm trying to say is that I'm working with a tense situation and a narrow time frame. A little cooperation would be appreciated.''

"You really intend to smuggle me out of the country.'' It seemed so improbable, perhaps because she'd grown used to thinking of herself as unimportant to anyone.

"If I have to. Our intelligence says your stepbrother may try to prevent your leaving. He could probably make it stick because of his position with the Taliban high command.''

"Intelligence?''

"I had the help of a good friend who used to be with diplomatic security before opening up shop on his own. And John was involved in the op up to his eyeballs until, well, until the last."

She shook her head. "So much trouble."

"You were John's kid, his pride and joy. He used to pass around pictures of you to everybody who'd take a look. Sometimes, especially after new ones stopped coming, he'd spread them all out and talk to you while he slowly drank himself into a stupor."

"Don't!"

He gave a moody shrug, remaining silent for long seconds. Finally he said, "I was just trying to tell you why I'm here, how I know you. Are you sure you really never heard of me?"

She almost denied it, but hesitated as a shadow of memory flickered through her mind. "I think...it seems as if the people who owned the lake camp where I stayed with my father one summer in Louisiana may have been named Benedict."

"You got it, sugar." His teeth gleamed white for a second in the dim light as he smiled. "Your dad used to borrow the camp. He had no real home, just a motel room for when he was stateside between oilfield jobs."

"It was wonderful there. And he did speak of his young friend who had loaned him the place, though you were still overseas, I think. Mostly he called you..."

"That damn Benedict kid. Right?"

The droll self-deprecation in his voice surprised her. She wasn't used to men who could laugh at themselves. "It was a cover for how much he liked you, I think."

He shrugged as if embarrassed. "I was fresh out of college along about then and had a chip on my shoulder the size of a derrick. John made sure I stayed out of trouble when I first hit the fields. Or tried, anyway."

"So you feel indebted, which is why you are here?"

"I wouldn't put it that way."

His deep voice carried a drawl, as if he was intent on hiding something strongly felt but private. Curiosity stirred inside her. That was unusual since to suppress all interest in men, how they felt and what they thought, had become a way of life. She wasn't sure she liked it, especially since she would probably never see Wade Benedict again after tonight.

"What I started to tell you, anyway," he continued, "is that I have two brothers with wives and a kid or two, plus three or four close cousins and a few dozen more that I like well enough to claim as kin. If it's family you're missing, you'll find more than you really want in my neck of the woods, around Turn-Coupe, Louisiana. Not that you're obliged to settle down there, of course. Once you find your feet, you can go anywhere that suits your fancy."

It sounded so reasonable, so exactly what she might have wished for at one time. Now it was impossible.

"Thank you very much, but, as I'm been trying to tell you, I can't go with you."

"You don't know what you're saying."

"But you do? You are so superior and wise that you are better able to judge what is good for me than I, a mere woman? Go—"

He put out his hand, laying his fingertips against the scarf she still held over her face, finding her lips with amazing accuracy. Surprise stopped her voice. In the sudden quiet, she heard what had alerted him, the creak of the hinges on the house door.

Wade Benedict glanced at her with a lifted brow. At her stiff nod, he removed his hand, then swiftly changed his position so that his body with its dark clothing shielded her, especially the light blue of the blouse she wore with her long skirt. They stood motionless in the dark blotch of tree shadow.

An oblong of light fell across the garden. Ahmad's stocky shape filled the doorway. Chloe tensed, expecting to be reprimanded for staying outside so long.

It didn't happen. Instead her stepbrother stepped out to the edge of the herb bed where he unbuttoned his pants and relieved himself of the endless cups of tea he'd drunk in his role as host. It was a favorite trick of his, that defilement, because he knew the garden was her retreat.

Once done, Ahmad turned, refastening his clothes. The kitchen door closed behind him, and she was left alone again with Wade Benedict.

They didn't move or speak for long seconds. With

every sense on high alert, Chloe could feel the breeze that stirred the leaves overhead, catch the scents including night-blooming jasmine, mint and the sour mulberries that had been crushed underfoot. She could also feel the body heat of the man who stood so close. If she moved her hand just a fraction, she could touch him. The temptation to do just that lurched through her so she clenched her fingers into a fist to prevent it.

When she'd first come here, when she'd been so dismayed and unhappy, she'd daydreamed in the way of teenagers that her father would come for her. He'd whisk her away, maybe knocking Ahmad flat in the process, and the two of them would fly straight back to America. The fantasy had always run headlong into the fact that she'd have to leave her mother behind if she went away, something that had been insupportable. She was reminded of that particular fantasy now, she thought, because the daydream beckoned once more and she was still constrained by ties of duty and affection.

Wade Benedict was not a figment of her imagination, however. He was real, and it seemed that he would not be easily deflected from his purpose.

"Close call."

Delayed reaction rippled over her so her teeth chattered a little as she opened her mouth to speak. "Yes."

He put out a hand as if to touch her, then drew it back again. "If this Ahmad character scares you so much I'd think you'd be dying to get away from him."

She pressed her lips together. Explaining further would be a waste of breath. She had to get rid of this man somehow, before he ruined everything. "It's a big step, a huge change. I...need time to think about it."

Doubt rode his voice as he asked, "How much time?"

"Thirty-six hours? I will meet you in the bazaar then."

"Why not tomorrow?"

"I can't go out any time I please, but usually try to teach two days per week. If I can't make it the day after tomorrow, it will be the day after that. If I'm not there then, you will know that I am staying."

"Now wait a minute," he began.

"It's the best I can do."

"Why do I have a feeling I'll be standing around again, waiting for someone who never shows?"

"If it happens, then you must accept that it was impossible for me to leave."

"Or that you prefer the devil you know?"

Her brow pleated in a frown. "Is that supposed to mean something?"

"You've been here so long that a lot of what goes on seems almost natural, part of a familiar rut that doesn't require you to think because somebody takes care of that for you. You're like a prisoner who has been behind bars so long that the outside world looks too big to handle. It's easier to stay put.''

"I told you why it's important to me.''

"Yeah, but is that the real reason or just an excuse? You're too bright to bury yourself here.''

She drew herself up, standing tall before him though the top of her head only came to his chin. "Think what you like. I have given you my answer. You must accept it or I will tell you now that I can't go.''

He muttered something that might have been profane as he lifted a hand to waist level, abruptly closing it into a fist.

Chloe flinched; she couldn't help it.

Wade lowered his hand, staring at her before he said in precise tones, "I've never hit a woman in my life.''

"No. I... It was just a reflex.'' His gesture had been one of exasperation. She saw that now.

"I know that, damn it all. What I don't get is you being so afraid and still...'' He closed his lips on the words and swung around, turning his back to her.

He was angry and perhaps wounded in his pride that she could imagine he would use force. It was astonishing, and also disturbing. "I'm sorry.''

"God, don't apologize. That just makes it worse.'' He stared up at the mulberry leaves above him a second. "Never mind. Be at the market two mornings from now, you hear?''

"And if I'm not?''

"I came here to take you out of this hellish country. You're going, one way or another."

That sounded like a threat. "What are you saying?"

He didn't answer, but only took a running step and leaped to catch a lower branch of the mulberry tree. A lithe swing and twist of his body, and he was balanced on top of the wall, a shadow among the rustling branches. Seconds later, he vanished.

Chloe was alone in the garden once more, with only her fears and regrets.

3

Wade Benedict stood on the far side of the stone wall until he heard a door open and close and knew Chloe Madison was safe inside once more. Or at least safe from any consequences of his visit, as far as he could tell. Only then did he move off into the night, heading for the dingy room he'd taken in a midtown hotel.

He kept to the backstreets, every sense on high alert. Curfew was in effect in Ajzukabad as in all Hazaristan cities, and he wasn't exempt because he was American. In fact, it might get him a cracked skull or trip to pokey even faster than normal. Anti-American sentiment was strong here since the U.S. attack on Afghanistan, and he could be targeted for that reason alone. A knife in the ribs while his wallet was lifted was also a definite possibility. All the public hangings and chopped-off hands in the world couldn't stop that ancient response to terrible economic conditions.

The last few minutes with Chloe Madison played in his head like a bad movie. He couldn't believe she'd actually thought he meant to hit her. That reaction told him more than he wanted to know about what her life was like these days. Leaving John's daughter in the house with that stepbrother of hers for thirty-six more hours really went against the grain.

The file on Ahmad indicated that he'd been brought up by his grandfather on a steady diet of Islamic fundamentalism that had been compounded by his introduction to the Taliban. From the mullahs at the school in Kabul where he was sent for his education, he'd been indoctrinated with the idea that women were immoral beings who must always be controlled, and that the U.S. was to blame for every bad thing that had ever happened in a Muslim nation. The result was a full-blown hatred of both women and all things American. His father's marriage to an American woman had been an insult in his view, a slur on the family honor. It was rumored that he'd rid himself of his stepmother by having her murdered in the street while his father was away. Evidence also suggested a connection to the al Qaeda terrorist network, one developed while he was in Afghanistan. It wasn't simply that Chloe's stepbrother had developed a fanatic streak with a vicious edge but that he'd found the perfect position for expressing it.

How much Chloe Madison knew or suspected about these things, Wade couldn't tell. She was uptight beyond belief, giving nothing away, letting no one get close. She understood the risks in what she was doing well enough, he thought, but had grown so used to them that they no longer had the power to scare her. She'd always been a gutsy little thing, according to John. Apparently she hadn't changed. The Benedict in him saluted that courage as well as her loyalty to her friends and attempt to better the situation around her. Still, her refusal to listen to reason made him nuts.

He didn't like this delay, not one little bit. It was too much of a reminder of another wait, another hostage situation, another woman. The sooner this was over, the better. Besides, other people were involved in the operation, and some of them had more important things to do than stand around while Chloe made up her mind.

Wade was almost abreast of the shop doorway when he saw the woman. She eased toward him like a sheeted ghost with one hand held out in traditional begging posture. She didn't stop as she came nearer, but brushed against him, reaching with her other hand under the cover of her burqa to brush across his groin. It wasn't the first time he'd been approached by a prostitute in a foreign city, but it was maybe the weirdest. Even if paying for sex was his style, he couldn't imagine taking up an offer from a woman whose face he couldn't see and whose body was covered from head to toe.

"No," he said with precision.

The woman gasped and instantly effaced herself. The movement was so swift that Wade felt a wrench of guilt. He hadn't meant to seem threatening. Prostitution was forbidden, he knew, but if the fear of being too forward could bring that kind of terror, then he didn't like to think what the penalty for being caught must be or how great the desperation that would force a woman out into the night.

The incident was a potent reminder of Chloe's reaction to his visit. She was probably right about the danger of contact from him. It couldn't be helped. There were precious few ways for a man to talk to a woman here, which meant that he was forced to take chances. He'd been rough on her, too, suggesting that she liked her virtual captivity. He'd hoped to jar her into commitment, or at least an admission that she wanted to go home. The trick hadn't come close to working, and for that she also had his grudging admiration.

It had been worth the chance of getting caught sneaking over the garden wall just to see her without that ridiculous getup. The proud way she walked within her flowing folds of cloth, as if refusing to acknowledge the handicap, intrigued him, but it wasn't easy to talk to a woman when you couldn't see her face. Of course, he still didn't really know what she looked like. She'd seen to that, as if covering her face had become some sort of protective instinct instead of one of the thousand and one rules she had to follow.

He'd give a lot to know exactly how the bright-eyed preteen with the million-dollar smile that he remembered from John's photographs had turned out. He wasn't like one of those hopeless guys in romantic movies who fell in love with a picture, but she'd always looked to him like a great kid who would grow up to be quite a package. The need to find out if he was right was beginning to nag at him. Just curiosity, brought on by the whole veil thing, the lure of the forbidden, the mystery and all that.

Not that he had much use for the exotic East, particularly this corner of it. Oh, he was impressed as all get-out by the wide deserts and mountain peaks so tall they punched holes in the sky. The endurance and fighting spirit of the people amazed him, too. But it was impossible to take a real liking to a place where maimed ex-soldiers and old women begged and died in streets that smelled like sewers, and the government was doing its level best to destroy all trace of civilized living.

Ahead of him in the darkness, he caught the glow of a flashlight and the sound of booted footsteps. Two uniformed policemen with cudgels swinging from their fists came into view. Wade slid immediately into the nearest alley. Pressing his back to the mud brick wall, he tried to make himself a part of it. It wasn't so much that he feared arrest as it was the need to avoid drawing attention to his after-dark activity. You never knew when the wrong person might hear about it. It was always possible, too, that his name could show up in some semiobsolete database of diplomatic security service personnel. That was one of the risks that he had weighed before agreeing to this operation. But of course that part of his past was the main reason

John Madison had tapped him for it in the first place. Well, that and the need for a man he could trust not to take advantage of the situation and, just possibly, of his daughter.

The patrol came closer. Wade reached to unsnap the shoulder holster nestled under his armpit and palm the weapon it held. The move was silent, practiced, natural. He could sense the familiar closing down of thought and emotion, of everything except animal-like nocturnal perception and steel-hard will. Even as the old readiness spread through him, he felt his gut tighten. Nobody had mentioned killing in order to get Chloe Madison out of Hazaristan, but the possibility had been understood. Wade could do the job if he had to, but he didn't like it, hadn't needed to worry about it for a long time.

One of the policemen laughed in a low rumble of sound that marked him as all too human. He and his partner were talking, their voices gaining in volume as they neared the alley. They strolled past with their turbaned heads nodding in unison and the sticks they carried tapping the sidewalk now and then in random patterns. They didn't even glance toward the alley.

Wade sighed and replaced his weapon as the pair's footfalls receded. He stretched his neck to relieve tense muscles while he waited to be certain the street was clear again. Emerging from the other end of the alley as a precaution, he made his way toward the hotel with all possible speed.

It was good to shut the door of his room behind

him and secure it for the night with his own hardware. The place was a dump, yes, but it was his dump for now, his little spot of America in this too-strange land.

He glanced at his watch with a frown. The timing was wrong for a call to the far side of the globe. It would jerk his old buddy and former boss, head of Vantage International Security on the Virginia edge of the Beltway, from a sound sleep. Wade shrugged, then hauled out the satellite cell phone from his black leather duffel that sat at the foot of the bed. Activating the built-in scrambler, he punched in the numbers.

It was picked up on the second ring. Nat Hedley's voice was a little husky but disgustingly alert otherwise. Wade wasted little time on preliminaries, but gave a succinct rundown of the problem and the delay it was causing. Then he waited.

"Christ, Wade, what happened to the famous Benedict charm? I thought that moonlight-and-honeysuckle drawl of yours was guaranteed to melt the pants off any female in ten seconds flat."

"This one doesn't wear any pants to melt."

"Found that out already, did you?"

"Drag that wad of fat cells that passes as your brain out of the toilet, my man. I only meant that underwear has never quite caught on over here as in the West. Besides, I don't think the lady has much use for men."

"You mean she's..."

"Hell, nothing like that," Wade said hastily. "She's been taught by experts to avoid contact."

Nat grunted his understanding, though he didn't sound particularly convinced. "So what's the plan?"

"I wait. That's if you can confirm that our transport out of here will do the same?"

"Done. But what if she won't budge after this deadline? If the hawks in Washington get their way, they'll be calling in air strikes on Kashi and Ajzukabad any day now."

"She's coming home. It was a promise when I made it, and it's still a promise."

"I heard that. But if she's not too fond of guys now, how's she going to feel after you bundle her off to the States when she doesn't want to go."

"Grateful?"

"Wouldn't bet on it. In my experience, females show gratitude least when you expect it most. Ouch! Maggie, hey! Stop it, woman!"

Wade grinned briefly as he listened to what sounded like Nat taking his lumps from a pillow being wielded by his wife and bedmate of some twelve or thirteen years. When he thought he might be heard again, he said, "Doesn't much matter what Chloe Madison thinks. She'll be safe, and that's the important thing."

Nat apparently lost the battle among the sheets, because it was Maggie Hedley who spoke in Wade's ear. "You be patient with that girl, you hear me,

Wade Benedict. Enough people have pushed her around without you doing the same thing.''

"I can't just walk away from her.''

"Now why? That precious Old South honor of yours? You gave your word, and that's it?''

"I promised John.''

"So what? She didn't ask you to make promises any more than she asked you to rescue her. And if she makes up her mind to stay, what's that to you?''

"You don't know what it's like over here. Women have no value, zilch, nada, none. A man can do anything to them and get away with it. Leaving her behind could be a death sentence. Or worse.''

"Nothing is worse than death, my darling man. But let me get this straight. You're worrying yourself to smithereens over what might happen to this woman you've barely met?''

Wade had known Nat and his wife a long time. He was fond of them both, particularly Maggie who made a mean lemon icebox pie and had an unerring instinct for finding the soft underbelly of the tough guys who worked for her husband. Still, he'd learned the hard way to tread warily when she was on the warpath. "I guess you could say that.''

"Attractive, is she?''

"Wouldn't know, though she was a cute kid from her photos.'' He gave Nat's wife the scoop on that part.

"Lord, you're worse off than I thought!''

"Now, Maggie," he began with exaggerated patience.

"Forget it. Bring her home by force, if that's what you have to do. But remember that you're supposed to be a gentleman. You can at least act like one, even if being one is too much for you!"

"Yes, ma'am," he said in his most deferential tone. It was a relief to hear Maggie laugh before she handed the phone back to her husband.

Wade clarified a few more details with Nat, then signed off and tossed the phone back into the top of his duffel. It bounced off a plastic carton of canned chicken with crackers, and he dug out that snack package. He hadn't eaten before positioning himself to invade Chloe's living space, and now his stomach thought his throat had been cut. It wasn't the first meal he'd made out of a can by far. Food wasn't too high on his list of priorities, and it was less trouble to eat in his room than hunt a restaurant meal. Besides, though he wasn't overly squeamish, he did have his standards, and the starvation rate in this part of the world made him wonder just what kind of meat might be on the menu.

Popping the top on the chicken, he fished out a chunk and balanced it on a cracker before wolfing it down. While he chewed, he unlaced his boots and kicked them off. By the time he had finished the sketchy meal and chugged a bottle of tepid water, he had undressed and was on his way to the shower.

He wasn't sleepy and there was no TV. He pulled

out the dossier on Ahmad along with a sheaf of other reports, and spent an hour or so going over them. They weren't exactly bedtime stories. The Taliban were a piece of work, like some hyperreligious motorcycle gang drunk on power and testosterone, getting off on their reign of terror. That they targeted women was typical of that kind of gang-bang mentality, Wade thought, but still enough to turn the stomach of a Southern good old boy brought up to revere the opposite sex. By the time he turned out the light, he had an even clearer understanding of the anger that drove Chloe Madison, since a savage need to punch out something or somebody thrummed in his own veins. If there had ever been a prayer in hell that he'd leave her behind to live out her life with these misogynistic psychopaths, there was one no longer.

The dream began as if always did, with a dance.

It was a lavish embassy function on a pleasantly cool night, as most nights were in Middle Eastern desert countries. A band played the kind of music that made a decent background for chitchat covering anything from casual flirtation and political arguments to megabuck business ventures and high-level diplomatic initiatives. The room smelled of flowers, American liquor and food, and though relatively few women were present other than embassy staff, the glittering jewelry rivaled the sparkle of the chandeliers overhead. Wade was officially off duty from his job of protecting the ambassador and his family and other embassy personnel, but attending such formal events as backup was always encouraged. Fading into the woodwork, holding up the wall at strategic posts was his specialty, so it was a surprise when the trophy wife of one of the middle-aged Texas oilmen in town snagged his elbow and pulled him out onto the dance floor. She'd had a bit too much champagne, maybe to drown whatever pain it was that hovered behind her strained smile. When she locked her arms around his neck and draped herself over him like some drooping lily, Wade didn't have the heart to push her away. A large part of that reluctance had been because he could feel the difficult breaths she took as she tried to control tears. Then, as he turned with her in the dance, he noticed that the husband was watching and he wasn't happy.

Abruptly he was transported to a mud hut on the edge of some small town. The place was an extremist stronghold where the vice consul was being held after being abducted from his car on a lonely road where he shouldn't have been in the first place. The oilman's wife, who definitely shouldn't have been there, either, was also in the dark hut.

Wade had just infiltrated the place, taking out the guard posted at the rear entrance and another one in the hallway. He could hear the rest of the terrorist cell in a front room chowing down, since it was Ramadan and they'd been fasting all day. He had exactly three minutes, an eternity of time, to get the kidnapped pair on their feet and out the back door. Then all hell was going to break loose as the Diplomatic

Security Service, under command of security chief Nat Hedley, swept out the snake's nest.

Wade moved soundlessly into the windowless cubicle of a room where the vice consul and the woman were laid out back to back on the floor. The embassy second-in-command was his first responsibility. A Yale man with a lanky build and perpetually arrogant expression, he was smart enough to wait for instructions after he was freed. Then Wade turned to the oilman's wife.

Her face was a ghastly mask of ruined makeup overlaying pain and terror. She was tied up like a bulldogged steer, her body bent backward in a bow. No way was she going to be able to walk out on her own. He cut her loose with a few quick slices, stifling her moan with one hand as he helped her straighten her body. Pulling her upright, he clutched her against him with a firm grip while holding his weapon ready in his free hand. He motioned to the Yale man to follow, then started back the way he'd come.

He heard the yelled order, first round of shots and slamming entry before his second step. Something was wrong; the operation was going down early. He put it in high gear as he half dragged the woman down the back hall.

The exit ahead was blocked by a man's figure. The compressed thump of silenced shots echoed off the walls. Wade felt the woman he carried jerk as the bullets hit her, felt the warm wet splatter of her blood. He raised his weapon, squeezed the trigger. Then a

*red and orange fireball lit the night and his world
went to pieces.*

Wade came awake so fast that he wrenched to a
sitting position on the mattress before his eyes
snapped open. His breath rasped in his throat. His
brain felt on fire. The purple blotch of scar tissue on
his left side and groove hidden by the hair at his tem-
ple burned with phantom pain. Resting his elbows on
his raised knees, he closed his eyes again and pressed
the heels of his hands hard against the eyelids. Then
he let his hands drop and shook himself like a dog.

Where that nightmare had come from was no mystery. He'd lived it. He'd also relived it during debrief-
ing, when he'd tried to explain that the death of one
of the hostages was no DSS failure but a setup, and
for months afterward. Why it had visited him again
tonight, years after he'd conquered it, was easy to see.
He'd failed once to remove a woman from danger and
was half-afraid that the same thing would happen
again.

The two cases were nothing alike, and Wade knew
it. There was no way in hell he could have guessed
that the oilman wanted his wife dead for a lot of
twisted reasons that had more to do with her habit of
asking strange men to dance than it did Middle Eastern politics or government security. It made no difference. He was still forced to second-guess his decision and actions that night, and to wonder if he
could make any similar situation come out right.

Wade sometimes thought the problem was that the

incident had never been resolved. Nat Hedley had raised ten kinds of stink over the foul-up, but it had done no good. There was considerable confusion, intentional or otherwise, about just who had triggered the op or been first through the hut's rear entrance. Wade had been out of it for days, in no shape for filing official reports, and the vice consul had seen nothing once he'd hit the floor at the first sound of gunfire. Accusing a wealthy and influential citizen who was a frequent campaign contributor of having his wife murdered had not been a popular idea, and the body had been released for shipment back to the States followed by cremation. Then a week later, the oilman, in the grip of apparent senile dementia associated with Alzheimer's, had shot himself. The incident was written off as an unfortunate accident during a hostage situation and no amount of requests for investigation could get it reopened.

Wade had resigned from the DSS, returning to the oil fields that he'd abandoned when Nat Hedley recruited him. He'd settled back into a comfortable routine of months overseas followed by weeks at home. Nat had left the service a couple of years later to start Vantage International Security, specializing in the rescue of Americans kidnapped or otherwise detained in foreign countries. And that had been that, until Wade got the call from John Madison.

In retrospect, Wade thought he'd gravitated toward John in those early oil-field days out of the need for something that he'd never gotten from his old man.

Why John, almost twenty years older, had taken him on, Wade couldn't imagine. He'd been a reckless kid and high-tempered, with more bravado than brains. It was a wonder he hadn't gotten himself killed a dozen times over. John's influence had steadied him, given him the grounding he'd needed to set himself straight.

A sharp knock on the door snagged his attention just then. He eased from the bed and stepped into his pants. Picking up his handgun from the bedside table, he crossed to the room noiselessly on bare feet. There was no peephole. It didn't take a lot of imagination to figure out what was happening in the hall, however, since the doorknob turned under his fingers as he touched it.

He pulled his hand back, then thumbed off the safety of his weapon. Carefully he reached down and set aside the stainless-steel bar he'd added to the hotel's flimsy security. Then he stepped to one side and waited.

The lock clicked and the door opened a crack. It widened. A man inserted his head and shoulders.

Wade grabbed the intruder's shirtfront and jerked him inside. Then he slammed him against the wall and shoved his handgun's barrel under the man's chin. ''You have two seconds to tell me what you're doing here,'' he said in a low growl. ''Start talking.''

''Release me, infidel, or you will be shot.''

''Be hard to give the order without the bottom half of your face.'' Wade's reply was in the Pashtu the man had used, since he'd picked up the rudiments in a two-week crash course, thanks in large part to past familiarity with Arabic. Catching a furtive sound from outside, he added, "Tell your buddy to step into the room where I can see him or this discussion is over."

The man he held stood rigid, resistance in every line of his body. The struggle between survival and defiance was almost palpable. Then he called out, "Enter, Zahir."

A slight figure slid around the doorjamb and stood waiting with his back pressed to the facing. A spate of Pashtu far too rapid for Wade to follow passed between the two men. As it ended, the smaller one looked at him and put his hands together and bowed in a gesture of respect. "Esteemed sir," he said in passable English. "We mean you no harm but only wished to make your acquaintance and discover the purpose for your visit to Ajzukabad."

"You picked a mighty strange time for a social call," Wade returned.

"This may be so. It was necessary in order to find you in your room."

That sounded as if they might have attempted to contact him earlier. It didn't mean they wouldn't have slit his throat, given half a chance, but seemed to hint at semipeaceable intentions. He indicated the bedside lamp. "Let's have a little light on the subject, shall we?"

The lamp gave off less light than a couple of good birthday candles, but it was enough to confirm his suspicions. He'd never laid eyes on the younger man who had flicked it on, but the one who had come through the door first was Chloe's stepbrother Ahmad. Wade released him and stepped back. Remembering just in time that the Hazari was supposed to be a virtual stranger to him, he said, "I saw you in Kashi, at the football stadium."

"And I you," Ahmad replied, then continued with his companion dutifully translating after him. "Who are you and what do you want?"

Wade gave his name, even as he wondered belatedly if he should have arranged for a false identity in case Chloe's stepbrother was the culprit behind the missing letters. No recognition appeared in the guy's face, however, which meant he either had no memory for names or was good at hiding reactions behind his beard.

"Why do you linger in the bazaar? Why do you watch our women?"

"Veils just plumb fascinate me," Wade said with his best dumb-as-dirt-drawl. "Can't for the life of me see how they breathe under them tablecloths, not to mention how they ever manage to cross a street without getting run over. Now I'd like to know why you've been following me."

"You must expect such things when you travel in a country that is at war."

Wade had expected them, as a matter of fact. That was why he'd gone a couple of miles out of his way to lose the tail before heading to the house where

Chloe lived earlier. "The idea makes me nervous. I'm a textile importer, not a spy."

Ahmad pursed moist, fleshy lips. "A textile importer. Yet you visit no makers of textiles."

"I'm told the choicest goods are made privately, by women working in their homes." At least that was what he'd read in the dossier compiled to go along with the reason for his visit as stated on his entrance papers.

"No such goods exist. Our women do not concern themselves with the sordid world of commerce."

"You mean they'd rather beg like those I've seen in the streets, or maybe starve?" This was twisting the lion's tail and nothing more, but Wade couldn't resist.

"You will do better to confine your inquiries to cloth and your purchases to normal markets where men may sit down with each other to reach a bargain. That is if you truly have interest in our goods."

With the threat of immediate death removed, Ahmad was fast reverting to bullying arrogance of the kind that usually covered insecurity, Wade thought. Behind his attitude was almost certainly the over-the-top zealotry that came from embracing a cause for the sense of belonging conferred by it. That was the same cult mentality that had produced the Manson murders and the mass death at Jonestown. Wade understood it well enough, since he'd come close to something similar before his disenchantment with the DSS. Any fighting force developed its own brand of brotherhood, as did most religious or ideological communities. Some were just more extreme than others. And the most dangerous members were those who had no thought or purpose not sanctioned by their leaders.

"Rugs, that's what I'm after," Wade said easily. "Though I've taken a liking to the embroidered women's clothes I've seen here and there. Know where I might find a source for quality goods along that line?"

"Hardly. And I must say you do not look the kind of man who would find them of interest."

Something in the stepbrother's voice really got to Wade; he just couldn't help it. Tilting his head, he asked softly, "You calling me a liar?"

"I've no reason to do that. Yet. But I am here to make you understand Taliban policy in respect to foreign nationals. You may come to our country, you may leave your money, but you may not comment publicly on our internal policies, interfere in our internal affairs, or attempt to contact a private citizen for any nonbusiness-related purpose. Is this clear?"

Wade glanced at the interpreter as the young man repeated his leader's nonsense. This Zahir was young, with dark, liquid eyes and a wispy beard that almost looked glued to his chin. His turban and uniform were carefully pressed, obviously new. Soft around the edges, he watched Ahmad with the kind of nervous awareness that suggested dependency. If Ahmad was aware of his regard or his favor, he gave no sign. Wade had heard a few things about the closeness of

Muslim brotherhood over the years, but saw little indication of that preference in Chloe's stepbrother.

"No problem," he said hastily as he saw that Ahmad was now waiting for his answer. The agreement cost him nothing since Chloe Madison was not, as far as he was concerned, a Hazari citizen.

"It's an excellent thing that we understand each other. Be advised as well that the faster you conclude the business that brought you here, the better it will be for all."

"I couldn't agree with you more. This just ain't a place many folks would want to linger."

It was possible that he'd overdone the hayseed cooperation, for Ahmad gave him a hard stare. "There will be no more warnings."

"None required." Wade moved to the door with a rangy stride and reached to pull it open. "But I should tell you that I'll be in and out a lot. You won't be surprised if I'm a tad hard to keep tabs on for the rest of my stay?"

Ahmad's eyes narrowed. He stepped through the doorway with his interpreter trailing after him, then turned back again in the hall. "I think you will find that the Taliban can lay hands on you whenever it pleases."

"They're sure welcome to try," Wade returned with his blandest smile.

As he swung the door shut on his visitors, however, his humor vanished. He stood staring at nothing until he could no longer hear their receding footsteps.

4

Chloe barely slept at all. Fury that Ahmad would keep her father's death from her churned in her mind. That he'd forced her to remain dependent while he planned to trap her in a marriage of his choosing then steal her inheritance made her long to thwart him. Most of all, she could not stop replaying the moments in the garden with Wade Benedict. He had destroyed her hard-won acceptance of her life, substituting visions of freedom and paradise that must remain forever out of her reach. Because he had presented this bright hope, her future now appeared more bleak. For this she was almost as angry with him as she was with Ahmad.

Morning brought the news that Ahmad was suffering the effects of his overeating the night before and would be at home all day. Chloe worked conscientiously around the house, completing her chores so nothing would prevent her from going to teach if the opportunity arose the following day. It paid off. Ahmad left early, and by midmorning she was at the house of Ismael's mother, Willa, where classes were held once every two weeks or so on a rotating basis with three other households. Treena had been left at home, as she didn't feel well. Ismael escorted Chloe for a dutiful visit to his widowed mother.

A woman of furious energy and intelligence, Willa had lost her husband to pneumonia and a young daughter to childhood illness, as well as her business. Considering her life over at forty, as few women lived much past that age in this part of the world, she had dedicated what time she had left to the underground women's movement. Besides allowing the school to meet in her sitting room, she kept a small beauty salon in a back closet where the forbidden cosmetics, facials, hair treatments and manicures could be had. Many women enjoyed its services as a comfort in their trials and as a form of secret defiance.

Chloe and the widow exchanged the ritual three kisses on either cheek of greeting, then settled to glasses of tea in silver holders while waiting for the pupils to gather. They spoke in strained voices of recent difficulties among their group, particularly of a woman they both knew who had had a thumbnail amputated for being caught wearing nail polish. After a few moments, Willa reached to stroke her fingertips across Chloe's cheek. "You look tired, my dear. Is all well with you?"

"Not exactly," Chloe answered with a wan smile before going on to tell her of the many things that were taking place.

The widow stared at her in consternation. "Oh,

Chloe. How we shall miss you when you are no longer with us.''

''I said the American has come for me, not that I would go with him.''

''How can you not? Unless…surely you cannot *wish* to marry the man chosen for you?''

''I have no need for a groom, no love for any man,'' she answered firmly.

''So you will defy Ahmad?'' Willa's voice was hushed.

''He hasn't yet presented a marriage. As long as he is only considering it, worrying serves no purpose.''

''But once he does present it, you will have no choice. Why not go away while there is time?''

''How can I when I am needed so badly here?'' Chloe waved toward the schoolroom.

''Have you thought that it might be kismet? This man who comes may hold your destiny in his hands. It could be you are meant to return to your true home, that you may be of more service there.''

''What are you saying?''

''Think, love. You are of that modern world so different and far away over the sea. You understand it. People there may listen if you tell them what we suffer here.''

''And they may not,'' Chloe said shortly. ''That world is also run by men who care more for rules and the rights of those in power than for the things endured by women.''

''They are not so hardened to suffering, I think.

Some have good hearts, or so I'm told. Do you not think that in this place called Louisiana, which you speak of from time to time, that you might find men who would become our allies?''

Was it possible? Could someone like Wade Benedict understand or care about their problems or be willing to help her effect a change? What a difference it would make.

Could she really return to Louisiana with a free heart? How she longed to see it again, to discover if it was really the earthly paradise that lingered in her mind. She had pretended to Wade that she barely remembered, but that had been mere self-protection. She could not let him know how often she returned in dreams to that camp on the lake where everything was lush and green, the days golden and long, and her father's love surrounded her like a benediction. If he knew, if the tall American even guessed, he would surely use it against her.

''But the most important fight is here!'' she argued, clenching her hands into fists as she sought to banish unwanted images of a placid lake and a man's naked face. ''It is here that we must make a stand.''

''Against Ahmad? He will break you. Have you learned so little of the power of the head of the family?''

''I've learned.'' Or rather she had learned to pretend, Chloe thought, to bow her head and do as she was told while hating with all her heart.

"Yes. Far better to bend and kiss the stick, then kill quietly while he sleeps."

Chloe met the other woman's eyes at those whispered words. They were not idle. They both knew one mad old woman who now lived on the streets after sewing her abusive husband into a sheet then beating him to death with a broom, and another younger one who had served hers arsenic after the battering he gave her killed her unborn child. Women could be pushed too far.

"And yet I fear for you," Ismael's mother went on after a moment. "You play the subservient female, just as we taught you with such care, but it isn't easy for you. Because of where you were born, you are too independent of thought, too fearless and quick to rash action. You will say or do something that will get you killed."

"Like my mother," she said, giving voice to the object lesson behind her friend's words.

"Just so. This wealth you have inherited is a gift from Allah. It could be used to aid our cause. It may be that it is meant for this purpose."

"You really think I should go?" Chloe reached for her mint tea, avoiding the other woman's gaze so her own would not influence the answer. The liquid in the glass reminded her of Wade Benedict's eyes. It also brought back the tea she'd had so often in Louisiana, cold, sweet refreshment served over tinkling cubes of ice. She set her warm glass down again without drinking.

"How can I say?" Willa answered. "You must search your heart, think carefully, and then decide for yourself."

It wasn't the answer Chloe wanted to hear. This was the morning she was to meet Wade Benedict in the bazaar. If she was to keep that appointment, then there was little time left for making up her mind.

A young girl appeared in the doorway just then. Her smile was shy, though her expression held determination. "Chloe, revered teacher," she said. "Your humble pupils wait for you."

It seemed very like an omen. Chloe smiled at Ismael's mother and gave a small shrug. Then she took the smaller girl's hand and walked with her to the classroom.

The lesson, a recitation of the capitals of the cities of Europe, was designed to broaden the horizons of those for whom Hazaristan was the beginning and end of the world. It went smoothly enough, with only a few stumbles over unfamiliar syllables. Looking around her at the earnest, shining faces, Chloe felt a rush of pride and love. They were so intelligent, wanted so much to learn. How any thinking person could dismiss these girl children as worthless, relegating them to a lifetime of nothing except tending babies and the houses of their fathers and husbands, was a fathomless mystery. To help them in any way she could seemed worth any sacrifice. If that made her a martyr as Wade Benedict suggested, then so be it. She was sorry if he was forced to wait again and go away empty-handed. He would recover, but these young girls might not survive the disappointments in their lives if they were not taught a sense of self-worth now. She had to save them, or at least try. Wade Benedict could save himself.

Then from the front of the widow's house came the chime of a brass gong of the type that had once summoned the elite to dinner during the British Raj. It rang out three times, the mellow notes hanging in the air like the prelude to some composition in a minor key.

Instantly Chloe made a slicing motion with her hand, cutting off the chant of capital cities. Taking up the copy of the Qur'an that lay beside her, she opened it to the prayer that was the opening *sura,* or chapter. She read the first line and the girls, like the perfect automatons the mullahs wanted them to become, followed her lead by chanting after her. Under cover of the sound, Chloe turned her small blackboard so it became a decorative mirror and deposited her lesson plan beneath the noisome chamber pot that sat behind a screen in a corner. By the time the door opened to reveal the police, there was no sign of anything taking place in the room except holy study.

The girls broke off recitation, screaming and hiding their faces as they saw the police with their raised sticks and ferocious glares. A red haze of rage rose in front of Chloe's eyes for the unnecessary use of terror tactics. Controlling it with strong effort, she spoke soothingly to her pupils then covered her own face and turned to meet this official threat.

"What is this gathering? What are you doing with these girl children?"

The demand came from the largest of the pair, a man wearing the special turban of the hajji, one who has made the pilgrimage to Mecca. "We pray, honored one," she replied at her most deferential.

"What use is prayer to such as these?" the second policeman asked with a sneer in his voice.

"The better to instruct their future sons. Surely this is a benefit to be desired?"

"It is not for women to instruct."

"True," she said gravely. "But may they not offer guidance? You must see that even females such as these children may learn to point out the many blessings of Allah."

The policemen could not disagree without suggesting that religious instruction in the cradle was useless, but neither could they agree without appearing to condone the interrupted study. They were silent for a moment as they digested the conundrum.

"I warned you that she has the tongue of a serpent."

It was Ahmad, speaking from the doorway. As Chloe lifted her eyes to meet his, he gave her a hard stare then moved into the room. Without stopping to think, she asked, "You sent these men here?"

He didn't bother to answer her, though a flush of

anger darkened his face. To the police, he said, "Be done with this farce. Send these vermin home."

"We found no wrongdoing." The features of the larger policeman mirrored belligerence, perhaps at the suggestion that he took orders from the militia.

"You wouldn't, since she is obviously too sly for you. Leave it to me, then. I know how to deal with her insolence."

Many of the girls were crying now, frightened by the loud voices and the threat of violence they felt in the air. One or two looked at Chloe with pity in their eyes that made them appear much older than they were. The last thing they needed, any of them, was to be exposed to more unpleasantness. In any case, the chance of learning anything useful today had vanished.

"You are dismissed, my loves," she said to them with a shooing gesture and valiant attempt at a smile. "Go with my blessing and the memory of all I've tried to tell you."

The room cleared in seconds. Her stepbrother gave her a snide look, then escorted the policemen to the front door where, Chloe thought, a bribe of the kind that usually oiled transactions in this part of the world was probably passed. From elsewhere in the house came the voice of Ismael's mother talking to the children, offering sweets and reassurance. At least no one had tried to detain them or subject them to the kind of interrogation that could leave scars.

Ahmad appeared in the doorway again within seconds. Pausing there, he said, "You are guilty, of course."

"Of what, please?"

"Don't play games with me. Your bitch of a mother taught you behind my back, and you think to deceive me while you follow her lead. I am not so easily fooled as the police. But you should be grateful to me. I could have had you beaten into this floor. I could have allowed them to take you away to be whipped, or worse."

She dared lift her eyes to his for long seconds. "Why didn't you then?"

"I have other plans."

"Such as?" The words were clipped as she set her teeth to prevent them from chattering.

He gave a short laugh, possibly at the idea that he might actually answer such an impertinent question. "Get your burqa. We're going home."

She was not allowed to take leave of her hostess, nor did they wait for Ismael to be summoned from the *hajra* where he was partaking of tea in solitary state while reading the latest newsmagazines from abroad. Ahmad marched her from the house, then moved off down the street leaving her to trail after him. She glared at his back through the mesh over her eyes, hating him and everything he stood for, despising the swagger of his walk, the set of his shoulders, even the way he wore his turban. It might be futile, but was better than dwelling on what he meant to do to her.

Inside the house, Ahmad snatched the burqa from her as she began to remove it, tossing it aside. Taking her arm in a hard grip, he dragged her through the house to her narrow room with its low cot and black-painted window. He shoved her into its dim confines, then let go of her so she stumbled and nearly fell.

"Remain," he ordered. "Since you have abused your freedom of movement, this will be your prison."

Chloe whirled to face him as she regained her balance. "What do you mean?"

"There will be no more visiting, no more teaching. You are confined to this room until I say you may go."

"When will that be?" From somewhere in the house came the sound of a door closing followed by low voices that might have been those of Treena and Ismael, but the sounds barely registered.

Ahmad's mouth curved like a scimitar within the cover of his beard. "When you are wed."

It was what she feared, the thing she most dreaded. "Who..." she began.

"That is my choice, but I promise you won't be pleased."

She faced him squarely with her fists held at her sides. "I won't accept him."

"You will, and soon."

"Why are you doing this? Why now?"

"You have gone astray like the stupid ewe that wanders too near the wolf's den. Your independent

ways can only bring you grief. I am saving you from
that.''

He believed that, she thought. He really did, which
meant he was light-years away from understanding
how she or the other women around him viewed the
actions of him and his kind. ''How noble,'' she said
in choked irony. ''And the money has nothing to do
with it?''

His head came up like a bull scenting danger at her
oblique reference to his honor, but he zeroed in on
the more concrete insult. ''Money?''

''The bride-price you will get for selling me.'' She
wasn't supposed to know of her inheritance, something she'd almost forgotten.

''You will not speak of things that do not concern
you!''

''I have no concern in where I am to live or with
whom? You're insane if you think...''

He lunged forward and slapped her, an openhanded
blow with the full force of his temper behind it. As
she stumbled back, tasting blood, he caught her arm
and gave her the return swing. She spun with the
blow's force, half-blinded by pain. As he let her go,
she struck the wall then slid down to a sitting position, holding a hand to her face. Willa had been right,
she saw in dazed recognition. She had never really
learned proper subservience, had reverted to independent thought all too readily under the influence of
Wade Benedict. This was the result.

''You will do exactly as I say, stepsister,'' he said,

looming over her. "You will do it now and for the rest of your life. You will obey my every command, answer my slightest wish. You will serve me. You will be mine to use and to chastise as I please, for I am the man chosen to be your bridegroom, my dear stepsister. I am the man you will marry."

"No!" The single word was so sharp with horror that it hurt her throat.

"Oh, yes," he said, his voice rich with anticipation.

A movement came at the open doorway and Ismael stepped into view. Concern was plain in his face as he spoke. "Ahmad? What passes here?"

"Traitor," he said in rough accusation as he turned to face this new target. "I trusted you to guard this woman, to see that she did nothing to shame my house and my name, and how do you repay me?"

"Your way is not my way," Ismael said simply, the words firm though his face had no more color than his white turban.

"Your way allowed this she-devil here to corrupt my sister with her foreign ways, foreign ideas. It permitted the women under your protection to spit on the laws of Islam and bring dishonor to this house."

"I see no dishonor."

"You are a fool," Ahmad shouted. "Next you will say you see no corruption."

"Treena makes her own decision, follows her own heart."

Chloe's ears still rang from the impact of Ahmad's

hand, and her heart beat so heavily that she could barely make out what the two men were saying. Still, Ismael's valor in daring to stand up for her and Treena warmed her heart.

Ahmad snorted in disgust. "I should kill you, and would if you were not the father of my future nephew. You will redeem yourself by chastising my sister as she deserves."

"She is my wife. I will decide when she requires punishment." Ismael moved forward a halting step. "She is my wife and I love her."

"You will do it or I will do it for you."

"She carries my son as you just said. She shall not be touched."

"I demand..."

"You demand?" Ismael interrupted. "You demand while speaking of honor, yet you intend to marry this woman in defiance of the laws as set down by Mohammed."

Ahmad glared at him. "There is no law to prevent this marriage. I spoke to the mullahs only this morning, and they explained the wisdom of the Qur'an in this matter. It is forbidden for two people to wed when they share a parent, but nothing prohibits a marriage of those joined by law alone with no blood tie between them."

"This may be law, but what of decency?" Ismael's gaze was troubled as he glanced from Ahmad to where Chloe sat, then back again.

"What of it?"

"Have you none? You have lived with Chloe as a sister, thought of her as a sister."

"Never!"

"I say you have, for otherwise you'd never have sought out the mullahs for an excuse to take her."

"Silence!"

"It's wrong," Ismael insisted, his gaze flicking again toward Chloe's bruised face. "It's a crime you will live to regret."

"What do you know of it?" Ahmad demanded. "You with your puny silver craft and crippled foot? You have never dared risk anything, never fought in battle, never given yourself and everything you are to a glorious cause. You are only half-alive and will never be more."

"I love and I make beautiful things with my hands," Ismael said in quiet assurance. "You hate and destroy. Which is living?"

Doubt cast a shadow across Ahmad's face for a single instant. Then he made a rude, dismissive gesture. "Words, nothing but words. What power have they compared to deeds that lead to paradise?"

Striding toward Ismael, he caught his arm, dragging him from the room. He slammed the door shut behind them. The rasp of metal against metal sounded as the key was turned in the lock.

Chloe let out the breath she hadn't realized she was holding. With trembling hands, she pushed back the thick mane of her hair. She had survived. It was more than she'd expected. The reason was most likely the money to come from her father's estate, but that didn't matter compared to the result.

She had stood up to Ahmad and lived to tell the tale. It felt good, more like her old self. She would probably pay for it eventually, but at least she'd had this moment.

Ismael had defied Ahmad as well. She hoped that he did not also have reason to regret it.

For long moments, Chloe sat staring at the wall, thinking of the two men. Ismael had appeared the stronger of the two in their exchange just now. Funny that she had never noticed. That strength came from inside, she thought, from knowledge of himself and the peace in his soul. Ahmad had neither of these things so was at the mercy of his impulses. Such a revelation didn't help, of course, when his impulse of the moment was to tie her to him with marriage.

What was she going to do? That frantic question beat into her brain. There was no answer that she could see. No possibility of escape existed. The one person who might be able to stop Ahmad was her stepfather, but any chance of contacting Imam in time was remote. He had not been home since her mother's death. His occasional messages were often weeks old by the time they arrived and getting word to him was almost impossible. Communication with northern border forces was never easy because of erratic troop movements and the general breakdown in government-sponsored services. Still it sometimes seemed to Chloe that he'd deserted them.

Regret for the lost opportunity offered by Wade Benedict touched her, but she refused to think of it. She wouldn't imagine what might have been or picture Wade Benedict waiting at the bazaar even now.

Or perhaps he wasn't there. Could be he had already given up, was walking back to his hotel, or packing his bag, arranging to be driven to the airport. Soon he would be gone and would never return.

She glanced around the small room, but there was no way out. The door was solid, the walls thick, the window made of small jalousie panes that opened only a few inches even when not stuck together by black paint. This wasn't the first time she'd been locked in, so all avenues had been explored and abandoned long ago. Even if she could leave the house, where could she go? There were safe houses operated by the RAWA, yes, but to be caught in the streets without a male guardian was as dangerous as what she faced from Ahmad. No, there was no way out.

Pushing to her feet, she moved to the water jug on the table beside her bed. She rinsed her mouth, feeling a cut on the inside of her cheek with her tongue. Wetting a cloth, she pressed its cool wetness to her face in hope of minimizing the swelling. Curling up on the bed then, she lay still and tried not to think at all as she waited for whatever was to come.

A soft call roused her. It was night, for she had

been staring into the darkness like a zombie for some time.

"Chloe? Are you all right?"

She sat up and swung her legs off the cot, moving toward the sliver of light that marked the locked door. "Treena? You should not be here. Ahmad is angry enough with you already."

"He has gone out. He has the key or I would have brought you food and water."

Chloe smiled with a shake of her head though she knew Treena couldn't see it. "You are so brave."

"I fear for you, sister of my heart. I am ordered to prepare a wedding feast."

"Then you must do it."

"How can you say that so calmly? I can't believe Ahmad is doing this thing! I could have sworn he would never..."

"What?" Chloe waited, a frown between her brows at the odd note in her stepsister's voice.

"Never marry."

"Because of his dedication to his cause?"

"Not really." Treena sighed, a worried sound in the darkness. "I love my brother. He was a sweet child, so sweet. I remember him dearly from when we were young together, the two of us left alone with our grandparents." A brushing noise came, as if her stepsister had leaned against the door. "I thought never to speak of what came after, of the thing that brought this hate and paranoia to him. Now I must, for I fear that he will kill you when the marriage contract is signed and he is your master. There will be nothing to stop him, Chloe, nothing.''

"I'm not sure what you're trying to say." Chloe pressed her forehead to the door, listening intently.

"It was the mullahs," Treena answered. "He was such a handsome little boy when our grandfather sent him away to school, such big bright eyes, sturdy body and gentle smile. Some of these religious teachers are holy men, but some...oh, some are not. Those who are most corrupt delight in making boys such as my brother fear and despise the love of women and the power it may have over a man. They enjoy training them to serve their needs in ways that...that make women unnecessary.''

"You are saying he has become a lover of men?''

"Not really, not in the way you mean. But he has no tenderness in him, not anymore. He cannot permit himself the love of a women from terror that she will drain his power, just as he was taught by those who see desire for a woman as competition for the adoration of their jealous God. He is consumed with rage as well, rage that he must feel desire at all, rage against those who hurt him, rage against his grandfather for allowing it to be done. Above all, he carries rage against his father who should have protected him but was away in the States getting married to one he could only hate.''

It was not a pretty description though it made sense in a dreadful kind of way. "So that's why your father gave in to him so easily, why he allowed him to take over.''

''From guilt and sorrow, yes.''

''But why hate my mother?''

''She was an enemy twice over in his eyes, both female and American, so a perfect target for his anger. To hate the mullahs would be a sacrilege. To despise his father and grandfather to whom he was so similar in nature was too much like hating himself. He had to have someone as a focus for all that rage.''

Chloe shook her head as compassion stirred inside her. For the first time, she has some small understanding of the pain she had glimpsed once or twice in Ahmad's face. ''People can't help the things that are done to them as children,'' she said slowly. ''But they can help what they choose to do later because of it.''

''Ahmad might have chosen differently, I think, if that had been all. There is also the matter of our father's second betrayal.''

''What do your mean?'' Her stepfather, Imam, was an honorable man. Chloe would have sworn it.

''He is not with the Taliban militia. He has no love of their policies or their methods, no heart for fighting their battles. After your mother was killed, he deserted. He has been seen with the opposition forces in the mountains.''

''He's fighting against the Taliban?''

''And against his son.''

What a terrible blow for Ahmad, Chloe thought, or

at least to his pride. ''Why haven't I been told this before?''

''My brother would as soon no one knew. But what about this marriage? You must not go through with it.''

Could she? If she could somehow manage to continue her teaching, could she force herself to take Ahmad as her husband with all the intimacy that implied? She didn't know, she really didn't.

''I seem to have no choice,'' she answered, staring into the dark.

''Even if he intends to kill you?''

''Surely he doesn't hate me that much? I've done nothing to him.''

''You are your mother's daughter. But it may be his notion of honor more than hatred. When the vows are spoken and your inheritance under his control, there will be nothing to prevent him from avenging what he considers to be yet another treachery.''

''You mean he...he will not want me? Even at first?'' It seemed vaguely possible, given what she'd heard.

''I fear he will not spare you this physical domination. Though whether from twisted desire or pure revenge is something only he can know. Still you have shamed him by your teaching. He cannot allow it to be seen that he has no control over the women in his house. Death is the ultimate control.''

''Dear God,'' Chloe whispered.

Treena was silent for long seconds. When she

spoke again, her voice held determination. "The American must be told."

"What can he do?" Chloe laughed without humor. "This is a family matter."

"I'm not sure. Still, he was sent by your father so stands as proxy for him. His presence added to this crisis, I think, since it forced Ahmad to take notice of your coming and going. The foreigner has a responsibility toward you."

"Ahmad won't see it that way," Chloe warned. "And he may consider any message to Wade Benedict as a greater betrayal than all the rest."

"He may, if he finds out."

"He will certainly guess if Benedict interferes." Privately she was sure that contact was useless. Regardless of what he'd said, it was doubtful he would risk a serious confrontation with Ahmad for the sake of a woman he barely knew.

"What Ahmad thinks of me matters little," Treena answered.

The apprehension that crept through Chloe's veins suggested otherwise. "But if he is so dangerous to me, will he spare you?"

"I am his sister."

"You are a woman."

"So I am, and a mother of daughters," Treena answered with resolution in her voice. "Some things must be done because they are right, not because they are safe."

5

The crash against the bedroom door brought Chloe around in a single wrench of tense muscles. She stood still where she had been pacing in the darkness. She'd heard no footsteps, no warning, yet it sounded as if someone was trying to break down the door. Before she could gather her thoughts for her next move, another blow struck the heavy panel. It swung inward, propelling a man into the room. He plunged to a halt then straightened, a tall, broad-shouldered silhouette against the light coming from the small anteroom beyond him.

Wade Benedict.

He'd actually come for her.

"Get your things and let's go," he said. "We don't have time to waste."

At that moment, Treena appeared behind him, coming from where she must have been standing back out of the way. "Hurry," she urged. "Ismael watches in case Ahmad returns or his guards discover that the American has eluded them. But he won't be able to stop them."

The noise had awakened the children in the next

bedroom where Treena and her husband slept, for they were crying. Their frightened screams, and the nursemaid's futile attempts to quiet them, made it hard to concentrate. They were also a reminder that she might never see them again if she went away now. These little girls, along with Treena and Ismael, were the only things she valued in the house. Everything else, the photo of her parents, the last of her mother's trinkets and jewelry, had been sold or destroyed. Regardless, she hesitated. She had been so doubtful that this man would come that she had made no final decision. Yet here it was upon her.

Hope was life and life was hope in her lexicon. If she could not expect to live long enough to fight for what she believed, then it was better to leave the battleground. In that case, there was no real choice.

"There's nothing I want to take," she said as she stepped toward Wade Benedict. "I'm ready."

"You will need this," Treena said, handing over the burqa that was draped across her arm.

"Yes, of course."

Shaking out the heavy folds, she lofted them above her head and let them settle around her while trying to position the mesh screen so she could see. She was still struggling with it when the commotion began at the front of the house. She went as motionless as a cloth-covered statue as she heard Ismael's voice, followed by that of Ahmad's in rasping command.

Her elbow was caught in a firm grasp and she was pulled in the general direction of the kitchen with its rear exit. She took a few blind steps, then bumped into Wade as he stopped abruptly. As she finally centered the small viewing window, she saw that they were in the center of the anteroom from which many of the rooms opened, and that the American was staring at the doorway that led into the *hajra*.

Chloe swung around in time to see Ahmad drag his brother-in-law into the room by the collar of his shirt, then give him a hard kick that landed on his maimed foot. Ismael groaned and would have fallen if Treena hadn't rushed forward to clutch his arm. As he regained his balance, she slid her hand down to hold his, keeping him close beside her.

Ahmad gave them a look of derision, then turned to Chloe. His gaze moved over the blue burqa that she wore. "Going somewhere, my bride?"

She refused to lower her eyes before him. "As you see."

"I think not." The purple mottling of rage suffused his face.

"There is only one way to stop me."

"My pleasure," he answered in a growl, then slapped a hand to the sheath on his belt. His knife flashed silver from hilt to curved tip as he drew it. Then he lunged forward.

Wade Benedict shouldered Chloe aside to face the bull-like charge. She whirled out of his way, coming up against the wall with her breath lodged in her throat. He had no weapon that she could see, no way to defend against that wickedly curved blade. She half expected to see him sliced open, but he sidestepped that first swiping blow. Circling Ahmad, he avoided the next slash with such smooth agility that he made it appear effortless. Swaying, leaping back from the plunging, roundhouse slices, he drew her stepbrother away from where Chloe stood. Then he skidded to a halt in a half crouch and whipped a hard arm behind his back. When he brought if forward again, a snub-nosed handgun was in his fist with the bore held rock-steady on Ahmad's chest.

Chloe put a hand to her mouth to stifle the sharp cry that rose inside her. Her gaze was not on the weapon, however, but on the dark wetness that cut across the front of Wade Benedict's black T-shirt, gleaming as it angled down to the waistband of his jeans.

Ahmad stopped. His eyes narrowed as he saw that his adversary was armed. Then his gaze fell to the evidence of injury. "This is interference that you are going to regret, American dog. I told you what would happen if you once more put your unclean hands on the woman who will be my wife."

"Your wife?" A sardonic smile curled the American's mouth. "Funny she didn't want to stick around for the wedding."

"Her desires make no difference."

"Lord, but you have a lot to learn about women."

"I know well how to treat bitches."

"That explains it," the American drawled. "Wrong breed."

Ahmad shifted the knife in his hand, as if itching for a target. Voice uneven, he said, "You show your ignorance now, for she has proved what kind she is by enticing my sister's husband with her evil wiles and woman's body. She used him to heap shame on my house. She holds him in such thrall that he even obeyed when told to send for you."

"No!" Treena cried.

The two men paid no attention. His gaze on Ahmad's face, the American asked, "And you still mean to marry the lady? Money has a way of overcoming principles, doesn't it?"

"So does revenge," Ahmad answered on a growl. "I guessed the vice in her, but now I am sure of it. I watched this house as Ismael left it on the way to your hotel, watched you arrive with him. For this added betrayal, the man who should have been as my brother will die with the woman when I am master of both her and her wealth."

"You needn't hold it against him, since I was on my way anyhow."

Even as Wade spoke, Treena released her grasp on her husband's hand and started toward her brother. "No," she said again.

"Don't!" Agonized supplication sounded in Ismael voice. He reached out to catch her arm, but she avoided him.

Ahmad barely glanced at his sister. "Fear not. You will also be avenged."

"I spit on your revenge," she said in a voice that

rang with fear and pride. "It was not my husband who helped Chloe deceive you, not his heart that wept tears for her future as your wife. I have been her accomplice and her savior. It was I who sent Ismael. It was I!"

Treena's advance had brought her within a few feet of Ahmad. Now he lifted his head, straightened slowly from his fighter's crouch to face his sister. His fingers gleamed white at the knuckles where they clenched his blade. "You," he repeated as if he'd never heard the word before. Then his face contorted with terrible, murderous anguish.

Terror engulfed Chloe. She opened her mouth to call out, but no sound emerged. Time slowed to a crawl. As she stepped forward with her gaze fastened on her stepsister's face, it was as if the air was as thick and viscous as oil. She saw Ahmad heave around and strike out in a sweeping, backhanded cut. The blade in his hand reflected a strange blue light in the dimness. It reached toward Treena. As it flashed past her throat, it left a red line in its wake.

Treena gave a bubbling sigh and lifted her hands to her neck. She began to fall like a marionette whose strings have been severed. Ismael caught her, stumbling to his knees as he eased her to the floor. A terrible cry left him as he covered his wife's hands with his own, pressing, trying to hold back the liquid red flow. It could not be done.

Treena caught his wrist as she gazed up at him. She spoke in a mouthing of words without sound.

"Our daughters, yes," Ismael said with strained comprehension in his voice. "To my mother. It will be done."

Treena tried again to speak.

"Yes, this day, my heart, my adored one. His reprisal shall not touch them. I promise it."

Treena didn't hear the vow in her husband's voice, or the love. Her valiant features went slack and her eyes began to glaze.

Ismael groaned, weaving where he knelt as he covered her eyes with his blood-red hand, smoothed down her slim shape to press his hand to her abdomen with its slight swell. Then he turned his head toward Ahmad. "You killed her," he whispered. Then he said again as wild sorrow infiltrated his voice. "You killed my wife, your sister. You killed my son, your nephew. What kind of honor, what vengeance, is this?"

Ahmad did not answer, didn't appear to hear for long seconds. He stood white-faced and slack-mouthed, staring at his sister on the floor with empty eyes. Then he whispered, almost to himself, "Her daughters. They are tainted as well."

Wade spoke then, his voice like iron as he pointed the handgun at Ahmad. "Hands up. Now. Where I can see them."

Ahmad shook his head like a boxer recovering from a knockout punch. As he looked at the American, recognition of his position came into his face, tightening the skin across the heavy bones. Slowly he obeyed the order, but the enmity in his face was frightening to see.

"Good. Now back up, nice and easy, until you're inside the room behind you."

It was a storeroom, and a good choice, Chloe thought as she fought the black horror that gripped her. The lock on her own room was broken, the largest chamber that Ahmad had taken as his own was more likely to have a weapon stashed away somewhere inside, and he could not be allowed near Treena's daughters. With a dazed glance at Wade, she said, "The key..."

"Get it."

Ahmad had it, of course, since he enjoyed control of all the rooms and their contents. She could smell his acrid sweat, nauseating and animalistic, as she moved closer to him. Fearful that he would try to grab her, she was careful not to block the firing path. She reached out from as far away as possible to snag the metal key ring from his belt, then waited until Wade motioned him into the storeroom.

"For this, you will surely die," Ahmad said as he obeyed the gesture. "You cannot escape your fate, just as my sister could not escape hers. I will finish you and all your tribe."

"You can try."

Wade moved close enough to catch the door and slam it shut, keeping his shoulder against it. Chloe inserted the key in the old-fashioned lock and turned it. Then she stepped back as if her stepbrother might be able to reach through the solid wood.

"Go," Wade said in low command as he nodded toward the doorway that led back into the *hajra.* "Move it."

It was necessary; she could see that. Still, she couldn't prevent herself from turning toward where Ismael still sat rocking his wife's lifeless body as if nothing else existed in his world. Then she looked toward the far bedroom where the children still cried without end.

"You can't help her," Wade said, his voice rough with something that had the sound of understanding. "You can't help any of them."

She glanced at him, noting almost unconsciously the pale line around his mouth and the haunted pain that darkened his eyes. "I know," she whispered, her own unbearable grief apparent in that soft acknowledgment.

"Then let's get out of here while we still can."

He gave her no opportunity to argue, but clamped an arm around her waist and swept her from the room. She didn't resist but moved beside him from the house and out into the street.

The night had the sooty blackness of the hour after moonset. It didn't seem to bother Wade. He paused long enough to search the area around him with a hard gaze, then started down the dusty street.

A yell rang out, followed by gunshots. Dust geysers

kicked up just behind them. Wade whipped around to
return the fire, even as they broke into a run.

"Ahmad must have had men with him earlier,"
Chloe said, her voice jerky with her effort to keep up
with Wade's long strides.

"Good guess." He caught her arm, increasing her
pace, even as he fired again. "Had to have been a
small detail or we'd have been goners by now."

"Maybe only Zahir, a friend of his." The random
pattern of the rounds and apparent lack of pursuit
made it seem likely.

"Yeah, we met."

"He'll release Ahmad."

"Better than coming after us."

The shots trailed to a halt, either from the discour-
agement Wade had offered or because they were out
of range. As they reached the middle of the next
block, he swung into a narrow, rutted alleyway that
was bordered by mud walls overhung by palms and
bougainvillea. Chloe could see a vehicle sitting in the
dark at its far end. They raced toward it. Some fifty
yards away, Wade pulled up and motioned to her to
stay put. She nodded her understanding even as she
fought to catch her breath. He approached the older
model Volvo on a careful trajectory.

Abruptly something burst out of a mass of wild
grape just beyond the car's left fender. Wade Benedict
hugged the wall, swinging his head in her direction
as if to make certain she was doing the same. She
shook her head, motioning toward the feral cat that

had stopped to look back at him from under the car's rear bumper. He made a low sound of disgust, then moved on again.

Chloe held her breath as she saw him bend to look in at the front window. She saw him stiffen. After a second, he opened the door and reached inside at an awkward angle to turn the key. She heard a click, but the ignition didn't engage. He closed the door then walked quickly back to where she stood.

"What is it?"

"Dead. Driver and car."

"I don't..."

"My transport. The driver had instructions to wait for us. Now we don't have to wonder why Ahmad was a little slow reaching the house."

She pressed her lips together until they hurt, closing her eyes for a second. When she thought she could speak without her voice shaking, she asked, "What now?"

"Guess." As he offered that laconic comment, he turned to put his back to the wall behind them as if he intended to hold it up.

"I have no idea. You said everything was arranged, that it would be easy, no problem."

"The arrangements were for two days ago. I changed them over to this morning because you said that's how long it would take on your end. You missed that deadline, too. So here we are."

A chill moved over her. "You're saying we're on our own?"

"And on foot."

It wasn't what she wanted to hear. "You and I, the two of us."

"You were expecting maybe the Green Berets and a Bell & Howell to zip you out to a waiting sub?"

"I don't. I mean, I just thought this rescue, or whatever you want to call it, would have a support team."

"So it did. Favors were called in and people paid off. There were a couple of places reserved in a truck convoy heading for the Pakistan border and on to the international airport at Rawalpindi. But that was then and this is now. They pulled out when you didn't show."

"Still you came when Treena sent for you?"

"I promised John."

She turned bodily to stare at him through the screen over her eyes, half-afraid there was something more, something about his reasons that she didn't know.

His eyelashes rested on top of his cheekbones and his hands pressed back against the wall behind him. She could hear his breathing, fast and shallow, as if against the bite of pain. Freeing a hand, she put out her fingers and touched the warm, sticky wetness at his waistline.

"Idiot," she exclaimed. "You're bleeding to death, and we stand here talking. What were you thinking?"

"That you have more to say for yourself now than when I first saw you," he answered with the ghost of a laugh.

"As if it matters!" Reaching up under her burqa,

she removed the long, veil-like scarf that covered her hair. She made a small tear with her teeth, then ripped the cloth in half and folded it into a long pad. Wrapping this into the remaining length, she freed her arms then pressed the makeshift bandage to Wade's side, circling his waist with the free ends.

He grunted a little as she pulled them tight to knot them. "Very efficient."

"I hope it does some good."

"Can't hurt. Thanks."

His breath felt warm against the top of her head, even through her burqa, as she bent to check her handiwork in the dark. The mild and almost disinterested sound of his voice troubled her since it seemed to indicate that he was either light-headed from blood loss or drifting into a form of shock. "It's nothing." She slipped her arm around his waist with a brusque movement, then turned him toward the far end of the alley beyond the dark Volvo. "Come, we have to find shelter."

"You have a plan?"

"I know where I may be able to find help, but it's several blocks. Can you make it?" He was too tall for her to support very well, but he seemed able to stand well enough. As he shifted his arm that she'd draped over her shoulder, his fingers dangled against the swell of her breast.

"I can if you can."

She thought there was humor in his voice, as if either her annoyance or her efforts to take up the slack in the rescue effort amused him in some way. There was nothing funny about it to her. She had to find medical attention for him, and soon.

Chloe guided the American past the Volvo without looking at it, then down one block and over another. From there, she veered into a path that led through the vegetable garden of an elderly couple she knew, then along the back side of a warehouse used to store sheep's wool and lambskins. The two of them came out onto a boulevard lined with compounds whose big houses were crowded with shade and fruit trees and surrounded by fences. Some were of mud or stone, some of iron that had been installed during Victoria's reign. It was an exclusive area, silent and aloof in its screened isolation, though jasmine vines and orange trees shared their scents with passersby.

Chloe's progress slowed as she stumbled with Wade from one patch of shadow to another, stopping for every noise and every passing vehicle, investigating every cross street before venturing to the other side. The entire night began to seem surreal, as if she might also be in some form of shock. That she was now dependent on the man who leaned so heavily against her was so unbelievable that it was hard to grasp. She wasn't sure where she was going or what she was going to do when she got there, had nothing with her except the clothes she wore. All she knew was that she had to keep walking, keep moving because to stop could mean the end of everything.

Ahead of them lay another wide intersection. At

one time, there had been a working stoplight, but now
it dangled uselessly on its wires so that crossing it
could be a distinct hazard here where every man felt
the right of way was his to take. She caught the gleam
of headlights as she approached. Narrowing her eyes
to peer behind them, she recognized a slow-moving
patrol car.

She swung back the way they had come, glancing
around in swift search of cover. There was none, at
least nothing that they could reach in time. The nearest alley was a block back behind them; a tall iron
fence set on a low wall of stone blocked off the closest screen of shrubbery. Still, she had to do something
fast.

There was only one reason for a man and woman
to be seen on the streets together in violation of curfew. It was prohibited and incredibly lewd, but more
acceptable to male officialdom than a man and
woman unrelated and unmarried being caught alone
together at night.

Dragging Wade into a patch of deep shadow, she
pushed him into place with his back to the fence. She
snatched up the hem of her burqa and skirt beneath,
raising them to her waist as she plastered herself
against him from her breasts to her knees. Galvanized
by the rumble of the patrol car's engine coming
closer, she lifted her arms behind his head and applied
pressure until he bent and hid his beardless face in
the folds of blue cloth that draped against her neck.

Brightness from the headlights struck the fence

rails beside them. The car stopped at the cross street and did not move on, as if the occupants had spotted them. This was the moment of greatest danger, when the police must decide whether to stop and punish a prostitute apparently servicing a client in this quiet neighborhood or move on and leave them in peace. It could go either way, for this was a respectable and affluent area where such things were not done, but it was also possible that the man enjoying her might be a resident of some influence. With a low moan of fear, Chloe moved against the man she held, desperately grinding her hips.

Then she felt him shift his feet to a wider, lower stance. He lifted one arm around her waist to support her and reached with the other hand to clasp her hip. He kneaded it as if in appreciation for the firm, resilient flesh, then smoothed down along her leg until he could lift her knee and settle the naked softness at the juncture of her thighs more completely over his groin.

A shiver of purest pleasure gripped her, spreading in a radiating wave from the center of her being to every inch of her body. The sensation was stunning in its intensity, shocking beyond imagining at such an inappropriate time and place. She wasn't alone in her reaction, either, for Wade's grasp tightened and he stopped breathing. At the same time, she felt distinctly the sudden increase of heat and hardness where they were most closely crushed together.

She stiffened, tightening her arms around him.

"Don't," she said in something near panic. "I was just trying to... I mean I only wanted..."

"I know," he murmured against her ear. "The idea is cooperation."

"Don't help so much!"

"I'm trying, but...there's not a lot I can do about it."

The rich timbre of his voice moved over her like a caress. She could feel her nipples tightening, stinging a little where they drove into the muscled planes of his chest. The layers of cloth between them seemed an unbearable impediment, and she was miserably aware of a strong urge to know what it would feel like to be pressed against him with nothing separating them except air and human will.

It was just physical reaction, she told herself a little wildly. That was all, had to be all. She was a normal woman who had been deprived of sensual gratification. That she hadn't missed it until now was an irony she might find funny someday. But not now. Not now.

"You'd better move a little more," he offered. "The patrol are gawking like a couple of hayseeds at a sideshow."

She jerked back automatically, but he immediately pulled her close again.

"There you go, like that," he answered. "You'll get the hang of it in a minute."

A small sound of distress left her, but she knew that he was right and they needed to pretend. As she moved against him again, she whispered, "I don't believe you're badly hurt at all."

"Some things are guaranteed to revive a man." He shuddered, grasping her thigh. "But I swear I ache all over, and I'm so weak in the knees right now that the only thing holding me up is this fence and a truly desperate need to see what you're going to do next."

"Nothing!"

"Now that's a shame."

The amusement in his voice had a strained edge, she thought, as if his teasing might be a defense against other thoughts, other needs. The urge to put a stop to it united inside her with exasperation and perversity until it became an ungovernable impulse. Turning her head, positioning the mesh of her burqa at the level of her mouth with an experienced movement of her chin, she caught the hair at the back of his neck in her clenched fingers to angle his head toward her. Then she pressed her mouth to his.

He certainly cooperated; there was no doubt about that. He slanted his lips to match the cool contours of hers from corner to corner, moving them in blind exploration. Their surfaces were smooth and warm, and sweet in a way she'd never experienced, never dreamed. The abrasion of the crocheted screen between them was both irritant and incitement. The moist and delicate probe of his tongue, tracing around and through the small, square spaces between the thread bars, touching the line where her lips came together only at intervals, brought the tingling need to tear away the barrier for deeper, more positive contact. She could feel every suppressed instinct and desire she'd ever had rushing through her, seeking an outlet. She was lost in the sensation, uncaring of where she was or what she should be doing. It was pleasure and terror and the remedy for both, the only possible antidote for the horror of violence and pain she had witnessed. And nothing had ever been so compelling in her entire life, nothing so impossible to resist.

6

The sound of the police car behind them changed as it began to roll again. The glow of the headlights shifted, moving along the fence railings and away from them down the cross street. Wade took a firm grip on his better intentions and lifted his mouth from Chloe Madison's lips. Bracing against the fence, he released her knee and raised his hands to clasp her shoulders and put her away from him. Then he did his best to ease upright without calling attention to the quivering of his thighs or the uncomfortable lump under the zipper of his jeans.

She stepped back and let the damn tablecloth she wore fall into place again, straightening its folds the way some women might try to tidy their hair after that kind of mind-blowing kiss. She didn't look at him, which probably wasn't surprising. The truly amazing thing was that she hadn't clobbered him.

He couldn't remember the last time he'd come so close to losing it. That pretense of lust combined with virginal sweetness had been mind-blowing. She had no idea what she'd been doing to him, he thought.

Sheer instinct and native talent had moved her. It had certainly been enough to rouse his interest.

She'd felt so good, so right. Concentrating on incoming sensations had allowed him to forget for a few seconds his involvement in the death of another woman. It would have been easy, so fatally easy, to take over, take matters where she really didn't want them to go in his need to lose himself in her. Lust was the greatest medicine in the world for pain and self-directed anger.

As she reached for his arm, he let her take it and settle it over her shoulders once more. He kept a little distance between them, however, so his thigh wouldn't be pressed quite so disturbingly against her hip. She set out with firm, purposeful strides, and he matched her pace, walking like a prize bull to market toward wherever she was going and whatever she had in store for him.

They came upon the house not long afterward. A bungalow like a dozen others they'd passed, it was set back behind walls of mud plastered over with molting stucco. Nothing moved under the trees that surrounded the house, and its windows, under deep eaves and wide verandas, showed no lights. Chloe followed the wall until it made a right angle, then moved on a few more yards until they came to a side gate. As she sank to her knees, Wade felt his heart lurch. Then she searched under a pile of stones covered with ivy and pulled out a key.

Moments later, they were skirting the side of the

house on a path that looked as if it might take them to a back entrance. They passed a circle of shrubs, a set of wicker lawn furniture arranged as if for some Victorian tea party, and an arbor with a white, sweet-scented vine tumbling over it. As they neared a wood-pile half-hidden under some kind of creeper, a night creature squeaked in alarm, then shot from under it. The streaking flight brought Wade around with a jerk that sent pain stabbing into his side and startled a curse from him.

"Mongoose."

Chloe's whisper was even, almost offhand. Either she had far too much control over her reactions or was so close to the breaking point that nothing had the power to make her jump. Wade thought it was probably the last. Lord knew she'd seen enough to try anybody's soul, especially this evening.

The events that had taken place in the house where she'd lived with her stepbrother were too fresh, too vivid in his mind. He shoved them away with an effort. He'd deal with them later, when time and distance had taken the edge off. Too many other things required his attention now, such as staying upright and alert enough to deal with any further surprises.

"Are you all right?"

"Yeah. Sure." Or at least he would be one day.

"Only a little more to go."

"Lead on," he said, keeping it light, keeping it cool. Keeping it together.

"Your side is really hurting, isn't it?"

She had it wrong, but her concern still touched him. "I'm fine."

"Sure you are," she returned in disbelief.

God above, but what if she'd died back there instead of her stepsister, paying the price for his lack of foresight. Losing John's daughter might have been more than he could take. Against his will, he saw again the flash of the knife, the blood. How could he have guessed such a thing would happen? How could he have expected any man, even a fanatic like Ahmad, to turn on his own flesh and blood. It was so unnatural that it was almost impossible to guard against it.

Don't think about it, he warned himself. Don't get lost in how or why, or what might have gone differently. Don't, please God, start comparing those few fatal seconds to the time with the oilman's wife, even if both had ended with a woman dying who should have lived. No, he wouldn't analyze or agonize, not yet.

In tones harsher than intended, he asked, "So are we going to knock or just stand here all night?"

"Anxious to find a place to sit down, are you? Or maybe lie down?"

"Either one will do." What he really wanted was to get her inside, out of sight, out of obvious danger.

"Right. There's a night watchman around somewhere. He should be checking on us at any second."

From the darkness in front of them came the noise of a man clearing his throat, a gravelly rasp that suggested age and maybe smoke-damaged lungs. He stepped into view then, flicking on a small flashlight at the same time so its light puddled around his feet. His face was like ancient wrinkled leather with his eyes set in the folds like jet beads. A gray rag of a beard dangled from his chin and his faded clothes looked as if he slept in them regularly. Regardless, the assault rifle tucked under his arm was polished by years of care and handling.

The old man played the flashlight over their faces with a brief query that was incomprehensible to Wade, though Chloe seemed to understand it well enough. Her greeting was pleasant and she stood still, barely squinting under the bright scrutiny.

"Ah, the American lady," the watchman exclaimed with warmth edging into his voice. "Welcome again to this house. And to the infidel also."

So much for finding a safe place to go to ground, Wade thought in moody silence. He hoped the old man was trustworthy, because he obviously knew Chloe and had heard of him. Not that Wade meant to depend on his discretion. He'd keep his eyes open just as he had on the little stroll that had brought them here.

Chloe explained their problem in a few short sentences. The watchman tipped his head as if pondering the options open to him. Then he gestured for them to follow and led the way into the house.

They wound their way through what appeared to be a storeroom, some brand of butler's pantry and a dining room. Crossing an antechamber, they emerged finally in a large common room where a fountain bubbled in a stone basin set into the floor of mosaic tiles and overstuffed furniture held down the edges of a Bakhora rug. The old man folded himself in half as he indicated the seating, then left them there.

Wade didn't much care for the setup. He looked at Chloe with raised brows.

"We wait," she said in answer to that unspoken query.

"For what?"

"Whatever comes. Patience is an Islamic virtue, one that you'd have to cultivate if you lived here."

He doubted it, but didn't argue since he could hear the brittle sound of strained nerves and exhaustion in her voice. It was no great surprise to see her move to an ottoman and drop down onto its cushioned surface.

"Sit down," she suggested, waving at the chair next to it. "Please. Before you fall down."

He perched on the edge of the sofa. Sinking into its soft maroon leather was a great temptation, but he didn't intend to get too comfortable in a place that he might have to leave on short notice.

The minutes slipped past. The water music of the fountain was soothing but served to mask sound. Wade thought he could hear the ticking of a large clock from the next room and also voices from some more distant area, maybe down the corridor where the watchman had disappeared. He'd have been more wary except that the dominant one sounded female.

Then the slapping of sandals on tile came toward them. A woman materialized out of the dim recesses of the house. Rotund, wearing a caftan of some silky fabric in purple and green, a profusion of clinking silver jewelry, and with her hair streaming around her in wild salt-and-pepper strands, she looked like an exotic witch.

"Forgive me for keeping you waiting. But fear not. I've made preparations, given instructions and all is in hand."

"Instructions for what?" Wade asked as he climbed slowly to his feet. His knees still worked, even if they did feel like overcooked spaghetti.

"For your care, tall one," the woman answered with a smile.

"And you are?"

It was Chloe who answered his question, leaving her ottoman and moving to stand close beside him as if to keep him from doing anything foolish. "This is Ayla, a friend who is also a widow."

"Yes, yes, it happens when twenty million men are killed in twenty years. But I do not repine. War is a horrible thing but may bring good on occasion."

It sounded as if she didn't exactly miss her husband, Wade thought with a glance at Chloe.

She nodded, as if anxious for him to understand and cooperate. "Ayla opens her home as a school, among other things. It's best that you know little more than this."

Wade wondered if they really suspected that he

might blab about the widow's activities if he was arrested. They had no idea how unlikely that would be.

"All right then?" the woman named Ayla asked as he fell silent. She gestured toward the corridor and stepped back. "This way."

Chloe moved to stand beside Ayla. He remained where he was, gazing from one to the other in perplexity as he waited for someone to lead the way.

"Please," their hostess said with another wave toward the dark corridor.

It flashed through his mind that a trap lay somewhere out of sight. Then he dismissed the idea as ridiculous. "Right," he said with a gesture for them to precede him. "Whatever you say."

"The way is to the left, two doors down."

He inclined his head. "After you."

"No, no, Wade Shah, after you."

The title of respect, a little like saying "sir," was really too much but gave him an inkling of the problem. He could feel his neck growing hot as he said, "Ladies first. At least that's how I was brought up."

"You are very kind, but I must insist."

"So do I." Wade folded his arms over his chest.

"You don't understand," Chloe said. "It's the custom for men to go first."

He'd noticed men striding along the street with women trailing after them, but he didn't intend to make a habit of it. "I do understand," he corrected, "but it's not the way we do things where I come from, and my Benedict ancestors would spin in their graves if I forgot it.''

"But you went ahead of me in the street earlier."

"Back there was different. It was dangerous for you to go first."

"Circumstances change the rules then?"

"Only when it comes to safety. Don't try to confuse the issue by comparing that time to this, because it's not the same thing. Now the two of you can go first or we can stand here for what's left of the night. It's all the same to me."

"You're being ridiculous," she said in controlled anger.

She was probably right, but this was one thing he was going to do his way. He only watched her without answering.

"What is wrong?" the widow asked, looking from one to the other of them as if trying to guess at the subject of their exchange in a language she apparently had trouble understanding.

"He is being polite," Chloe told her with a dark glance in his direction. "In his own stubborn American way. It may be best to humor him."

"How so?" The widow's frown deepened.

"Like this," Chloe said, and led the way down the corridor with her head at a regal angle.

The widow still seemed confused and reluctant until Wade took her arm and moved her bodily along with him. She got the idea, finally. Which was just as well, since she released herself and took his arm to support him after the first few steps.

Any satisfaction he might have felt was short-lived. The room they entered looked like a hospital unit. There was a high bed with a length of plastic covering the white sheets, gooseneck lamp, sink with running water in the corner, and rolling table with medical supplies laid out in an orderly row. Completely missing from the setup, so far as he could see, was any trace of tetanus serum or antibiotics. He hoped like hell that Ahmad kept his knife clean.

"Sit here on the bed, if you please," the widow said to him. As he levered himself up onto the high mattress, she turned to Chloe. "Shall I put in the sutures, or will you?"

Indecision hovered in Chloe's face. "It may be better if I do it," she answered finally. "You can always take over if it's more than I can manage."

"Let me get this straight," Wade asked, just to be sure he had the gist of the exchange in Pashtu between the women. "One of you is going to sew me up?"

"We can't risk going to a hospital since we don't know what has happened with Ahmad or who may be searching for you. Anyway, the care you'd have here may actually be safer. This isn't exactly a throwaway society where disposable needles hit the trash every two seconds."

"I noticed," he said dryly.

"Ayla's husband was a physician and this was part

of his private clinic where she used to assist him before the Taliban came. She can take care of you now, if you prefer.''

"I don't think I do,'' he answered. It was probably stupid but, all things considered, he'd rather put himself in the hands of someone he knew.

"Good. She has other arrangements to make. We must be gone from here before daylight.''

He blew out a short, hard breath, then gave a firm nod. "Right. Let's do it.''

"Yes.'' She signaled an okay to the widow where she hovered near the door. Ayla whisked herself from the room with more grace and dispatch then her round shape suggested. Chloe moved to close the window blinds then, and bring the lamp closer. She placed a trash can at the bed's edge, then stepped nearer to where he sat on the mattress.

For a moment, Wade was sure she had no idea where to start. Then she flexed her fingers and shook them as if to release tension. With only a brief glance that didn't quite connect with his eyes, she reached around him and began to loosen the scarf she'd applied as bandaging.

She had to lean over his knees so her pelvis pressed against them. It was interesting for him, but bound to be uncomfortable for her. With a hand at her waist, he moved her back a little as he spread his thighs, then guided her into the opening.

She was stiff and unresponsive for a long moment. Her gaze through the mesh over her eyes was questioning. Abruptly he realized that the position was a copy of the one they'd shared earlier. That memory flared like a hot coal in his mind, though he tamped it down with an effort. "Just trying to help."

She made no replay, but went back to her job.

Wade sat still while trying to breathe normally against the rise of pain in the gash as pressure was released. He could feel the warm ooze of fluid again and the beginning of a throbbing ache that he knew would get worse before it got better. Then as she pulled free one end of the cloth that was stiff with drying blood, he stifled a gasp.

She sent him an upward glance. "Sorry."

He needed a distraction. The combination of Chloe's nearness and what was happening at his waistline wasn't helping his equilibrium. His strongest impulse at this moment was to lean forward and gather her into his arms, then lie back on the bed with her and drift into sleep.

Tweaking a fold of her burqa that was draped over his knee between two fingers, he said. "Your friend, the widow, didn't seem to mind me seeing her face. How come you're still wearing this tablecloth?"

"My hair would be exposed without my scarf. Besides, the front of my skirt is stained with your blood."

"Ayla's hair isn't covered."

"This is her home and she has no male relatives to care."

"You're also unattached now," he pointed out in

his most reasonable tone. ''Anyway, you'll probably never see any of these people again once we leave here. What does it matter if they know we've been a little closer together than might be acceptable?''

Carefully she peeled away another section of make-shift bandaging that was stuck like glue. ''We aren't gone yet, and we need their support. Ignoring their conventions isn't the best way to get it. And if we give them proof of wrongdoing then are taken by the police, we could be executed for...for what they think we have done.''

''We'd be innocent.''

''Tell that to mullahs who pass sentence.''

''You're sure it's not something else?''

''Such as?''

''Maybe a way to hide in plain sight?''

Her movements stilled. Resentment, or something near it, flashed at him from behind her little screen. ''From what?''

''I'm not sure. Unwanted attention maybe?''

''Yours, I suppose.'' The comment was dry.

''Or any other man's.''

''Brilliant deduction,'' she said in cool irony, ''and isn't it nice how well it matches Taliban edicts?''

She unwound the last of the scarf and tossed it aside as she finished speaking. It might have been an accident that she avoided his gaze by turning away to wash her hands, but he didn't think so. If the burqa wasn't a personal choice, then he could think of only one reason why she might cling to it.

He didn't much care for where that idea led him. Calling her on it didn't seem like much of a plan, however. If she was thinking of staying here, in spite of everything, then there had to be a better way to put a stop to it. She didn't respond to pressure tactics too well, as far as he could see.

Chloe dried her hands, then turned to him again. Stepping close, she griped the fullness of his T-shirt and began tugging the knit fabric from his jeans, a little here, a little there. The slow process as she tried to keep from hurting him was not comfortable. She was driving him crazy by inches.

Wade put his hands on hers to stop her. Then he grasped the back of his shirt and pulled it free of the long slash in his side in a single excruciating movement. While his body was still numb with the shock, he stripped the bloody mess off over his head.

"That must have hurt." She took the shirt and dropped it into the trash.

"Get it over and done with, that's my motto," he said, and immediately clamped his teeth together to keep them from chattering as he shuddered with reaction.

"So macho. You do know you've made it bleed worse than ever."

"Never mind. Just get started."

"There's no anesthetic," she said in doubtful tones. "I'll try to be as quick as I can."

"Fine. Just don't reassure me anymore, will you? Or I may back out altogether."

"You can't!"

Her lack of tact was, he thought, a measure of her concern. He must be worse off than he'd thought, not that he wanted to inspect the damage. In his driest tone, he said, "That was a joke. Sort of."

Reproof was in the glance she flung in his direction, he suspected, though he couldn't be sure because of the damn screen. The barrier was absolutely maddening, almost more so than the pain in his side. He had to fight a wild need to bodily drag all that extra cloth off her. As a substitute, he made a silent vow to talk her out of it as soon as he could manage it.

He realized after a second that she hadn't looked away from him. She stood unmoving, her gaze focused on his chest and shoulders. As the seconds ticked past, it seemed he could feel it on his skin. Simple reaction made his flat nipples tighten into knots.

"What?" he asked, unexpected self-consciousness making his voice sharp. "You never saw a half-naked man before?"

"No. At least... No."

"Never? Not even in the States?"

"At the swimming pool and the beach." She gave a slight shake of her head. "They were only boys."

It was a nice distinction, one he might appreciate at another time. For now, all he could think of was the obvious question raised by her admission. He opened his mouth to ask it, then closed it again.

Whether she was still a virgin, technically or otherwise, was none of his business.

Something of his thoughts must have shown on his face, for she backed away a step. Then she turned abruptly toward the sink to scrub her hands again.

The old watchman appeared at that moment. He carried a pot of water from which steam rose to wet his face. He said something to Chloe, but his voice was so low and rasping that Wade didn't catch it. Then he set down the pot, sent Wade a look of pity that needed no translation, and went away again.

"He wanted to know if he should hold me down?" Wade asked in a lame attempt at humor.

"He said a car will arrive shortly to take us to a safer place," she answered as she began to remove sterile scissors and needles from the scalding water with a pair of tongs. "The driver should be here by the time we're done." She paused. "I don't suppose there's anything you absolutely must have from your hotel?"

He thought of the satellite cell phone in his suitcase. Nat would be waiting for a report. There were arrangements that still could be made, given enough time. Yet it seemed the best way to make sure that Chloe got out of the country was to let her call the shots. She hadn't done badly thus far. "Nothing," he answered. "At least nothing important enough to risk going after."

"Good. That's good."

Turning from the instrument table, she indicated

that she was ready. Wade lay down on the plastic sheet. As she lifted his feet to the mattress, he rolled to his side, facing her. He bent his arm and rested his head on it, making himself as comfortable as possible. Then he closed his eyes.

The smell of some strong, old-fashioned soap filled his nose as he breathed deep, trying to relax. Seconds later, he felt the heat of a wet cloth moving over his bare skin. It was soothing as it passed over sensitized nerves, wiped away the itch of dried blood. He thought she followed the path of the cloth with her fingers, trailing them over the muscles of his abdomen and along the dip of his waist to his back. Whether from that touch or because of cool air brushing over damp skin as she shifted, he broke out in a rash of goose bumps along his backbone and the tops of his shoulders.

All pleasure in the experience suddenly vanished as she began to clean the wound, making a thorough job of it. It was a drastic reminder of what would come next.

The first piercing stab of the needle was the worst. Wade went rigid, feeling it in every atom of his being. Then he forced his mind to let go of the pain. He breathed deep, not fighting it but allowing it to flow through his body and away from him. After that, he lay perfectly still while she fastened his flesh back together like sewing a ripped seam.

Finally it was done. He was strapped up again with enough gauze and tape to wrap a mummy. The widow

Ayla returned for this last stage, bringing with her glasses of hot sweet tea for both him and Chloe. When he had drunk down this primitive form of glucose, she and Chloe pulled a baggy shirt with a deep neck slit and no buttons on over his head so he would put no strain on his stitches. Then they left him alone to exchange his jeans for a pair of khaki pants that looked like a designer knockoff. No underwear was provided to take the place of his blood-caked briefs. He raised a brow, but ignored the oversight since complaining didn't seem worth the effort.

The tea should have been sweeter and stronger. He was sweating by the time he was dressed, and needed help to walk across the room to the door. He said a polite and fairly coherent thank-you to the widow for her help and hospitality, or thought he did, then accepted the support of both Chloe and the watchman to the waiting car. The driver held the door open, and Wade slid gratefully onto the seat.

After that, everything came at him in flashes, like photo slides blinking one after the other across a screen. There was a gate that they rolled through without stopping. A fortress with gun-toting guards posted on the roof. A young woman with voluptuous breasts emphasized by a bodice embroidered with blue flowers and carrying a toddler on her hip. A pallet filled with down in a room with no windows. A taste of bread and chicken broth swallowed in darkness. Quiet, peace and sleep.

The dreams came then. Never quite the same, they

were also never really different. Sometimes the oilman's wife died from a knife slash to the throat instead of gunfire. Other times, it was Chloe who died. Or Ayla. Or the woman with the blue rose bodice. Or the stepsister whose children cried in the night. All the visions were filled with endless blood and pain. And in all of them, he was running, running, but unable to stop what was coming, yelling warnings that could not be heard.

Now and then, someone would come and lie down beside him, someone with a woman's soft body and sweet, clean scent. She held him against her, smoothing her hands over his shoulders and down his back, or else she would turn her back against him and allow him to hold her. She didn't move, even when his lax fingers cupped her breast as they fell naturally into place over her.

He knew the woman in his dreams, knew the shape and feel of her body and the balm of her touch. Knew her name and the secrets of her mind. He wanted her, needed her with a raw desperation that ate at him, clawing into his side. He was aware, with the wisdom of dreams, that to say so, to speak her name, would be to make her disappear. So he was silent. And while she was there, the nightmares remained at bay, as if she had some magic to banish them and allow him to sleep.

But often he woke alone, staring into the dark with his clothes wet with sweat and thirst like an ache in his throat. In those few lucid moments, he realized that his companion of the night was gone, and wondered if delirium had played tricks on him and Chloe had never been there at all.

7

"How long have we been here?"

Chloe turned quickly at the low-voiced question. Wade was watching her, his gaze troubled yet clear. She hadn't realized he was awake. Leaving the pallet she'd been straightening, she took the few steps that separated their sleeping places and went to one knee beside him. "Not quite forty-eight hours," she answered, reaching automatically to lay her fingers on his forehead. "You seem better this morning."

His smile had a rueful twist. "I've felt worse."

"I think your fever is lower."

"Could be."

She removed her hand and sat back. There was a pause. His gaze flicked over the veil-like scarf that covered her hair and the lower portion of her face, then returned to her eyes. All the things that had passed between them hovered unspoken. She thought that he meant to make some comment, and waited for it, trying to decide what she'd say.

It had not been an easy time. She'd slept only in snatches and mostly at his side since that was the only way he remained calm. Some of the men in the compound had taken care of his more personal needs, but she had sponged him to keep down the fever, given him water and spoon-fed him at intervals around the clock. She'd listened to his disjointed ramblings and held him with almost guilty closeness. Never had she known a male as she knew this one, though she really didn't know him at all.

Apparently he was as reluctant to bring things out into the open as she was. He glanced beyond her shoulder for a second before he spoke again.

"What's been going on? Have I missed anything?"

She weighed her answer, trying to decide if he was well enough to hear it. He needed to be, and soon. They couldn't stay where they were much longer. "The police are looking for you," she said finally. "You are accused of abducting me from my stepbrother's house."

"Figures."

"Yes. Ahmad is hiding the fact that I left of my own will and with a strange man. That leaves marriage as an open option should I be returned to him. Naturally he can pretend to discover my crime afterward as an excuse for getting rid of me."

"Once he's gained control of the money from your dad."

"Exactly." She hesitated, then added, "The police also think you killed my stepsister when she tried to stop this kidnapping."

The little color he had receded from under his suntanned features. "What about her husband? Is he saying nothing?"

"It seems so."

"Meaning?"

It was a question she'd been trying to answer for herself without much success. "Ismael loved her, I'm sure of that much. He may be protecting his children, since he knows that Ahmad will make them orphans if he finds out the extent of his cooperation with her activities. Only his mother would be available to look after the girls then. Ahmad could, and probably would, take them from her."

"You think he'd really kill kids?"

"Who can say?" she answered with a tired sigh. "They may be literally the children of a she-goat in his mind, and therefore tainted. But he could also take them to be brought up as good little Muslim girls by the grandmother and grandfather who raised him, and that would be merely a different kind of death." Her stepfather, Imam, might have intervened, since he was still officially head of the household. But his connection with the opposition forces in the hills made him a traitor who could be shot on sight if he left their mountain stronghold.

"This stepbrother of yours is psychotic," Wade said in disgust.

"You could say so. Others might call him devout and a good patriot, though extreme. He's declared a jihad against you."

Wade lifted a brow. "I thought that was some kind of holy war."

"Yes, though it's broad enough to include war against any infidel. It can also mean a struggle or crusade against evil in any form. You are not only an unbeliever but have impugned Ahmad's honor and defiled his house, and for that you must die."

"As slowly and painfully as possible, I suppose?"

His voice was flat. It was a good indication, Chloe thought, that he understood the seriousness of the threat. "Just so."

"It seems like cheating for good old Ahmad to bring the police into it. What kind of revenge is it if they chop off my head for him?"

"The main thing is that it makes getting you out of Hazaristan more difficult."

"Just me?"

He was sharp, regardless of his bout with fever. "Us. I should have said us."

"What about the people who helped out the other night?" he asked. "No repercussions for them?"

"Everything has been quiet with Ayla and her watchman. Not even a visit from the police."

"That's good. I'd hate to repay her by causing her arrest."

"She requires no repayment."

He gave her a straight look. "Maybe I need to make it."

"Your code, of course."

"Simple gratitude," he corrected.

She saw that perfectly well, since she felt the same about all that had been done for her over the past few days. It just wasn't what she'd expected from him. "The sooner we are away from here, the better it will be for everyone."

"Ready when you are."

"You're sure?"

A wry smile tilted one corner of his mouth. "You don't believe me?"

"You've been extremely ill," she said. "A little fever isn't unusual with a wound, but I was afraid I hadn't cleaned it well enough, or that the infection would turn into blood poisoning."

"You did fine. Don't worry. I'll make it."

Something in his voice snagged her attention. She studied his features, half-hidden now behind a two-day growth of beard that gave him the raffish look of a bandit. They seemed refined by fever, but gave nothing away. After a moment, she said, "We'll go this afternoon then. If we time it right, we can reach the border checkpoint just before the guard changes, when they are less likely to inspect papers too closely."

"Assuming we have papers? Other than American, I mean."

"That's been taken care of. We travel as Saudi nationals."

"I can handle that."

"We'll be taking the higher route through Azad Pass at the Pakistan border. It's the one favored by refugees because of the camps set up by the Pakistani government, so we should have plenty of company. Once over the border, it will be easy enough to reach Rawalpindi.''

"I'm impressed.''

She looked for mockery, but found none. "It's been done before. Taking people out, I mean. Besides, we've had plenty of time to think about it.''

"You had help?'' His gaze was steady as he waited for her answer.

"From the women who run this safe house, the Revolutionary Association of the Women of Afghanistan.''

"A scary thing, revolutionary women.''

"Yes. We hope so.'' In an effort to gloss over the moment, she went on quickly. "You should eat something to rebuild your strength. Are you hungry?''

"I could eat a horse. Not that it would be my first choice on the menu.''

"Don't worry,'' she said in dry reassurance. "It's far too great a delicacy these days to waste on an American.''

She turned away and left the room. Her smile faded as the heavy door clicked shut behind her. She had been half-afraid to broach the escape plan to Wade Benedict, afraid he'd refuse to consider something that didn't involve fast transport, heavy weaponry and him in control. It had gone well, almost too well. She'd think he was up to something except that she didn't see how that was possible.

There was one part of the escape plan that still had to be implemented. She'd thought it best to put it off until just before they left the fortress. Wade wasn't going to like it, she knew, but maybe waiting until it was too late to change the plan would make it easier to gain his cooperation. She could only hope.

"Not just no, but *hell* no!"

Wade wadded the burqa that Chloe had just handed him into a ball, then slung it across the room with such force that it bounced off the wall. She glared at him and went immediately to pick it up.

"You must wear it," she declared, thrusting it toward him again. "The guard at the checkpoint won't look twice at yet another woman covered from head to toe."

"That's because no man would be caught dead in one of the things."

"You'd rather take a chance on being spotted with your height and puny excuse for a beard?" she demanded with a wave toward his dark stubble. "Especially when the guard may have been warned to watch for Americans?"

"It's better than hiding behind women's skirts," he answered with dogged illogic.

"You won't be hiding, just escaping notice."

"Oh, sure. And a funny-looking female I'll make, standing a head taller than you."

"You won't be standing. You'll be in the back seat pretending to be carsick or pregnant or whatever you like that will allow you to slump in your seat. Anyway, the major part of a man's extra height is in his leg bones. We'll look more equal sitting next to each other.''

He crossed his arms over his chest and tucked his fingertips into his armpits. ''I won't wear it.''

''You have to,'' she cried in angry desperation. ''There's no other way. So you don't like it, so what? I don't like it, either. No woman likes it, but we have to put up with it all the time. I don't see why you can't endure the hateful thing for a couple of hours.''

He stared at her for long seconds. ''Whose idea was this?''

''Several of us decided on it.''

''Including you.''

She lifted her hands and let them fall so the burqa slapped against her knee. ''There's nothing personal about it!''

''You're sure it's not because of what I said the other night?''

''Absolutely not.'' That much was true, which didn't mean it hadn't occurred to her that he'd be getting a taste of something he was so sure was a deliberate choice.

''I suppose you'll be covered up head and ears, too?''

''Of course.''

He stared at her for long seconds, the intensity of his gaze an indication of the swift pace of his thoughts. Then he put out a hand and snatched the burqa from her, shaking it out like a bedsheet. It hung in his hands, an enormous spread of cream-colored fabric since it was long enough to cover him to the ground. His reaction was profane. He rolled it up with a winding motion and shoved it back at her again.

"No."

"Yes!" She pushed it against his chest. "If I'm to get you out of this country, you have to help."

"I'm supposed to be taking you out of here."

"Well, you can't. Maybe that's my fault. Maybe it's bad luck, bad karma or just bad timing. It doesn't matter because nothing can change it. We have to go on from here. And wearing this damn burqa is the best way to do that."

He fastened his gaze on the veil across the bottom of her face that wavered with her every angry breath. Slowly a look of consideration tinted his hazel eyes a darker shade of green. "I'll make you a deal," he said at last.

"A deal?" Every ounce of the wariness rising inside her was in those words.

"That's right. It's fair enough, I think, considering what you want me to do."

"What is it?"

"I'll put this thing on if you'll take yours off."

"My burqa?"

"And the scarf thing, veil or whatever you call it that you're wearing."

She lifted a hand to the cloth cover. "No, really. I need camouflage, too."

"Doesn't have to happen now," he said with a magnanimous gesture. "But the minute we're safe on the other side of the border, off it comes."

It was a reprieve, though he didn't know that. Any unveiling would be minimal, since she had every intention of leaving him in Pakistan and returning to Ajzukabad with the driver.

"Fine," she said.

His features went blank with surprise. "That's an agreement?"

"Yes."

"You'll get rid of everything, let me see your face with nothing in the way?"

"I just said so, didn't I?" she demanded in irritation. "Though I fail to see why it's so important to you."

"I don't like people keeping things from me."

Uneasiness shifted through her. He couldn't know what she had in mind. Could he? "I'm not."

"Aren't you? Then take it off now."

"I don't have time." She dropped the burqa on the pallet and moved toward the door. "You might want to get ready, too. We leave in ten minutes."

His comment, and expression when he made it, remained with Chloe during the long ride to the border. All she wanted to keep from Wade was her intention to go back to Ajzukabad. Well, and how much she knew about the things that haunted his dreams. And yet, she'd felt such instant resistance to letting him see her naked face. Why was that? Vanity, maybe,

the fear that he'd be disappointed? Or was it nothing
to do with him personally, but reluctance to expose
any portion of herself to any man? Was it not so much
her physical appearance she was keeping to herself as
the thoughts and feelings that might show in her face?
She'd grown so used to concealing these things, to
pretending to be a passive nonentity in a world of
masculine violence. The burqa had become a mask of
compliance she wore while going about her subver-
sive activities behind it. To be forced to cast it off
and stand with all her resentment and animosity in
plain view was like being stripped naked. It might be
all right in another place and time where everyone
wore the same open face, but not here, and not now.

The town fell away behind them. They began to
climb the lower reaches of a mountain range that
blended eventually into the Hindu Kush. The sere
hills rolled ahead of them in shades of beige and gold,
ochre and brown that complemented the dusty green
of juniper and pine forests. Behind these rose the
misty, cloud-shrouded ranges of some of the tallest
mountains in the world. High in their blue and purple
fastness lay a handful of high-altitude passes through
the mountains that had served as trade and invasion
routes for centuries, and still did. One of these, the
Azad, or Free, pass carved out during the wars of the
British Raj, was the route they would be taking.

Their transport was a station wagon, a big, lum-
bering model almost forty years old. Such vehicles
were popular for their durability, but also because

they provided maximum passenger and cargo space. The driver was Kemal, a Tajik who spoke Dari Persian instead of Pashtu. A large man with the thick, blond-streaked hair of his kind, he slouched behind the wheel in morose silence, perhaps from fear or resentment at being assigned to drive two Americans to safety. He sent the station wagon along at a pace that threatened to destroy the tires as they bounced into the holes that pocked the pavement, and would have gone faster if not for the sharp complaints of the young woman beside him. This was Freshta, one of the most daring of the RAWA operatives. She was with them to smuggle out of the country a video showing a woman being executed for the crime of adultery. Once in Pakistan, she would put it into the hands of RAWA members who would see that it reached Western journalists sympathetic to the cause of the women of Hazaristan.

Chloe sat on the middle seat with Wade who was every bit as moody as Kemal. He wore the burqa as if it were a penance, staring through the mesh screen like a hawk through the bars of a cage. His smoldering irritation might have been comical if it hadn't brought to mind the anger she'd felt when she first put one on. In any case, she didn't dare smile for fear he might snatch the despised garment off and throw it at her.

"Are you okay?" she asked, largely as an excuse for staring at him.

The look he gave her was more than a little sardonic.

"What I meant was, no dizziness or nausea? No bleeding because of the jolts?"

"No."

The clipped sound of his voice scraped on her nerves, but she did her best to ignore it. He wouldn't be here if not for her, she reminded herself. If she had sent him on his way instead of dithering over whether to go or stay, he'd never have been hurt. She felt guilty that he'd come so far, gone to such expense, for nothing since she couldn't go back home with him. He'd brought the news of the inheritance that gave her the promise of independence as well, and she owed him for it. More than that, he was an American, her countryman. She refused to allow him to make her forget her obligation to him.

With the barest of glances in her direction, he asked, "How far do we have to go?"

"A couple of hours to the border, and the same to Rawalpindi on the other side. Everything will be all right once we reach Pakistan."

"So we're still flying out?"

"I found the plane tickets in your jeans pocket."

He gave a curt nod. "Your arrangements aren't too different from what I'd planned."

"They wouldn't be, I suppose. There are a limited number of possibilities. The main problem will be the border crossing."

"Right."

"We've done the best we could."

He made no answer. When she glanced at him, he was staring out the window again at the saw-toothed peaks that loomed ahead of them.

Time wore on. They left the river valley and began to ascend into the pass, winding along in a north-westerly direction over switchbacks that terraced the rocky brown slopes. As the climb grew steeper, they caught up with more slow-moving truck traffic and had to gear down to accommodate it. The trucks were hampered not only by the climb but also by the refugees that clogged the road, some alone, some in family groups, and many of them with everything they owned piled into ramshackle trucks or on handcarts, donkeys, camels and the occasional goat. The two hours Chloe had predicted became three as they crawled along, sometimes coming to a complete halt for moments on end.

The heat inside the station wagon grew stifling with the lack of air movement through the windows. The elevation of the pass wasn't high enough, at just over three thousand feet, to gain much in the way of mountain coolness, and the stone walls rising around them trapped and held the sun's warmth as well as blocking any breeze. Breathing became more difficult under Chloe's burqa, and she knew it was the same for Freshta and particularly Wade since he wasn't used to it. The smells of sweat, musty upholstery, exhaust fumes and the animal dung along the roadway didn't help matters.

The distance they advanced between stops grew shorter and shorter. The station wagon began to make ominous rattling sounds. Kemal got out the next time they came to a stall and poured water into the radiator from a plastic jug carried in the cargo area. They drank from the same jug, letting the cool liquid slide down their parched throats. Afterward, they inched along another few miles. Every now and then Kemal tapped the gauge on the dash panel and muttered into his beard.

The stone walls became cliffs that towered higher around them, far too high to climb. The sun slanted down below the peaks in the west, so the black shadow of the mountains inched lower on the near wall. The border station would close soon.

Then it loomed ahead of them. They crept closer, and the traffic line halted again. Kemal opened the door and got out to stand staring up the road. His eyes narrowed and his eyebrows drew together in a straight line at the edge of his turban.

Chloe looked at Freshta, who understood Dari Persian, as well as a half dozen other common dialects. Instantly the operative put a sharp-voiced query to Kemal. The exchange that followed was brief, with a sound that sent apprehension singing along Chloe's veins.

"Well?" she asked, suddenly breathless.

"The guard has stopped a truck and made the driver show his papers while they search the hold in back," Freshta answered.

"And that's all?"

"By no means. They have made the woman who rides with him remove her burqa, so she may be searched as well."

8

The station wagon crept forward again. Wade stared at the cliffs, but they offered no way out. They couldn't turn back without attracting the kind of attention they didn't want. The best thing seemed to be to keep going and hope the border guard was doing random searches. He couldn't remember the last time he'd felt so helpless. His own fault, of course, for leaving the details of getting out of the country to other people. Not that he'd have been able to arrange it any better.

It was infernally hot under the glorified bedsheet he wore. He didn't mind that so much as the lack of ventilation. His own body heat was trapped under the confining cloth, and the constant trickle of sweat made his wound itch and burn. On top of that was the sheer confinement, giving him the urge to yank it off and devil take the consequences. The surprising thing to him, after just a few hours of it, was that Hazaristan women hadn't risen as a body and murdered every man in sight. The burqa rage in this country had to far surpass any amount of U.S. road rage.

Chloe seemed all right with it. In fact, she was

amazingly calm about their slow creep toward possible arrest. No doubt years of wearing a damn burqa did wonders for self-control. It sure kept anyone from actually seeing you sweat.

While these thoughts ran through one part of his mind, another section was busy with contingencies. He grasped the weapon tucked into the waistband of his pants, testing to see how hard it would be to bring it into play. As Chloe glanced his way, he asked, "Kemal is armed, I suppose?"

"You can be sure of that."

"He know how to use it?"

The look she gave him was cool. "I'd say so. The men of his family have been fighters for generations."

"Why isn't he in the army then?"

"He was, until a Taliban unit overran his village a few months ago. Everyone in it was rounded up and shot for aiding the opposition forces. He lost his grandfather, his mother, two younger brothers, a sister and three nephews. Not unnaturally, he deserted when he heard. An older sister had been working with the RAWA, so here he is, aiding us while also acting as liaison between the organization and the opposition."

Wade considered asking if the woman called Freshta had a similar background, but thought better of it. It seemed everybody had a horror story. "I didn't realize the two groups had the same aims."

"They don't always. Some of the opposition leaders are as rigid in their interpretation of the Qur'an as the Taliban. Still, the relative easing of restrictions in Afghanistan gives us hope.''

There it was again, her alignment with women like Freshta. Wade let it pass, however, since his mind was on other things.

The big truck in front of them blocked his view of the border station. All he could see was a couple of people standing on the side of the road as if waiting for the search to be over. The driver was watching them, too, his eyes narrowed and his fingers drumming on the steering wheel.

"What are the chances of Kemal opening fire if something starts going down?" he asked Chloe in a low murmur.

"Excellent. His job is to protect us as well as take us across the border.''

Her tone suggested that she considered it a reasonable arrangement. She apparently figured he was in no shape to use a weapon. He'd be the first to admit that he wasn't in top form, but he was stronger than he'd led her to believe. That was the way he intended to keep it for a while longer.

He suspected that the past two days at the RAWA stronghold had left Chloe feeling even more grateful than she had been before, and guilty that she was running out on her friends. He could almost see her withdrawal into the dedicated mind-set she'd shown during their meeting in the garden. If he was a betting man, he'd put money on her planning to get him out of the country and on a plane home then go underground to defeat the Taliban. That might be noble, but he couldn't let it happen. If he must play the invalid to keep her off guard, then so be it.

She seemed less wary of him while he was down, so to speak. He didn't mind reining in his normal fast rate of recovery if it allowed him to get closer to her. The time might come when he'd need every advantage he could find or manufacture.

The truck ahead pulled into place for its turn, and Kemal eased the station wagon another few yards forward. They watched as the driver was ordered out and patted down for weapons. Freshta exclaimed under her breath, then spoke to Kemal in sharp tones. The driver spread his hands in the universal gesture of helplessness. A second later, he reached down and felt under his seat as if checking a hidden weapon. Wade felt his stomach muscles contract. The prospect of a gun battle was all right, but he didn't care for the idea of the two women being caught in the middle of it.

The truck driver was given the all clear. He climbed back into his rig that was large by Middle Eastern standards, but was like a toy compared to its American equivalent. As the guard waved him on, he pulled across the border and rumbled away, leaving the station clear.

Chloe reached out to put a hand on Wade's arm. "Lie back," she urged. "Close your eyes and act sick."

Playacting went against the grain. It might be worth it to prevent a confrontation that could get the women hurt, however. Besides, it was hard to resist the appeal in her eyes. He slumped down lower in the seat and closed his eyes.

Kemal pulled forward. Wade heard the border guard speak from a position near the driver's side window. A rustling sound indicated that their identification papers were being handed over. During the pause while they were scrutinized, Wade noticed the calls of birds. Somewhere a donkey brayed then fell silent again.

"Out," the guard commanded. "Out of the vehicle."

"Wait," Freshta began.

"Do not speak. Out. The women will remove their coverings."

Wade heard the swift intake of Chloe's breath. No one in the station wagon moved or spoke. The magnitude of this disaster seemed to hold them in its grip, as though it had taken away their ability to react.

He put a hand to his side, then began to sit up. "Kemal," he began, searching for the words in Pashtu that would alert the driver to be ready to make a move.

Abruptly Chloe swung toward her door and shoved it open. She erupted from the vehicle in a flurry of blue fabric. Screaming like a madwoman, she flew at the guard. With her face inches from his, she railed at him, calling him a defiler of women who sought to breach the sanctity of the veil for his own lewd and immoral purposes. Advancing on him, she demanded to know how he would feel if the women of his own family should be subjected to so shameful a necessity.

The guard blustered and waved his arms, but backed away the whole time. He was obviously demoralized, as if he'd never seen a woman in a temper before, never had one dare take him to task.

Chloe stalked him, talking faster, louder, waving her arms so her burqa flapped as if she would take flight. It looked as if she meant to chase the man back into his own guardhouse. Wade felt a warning tingle run down his spine. She was getting too far away from the station wagon and too near the guard. The man's face was turning red, and his frown growing blacker.

With his pistol gripped tight in his hand, Wade spoke in an urgent undertone to the woman called Freshta. "Call her back," he instructed. "Do it now. Tell her that I need her."

"It will be as well," the young woman answered in concern. Lifting her voice, she did as he'd suggested.

Chloe glanced back at them, then turned again to the guard. With a final gesture of angry contempt, she snatched their papers from his hand, then turned her back and strode toward them. Flinging herself in at the open door of the station wagon, she slammed it shut. Even as the sound echoed off the stone walls around them, she touched Kemal's shoulder. "Go," she said. "Drive away. Now!"

The driver said something incomprehensible,

though the way he gripped the weapon he held in his lap spoke volumes.

"He says the guards will begin to fire at any moment," Freshta translated.

Chloe put her hand on the woman's shoulder. "They won't if we go now. We have the initiative. Tell him. Please."

She was right, Wade saw. Their window of opportunity was getting narrower every second, however. Already, the guard was walking toward them again.

As Freshta spoke to the driver in a fast undertone, he began to wag his turbaned head.

Wade had had enough. In hard, but low command, he said, "Drive!"

The driver recognized the tone, if not the meaning. He flung down the pistol and jerked the station wagon into gear. They untracked with a screech of rubber.

Regardless, the Tajik had the presence of mind not to turn the departure into an escape. After that first jerk, he pulled away like a man on a family outing.

They seemed to move too slowly, in fact. The contrast between the instinct for speed and the actual turning of the wheels made it feel as if they were crawling. Wade strained for the sound of a shout, a shot, anything that would indicate an alarm. At the same time, he fought the urge to pull Chloe down beside him so she wouldn't make quite such a good target.

Freshta began to turn in her seat. "Don't look

back,'' Wade warned. "Act as though we have a perfect right to leave.''

"Just so,'' she said with a judicious nod, and faced forward again.

Chloe was staring at him. He risked a glance, half-afraid of what he might see.

"You're giving the orders now?'' she asked, her voice quiet.

"All I wanted was to get you out of there, pronto, before that goon recovered from the shock of seeing a woman turn into a witch in front of his eyes. You won, hands down. No use pressing your luck.''

"I thought...'' She stopped.

"What?''

"That you might be afraid I'd be hurt.''

She was trying to see past the screen that concealed his features. Well, good luck to her. "I guess you could say that.''

"Then I should thank you.''

He was stunned into a long silence, during which they drove ever farther into Pakistan. "That's it?'' he asked finally. "You're not mad because I horned in on your rescue operation?''

"You gave the orders that were required. You backed me up when I needed it. I'm grateful.''

He laughed and gave a slow shake of his head.

"What's so funny?''

If she could be that forthcoming, then so could he. "Not funny, but amazing. What you did back there was one of the bravest things I've ever seen. I've known combat veterans who'd have thought twice about charging an armed guard with only words for weapons.''

She looked down at her hands. ''I was just so mad that I...that it went all over me. The idea that he would take away the burqas the instant they might cause a problem, or that he could prevent us from leaving a place where staying is a daily penance, just made me crazy.''

''Whatever the reason, you did it. You got us out.''

She met his gaze there in the moving station wagon as the Hazaristan border fell away behind them, met and held it without instantly looking away as she usually did. The color of her eyes was a deep aquamarine-blue, he discovered, and almost crystalline in their clarity. She saw him, saw through him, as no one else ever had or would, or so it seemed. Deep inside him, something stirred as if in ancient recognition. And he wanted her as he'd never wanted anything or any woman in his whole life, wanted her with a pure longing that transcended physical desire to become soul-shattering necessity. He stared at her transfixed, aware that here and now, when he was most profoundly glad to be a man, he was dressed like a damn skirt-bound woman.

''I was terrified,'' Chloe said, her voice scarcely above a whisper.

It was then that he noticed the fine tremors that shivered along the folds of cloth covering her. Brave beyond words while she needed to be, she was paying the price now that the danger was over.

He reached out and touched the shape of her arm under her burqa, following it to the elbow and along her forearm until he could grasp her hand. With a tentative, inviting movement, he tugged her toward him.

Her gaze became valley-deep and edged with pain. Seeing it, he knew beyond a doubt that she meant to leave him. Still, he didn't look away. And after a second, she moved to his side, fitting herself against him while being careful of his knife wound. She relaxed by degrees, letting him hold her while they wound down out of the rift of the Azad Pass. He'd thought she might cry, but she did not. Together, they lay back, their eyes wide as they stared at the road ahead of them.

The station wagon had covered no more than fifteen miles when white, smokelike steam began to seep from under the hood, streaming back with the speed of their travel. It smelled of hot metal as it swirled in at the windows, and its pungency stung their eyes. Chloe sat up, and Wade followed suit. Kemal slowed, staring anxiously ahead as if in search of a place wide enough to pull off the road. Before one appeared, the engine died.

The Tajik steered onto the narrow shoulder as they rolled to a stop. He sat for a moment with disgust printed on his face. Then he slammed the heel of his hand against the steering wheel. Opening the door, he got out and stalked to the hood. He popped it loose, then flung it upward on its hinges.

Steam boiled out in a dirty cloud. The driver jumped back with an exclamation followed by a string of obvious invective. Freshta gave a nervous laugh, then bit her lip. With a worried glance over her shoulder in Wade's direction, she said, "You must know something of American machines. Is this one on fire, do you think?"

"Running hot again," Wade answered. "I'd say the head's probably cracked."

"A serious matter then?"

"Can't drive with it, if that's what you mean. The engine will have to be replaced."

Freshta looked at Chloe, apparently for enlightenment. As the concept was translated, she said, "I fear this will be difficult, since a similar vehicle that has been smashed must be found. It will take time, much time."

That made sense. Not too many automobile parts stores or even wrecking yards in this neck of the woods. "Looks like we're stuck."

The verdict was pretty much complete as Kemal returned to lean in the open door with his hands braced on either side. With fatalism in his face, he spoke to Freshta, and she sighed as she translated verbatim, "She does not go."

"Mind if I take a look?" Wade opened his door and unfolded himself to his full height.

Kemal turned and put his back to the brace between

the doors while he took a cigarette from his pocket and lit it with a kitchen match.

Taking that for permission, Wade took a step toward the front of the vehicle. The damn burqa tangled around his ankles, and he stopped, ripped the thing off and slam-dunked it into the back seat. Then he walked with his own free and natural stride to where the wagon's hood yawned open.

The head was cracked, all right. The valves had seized up as well. From the heat still rising off the engine, he wouldn't be surprised if the whole, blessed thing wasn't half-melted.

They were on foot.

One of the other doors opened and closed. Chloe moved from behind the screen of the hood, coming to stand beside him. "Well, what do you think?"

He gave her a crooked smile. "She's most definitely not going to go."

"I was afraid of that."

"Right. Where's all the GPS monitoring and cell phone wizardry when you really need them?"

"Put those out of your head," she said. "Try to think as if we'd gone back in time a couple of decades."

"Or more," he agreed, nodding toward where a man led a donkey burdened with a rolled rug, two clay water jars, and three bright-eyed youngsters under six years old along the opposite side of the road. "So what do we do now?"

"Don't ask me."

"It's your party."

"It wasn't supposed to end this way," she said in brooding irritation. "Besides, I know nothing of this area."

"Well," he drawled, glancing around him in the fading light that was drenched in sunset colors, "we might flag down a passing camel. Or maybe you could show an ankle so we could hitch a ride—that's if you can pick out a driver who isn't a psycho with a grudge against Americans."

"This isn't funny!"

"Who's joking?" It was a serious business in all truth, though he was painfully aware of an odd euphoria running like wine in his veins. He wasn't sure if he was light-headed still from loss of blood, exhilarated at being out of Hazaristan, or if it had something to do with the woman beside him. Whatever the cause, he liked the feeling.

"There are four of us. We'll have to wait for a truck at least."

"Or we can start walking. But if we're going to strike out on foot, it's time to lose the burqa."

"Not that again!"

He wasn't going to be deterred, not this time. "You aren't on Hazaristan soil anymore, and no one is looking. Take it off."

"Don't be ridiculous."

"We had a bargain."

She gave a long-suffering sigh before she said, "Pakistanis aren't a lot more progressive about women and their bodies than the Hazaris. Besides, half the men passing on this road are either Hazara or Afghans, as is Kemal.''

''What's that got to do with it?'' Wade thought he knew, but was in no mood to be helpful.

''You might want to think twice about setting up a situation where you have to defend my honor.''

She did have a point, as much as he hated to admit it. Before he had to capitulate, however, Freshta made her way around the station wagon's hood to stop beside them.

''Kemal and I have been talking,'' she said without preamble.

''That right?'' Wade glanced to where the driver had moved into view. The Tajik's features were grim behind his beard, which might or might not mean anything. ''And?''

''We see no reason for the two of us to go forward when we will only have to retrace our steps again.''

''Freshta, no,'' Chloe protested.

''Hear me out, please,'' the Afghan girl said, her gaze earnest through the mesh of her burqa. ''This is no easy decision.''

''If it's what I think...''

''Please,'' Freshta said again, then went on as Chloe fell silent. ''The way to Peshawar is clear. You have no need of a guide. It will be easier for only two people to find someone to take them, as well, so we four would likely have to split up into separate vehicles. We will leave you here, then, Kemal and I, while the two of you go on together.''

It made sense to Wade. As he shot a look at Kemal, the driver gave him a nod as though to say the plan suited him, too.

Chloe didn't appear to see it. With her gaze on Freshta, she asked, ''You would leave me to care for a wounded man?''

''He isn't so bad, I think. You must trust that he can manage this short journey.''

The Hazari girl was on to him, Wade thought, though he wasn't sure how he'd slipped up.

''And what of being caught alone with him?''

''You are in Pakistan where such things may be frowned on but not punished by death,'' Freshta said evenly. ''Soon you will be in the United States where they don't matter at all.''

''What if Ahmad learns of our leaving and follows us?''

''You must trust your American to protect you.''

Chloe's expression showed little confidence, but she didn't pursue it. Instead she asked, ''And what of your mission?''

''That I will entrust to you.'' As Freshta spoke, she lifted the skirt of her burqa and took a small flat package from the sash that was wrapped around her waist. She held it in her hands for a second, then extended it as if completing a ceremony.

Chloe made no move to accept it. She gave him a brief glance, Wade saw, as if she doubted the wisdom of allowing him to see the transfer. That sharpened his interest so he looked more closely. The package seemed about the size and shape of a video, but could be anything, even a nice, neat bundle of explosives. If it was dangerous, however, Kemal didn't seem worried. The driver stared down the road as if bored with women's chatter.

"Take it, Chloe. You must."

"I can't," she said. "I have no idea who I should give it to, or how to find them."

"I could tell you what has been done in the past, but it no longer matters," Freshta said quietly. "It will be much better if you take it to the States with you. There you may find a respected journalist who cares enough to make it the sensation that it deserves."

"Oh, but I didn't intend..."

"I know. I am aware of your dedication, your many good deeds and great heart. We have spoken of you among us, Ayla and I, and also Willa who is mother to your dead stepsister's husband. We have thought long and well, and this is what we decided between us. This mission was never mine, Chloe. It was always to be yours."

"No."

"Yes. Attend me, my sister in our cause."

"But if I go now, I may never be allowed to return."

"So be it. Some things are meant in this life, and perhaps it was kismet that brought you to my country, to suffer with its women so that you might do this thing now. No, truly," she said in haste as Chloe tried to speak. "If you return to Hazaristan you will die. You are too different to escape notice for long. Someone, somewhere, will betray you for favor, money or hope of paradise, and that will be the end. If women like me wish to risk our lives, this is as it should be. This is our land, the country of our birth and our hearts, and we have no wish to leave it for another. But it is not your country, our Chloe. You belong to America. Go there where women are free, and do what you may to help us be free also."

Chloe lifted her head. With what sounded like tears clogging her voice, she said simply, "If it pleases you, sister of my heart."

It was then that Kemal gave a grunt of impatience and pushed away from the stalled vehicle. His attention was not on the women, however, but fixed on the road ahead where a truck, indistinct in the growing dimness except for the twin beams of its headlights, came toward them on its way up the pass. Striding out onto the pavement directly in its path, the Tajik held up his hand like a traffic cop in a silent movie.

For long seconds, there was no sound except the whine of the diesel engine. Then came the hiss and squeal of air brakes. The truck was stopping.

With an imperious wave in Freshta's direction, Kemal called out to her.

"Yes," she replied, though with little obedience in

her tone. Turning back to Chloe, she thrust the package into her hands. Then she enveloped her in a swift hug that included the ritual kisses on the cheek of farewell. With the glint of tears in her eyes, she murmured softly, "Allah keep you, my friend. Live well and be happy."

"And you," Chloe replied.

Freshta looked at Wade. "Keep her safe."

Where the impulse came from, Wade wasn't sure, but he lifted a hand to his heart and inclined his head in a gesture he'd seen many times in the Middle East but never thought to copy. It seemed right at the moment.

Freshta smiled, for the brilliance of it shone behind her mesh screen. Then she turned in a whirl of cloth and ran for the truck that was rolling to a halt. Kemal helped her into the cab, probably for the sake of speed and because he wanted the window seat, since he slammed the door and draped an arm outside it. Then the truck pulled away. It picked up speed, grinding off with a clash of gears toward the Azad Pass and all that lay beyond.

Wade looked at the woman beside him. She stared back, her gaze unreadable.

So here he was, Wade Ethan Benedict, in the middle of a foreign country with no plan, no transportation, and no idea what to do next. He had about two-thirds of his normal strength, a single weapon with limited ammo, and he was stranded alone with a woman who considered him a liability and wanted desperately to be somewhere else. Night was coming on like a freight train, and the only shelter in sight was a crippled vehicle that, come good dark, was going to be a magnet for every thief and bandit in these hills.

On top of all this, he had a strong suspicion that he'd lost it, gone over the edge to stare lunacy in its grinning face. Because the main thing he felt bubbling up inside him was not gloom or doubt or even worry, but an enveloping tide of pure, outrageous joy.

God, but he was happy.

9

"What's so funny?" Chloe demanded.

"Nothing, nothing." The smile that curved Wade's lips vanished. He turned away from her, gazing around with an appraising stare at the darkening shapes of the rolling hills and the ever-present sawtoothed line of the Hindu Kush behind them.

She wished that she'd been less waspish. It wasn't his fault that everything had gone so terribly wrong, or that she felt forsaken. Of course, none of it would have happened if he had never come, or even if he'd left her alone when she'd asked.

Freshta and Ayla were sure the chain of events that had been set in motion was fate's hand at work. Chloe wished she could believe it. It seemed to her more like the hand of Wade Benedict.

Abruptly he moved with a lanky stride to the rear of the station wagon. Opening the cargo hatch, he rummaged inside, taking out and stacking what he found on the ground. The first thing was a bag made of carpet scraps that clanked with the dull metallic sound made by tools or cooking equipment, or both. On this was stacked a prayer rug and a stained wool blanket. Rolling the last two items together, he handed her the bundle.

Chloe took it automatically and tucked the video package that she still held into one end. Wrinkling her nose at the smell of goat and old cigarette smoke that clung to the wool and leather, she asked, ''What is this?''

''Camping gear.'' He removed the five-gallon water jug that Kemal had used earlier, then closed the hatch door.

''Camping,'' she repeated in flat tones.

''Call me chicken, but getting into a truck with some stranger on a deserted road at night, like your friend, just doesn't seem too bright. I might chance it on my own, but not with a woman.''

''I can take care of myself, thank you.''

''Famous last words. And I'm in no shape to ride to the rescue like some hero in the movies, thank you very much. Good old Kemal carried survival gear, as most folks do that live in mountain country. We'll camp for the night, and try for Peshawar in the morning.''

''Let me guess, you were a Boy Scout?''

''My brothers and I practically lived in the woods around our house when we were kids.''

''This isn't Louisiana.''

''That just means there are no mosquitoes and we won't be panting for air-conditioning.''

The last was certainly true. The air had grown noticeably cooler since the sun dropped behind the mountains. "We could sleep in the station wagon," she said with a troubled glance at the dust being chased across the road by the evening wind.

"Yeah, but the bandits and strip thieves might disturb your beauty rest."

"Strip thieves?"

"With car parts being scarce around here, I think you'll find this heap a skeleton of its former self come daylight."

"You're forgetting the nasty habit they have of cutting off the hands of thieves."

He gave her a judicious look. "First you have to catch the thief. And I'd say the prospect of losing a hand makes leaving witnesses out of the question. Do you really want to chance it?"

Camping suddenly didn't seem such a bad idea. "I suppose you've got the perfect site all picked out?"

"Over there." He tipped his head toward a stand of deodar cedars a fair distance away. The trees, ghostly in the fading light, clustered on a slope that was protected from the rear by a steep outcropping of rock but open on the remaining three sides.

"All the comforts of home," she said dryly. "Carry on, O Fearless Leader."

He picked up the water jug and the tool bag. With a hint of challenge in his eyes, he said, "After you."

If he thought she was going to argue with him, he was in for a surprise, Chloe thought. With a single speaking glance, she tucked the rolled blanket under one arm, picked up the skirt of her burqa and set out for the cedars.

By the time night had fallen around them, they sat on either side of a small fire sipping tea. Wade had built a fire pit of stones and kindled the blaze inside the concealing ring. It was Chloe who found the matches to start it with, however, in the bag of tools and utensils. She also discovered the packet of tea, tin can used for boiling water and plastic cup. And it was she who laid out the prayer rug on one side of the fire and the blanket on the other.

"Not exactly home," Wade said in wry comment as he glanced at her across the flames, "but not too uncomfortable, either."

Firelight reflected in his eyes and glinted for an instant on the whiteness of his teeth as he smiled. Abruptly she was aware of just how big and masculine he was, how attractive, and how alone they were there under the cedars. He seemed more relaxed than at any time since they'd met, as he lounged across from her with one knee drawn up to support his wrist and the hot tin can of tea that he held between his thumb and forefinger. He'd regained his normal color, so his skin appeared sun-burnished, and the rough, windblown waves of his hair shone with vitality. He didn't look at all like the man who had been lost in a feverish nightmare only the night before.

Realizing she was staring, she looked away. Her gaze fell on the leather bag that lay beside her.

"Would you like a snack? I found this with the other things."

"What is it?"

"Walnuts, seeds, dried fruit and maybe bits of meat, the Hazara version of trail mix, though a good bit older as a tradition."

He held out his hand, and she poured half of what was in the bag into it. "Interesting," he said as he stared down at it. Then he piled it carefully on the rug beside him. "Maybe later."

She wasn't really hungry, either, but sorted out a piece of what she thought was apricot. It was hardly a gourmet treat since it had been sun-dried without benefit of sugar or preservatives, and had dark spots whose origins she didn't want to speculate on. Still, she tore off a small piece with her teeth and began to chew it. The concentrated scent of apricot blended with the smells of burning cedar and wild sage from the mountain slopes, creating an incenselike fragrance.

"I expect camping out when you were a kid was never quite like this," she commented.

An odd expression crossed his face, then was gone. "Not quite. For one thing, no girls were allowed. Not that any ever applied."

"No girls in your family?"

"Not back then. Boys only, Adam and myself, Clay and Matt. The last two were twins."

"Were?"

"Matt died, killed in an oil rig explosion."

"I'm sorry." Her voice was soft as she spoke, perhaps in response to the spasm of pain that had crossed his face.

"It was a long time ago, over ten years. He has a daughter, a neat kid named Lainey. She had a kidney transplant a while back, but is doing fine so far. Clay gave her one of his, since he was the best donor match."

"That was…kind of him."

"Pure self-preservation, if you ask me. He loves that kid as if she was his own, would die tomorrow if anything happened to her. Doesn't hurt that he feels the same about her mother."

"Meaning…"

"He married the woman Matt loved, yeah. As twins, they always did have the same tastes in food, cars, women and so on. Stands to reason, I guess."

"What about your other brother?"

"Adam? His wife's psychic, reads his mind. It's downright weird, or might be if he didn't enjoy it so much."

"Enjoy?"

"You don't want to know."

From the hint of a salacious twinkle in his eyes, she thought he was probably right. On the other hand, talking seemed more comfortable than silence. Searching for something to keep it going, she asked, "No other nephews and nieces?"

"Not so far, but lots of baby cousins."

She sat listening as he went on to tell her of his

cousins Kane, Luke and Roan and their wives and offspring. He spoke also of the town of Turn-Coupe, the people who lived there, the courthouse square with its Confederate and Vietnam Veterans Memorials side by side, the annual pirate's day festival and the lake and its swamp areas. She paid attention to what he said, but most of all she listened to the rich timbre of his voice with its warm edging of nostalgia and affection. Whether he knew it or not, he loved his people and the place he had been born, and he missed them.

"Why did you leave Turn-Coupe?" she asked when he finally fell quiet.

He lifted a shoulder. "It's a long story and not especially interesting. Besides, I've talked enough."

"What else do we have to do, after all. I'd like to hear it."

He met her gaze through the blue streamers of smoke that shifted between them. Their depths were dark, yet alive with rigorously suppressed inclinations. An odd shiver moved over her, while deep inside she felt the rise of something similar to anticipation. Her heartbeat accelerated, and her lips parted for a quick, sharp breath.

He switched his gaze to his tea, swirling it in the tin can. His expression hardened, becoming distant.

"Of course, if that's too personal..." she began.

His lips flattened for a second. Then he twitched a wide shoulder. "Not especially. It's the usual family saga. Adam was the oldest son, the steady, hardworking one who did well in school and tried his best to please. Being the second son and middle child, I had to be different. I was the rebel, stubborn, touchy, a sore-headed pain in the...well, a pain. Our dad wasn't an easy man. He was a perfectionist, with a high-handed conviction that there was only one way to be, one way to do things, and that was his way. The twins were younger and had each other, so were able to get by. All of us spent a lot of time in the woods and swamps, keeping out of his way. Didn't always work. To say Dad and I butted heads would be an under-statement. His best way of trying to make me see reason was with a belt. That was the main reason my mom left him when I was a teenager, I think, and the only person stunned by it was Dad. Instead of trying to work it out, he did his best to make the breakup her fault. And of course we all resented him for it, especially me.'' He paused. ''See, I told you it was boring.''

''No, really it isn't.'' She was intrigued by that glimpse of what he'd been like before he'd developed the tough exterior that he'd worn when she'd first met him. It helped, too, to know that seemingly perfect families, as she'd somehow pictured the Benedicts when she'd stayed at their camp with her father, could have problems. The fact that his parents had been divorced as her own had been gave her a feeling of common ground. ''So is that why you left, because you couldn't get along with your dad?''

''That was the biggest part of it. But I was sick to

death of Turn-Coupe, too, and dying to see the world. I lived with my mom in New Orleans for a while, but didn't get on too well with her friends—she's an artist and seems to collect weird types the way some women collect china plates or figurines. I got an apartment, took a job tending bar at night, earned a degree. About the time I graduated, a recruiter came around offering premium salaries for engineers willing to live and work in the Middle East. So off I went.'' He glanced at her. ''You sure you want to hear this?''

Instead of answering, she asked, ''You didn't join the military?''

''What makes you think that?''

''The way you act now and then. Well, and you had nightmares about some kind of plan or operation that went wrong. It sounded as if it might have a military connection though it was confusing because there was a woman involved.''

''Jeez,'' he whispered, raising his free hand to his face, rubbing it with a force that distorted his expression, for a second, into a mask of tragedy.

''I'm sorry. I shouldn't have mentioned it.''

''Hell, why not?'' He expelled a short, hard breath. ''Could be you have a right to know the quality of the protection you're getting here.''

She didn't like the self-contempt she heard in his voice, or the force with which he flung the remains of his tea into the fire. Still, she wasn't sure she could stop him now if she tried. She was silent, waiting for him to go on.

"What I joined was the Diplomatic Security Service, a division dedicated to the protection of diplomatic personnel and their families abroad, with sometimes the occasional senator, congressman, head of a multinational corporation or heavy campaign contributor who takes a notion to visit foreign posts. I was recruited for that, too, on the basis of a little skirmish in Saudi Arabia between a diplomat's teenage son and what I thought were a couple of pickpockets. They turned out to be terrorists, and I happened by in time to keep him from getting blown to bits in a car bomb attack. The kid made sure I got a formal thanks and an informal visit from the director of security at that time, a guy named Nathaniel Hedley."

She had a feeling that there'd been much more to the encounter than he was telling, but she let it go. "You had an oil-field position by then, I imagine," she said. "Why did you agree?"

"Ego, I suppose," he answered with a twist of his neck, as if trying to relieve its stiffness. "I was young enough to be flattered by all the fuss and glamour, rubbing elbows with the moneyed folks and political movers and shakers. Then there was the high-flown language about a career dedicated to serving and protecting the men and women who furthered U.S. interests at home and abroad. I was a sucker for ideals, of one kind or another, back then. Of course, the briefing from veterans and the training I had to go through knocked a lot of that out of me, but it took a real mess to get rid of what was left."

She thought it was possible that some remained, or else why would he have ventured virtually alone into a country like Hazaristan at the behest of a friend? Why would he risk so much to carry out a mission that had been useless from the start?

"What kind of mess?" She drank the rest of her tea and set the cup aside.

"An ugly one," he answered quietly. "A Texas oilman flew in to visit the ambassador and, not incidentally, get some kind of angle on an upcoming meeting of OPEC. He brought his wife with him, a former model that he sent to Switzerland every year for the latest nip, tuck and mud bath. Oh, and decked out in Paris and Italian originals that he set off with a tasteful dollar sign made of diamonds pinned smack dab in the middle of her chest. I don't have to tell you, I'm sure, that he was old enough to be her grandfather and she was his second, or maybe third, trophy bride. He was busy making more money, she was bored, and so she entertained herself by swimming in the nude and asking unattached men to dance. But it turned out that she'd had a former lover who was a lawyer draw up her prenuptial agreement, and if the rich old coot she'd married decided to throw her out, it was going to cost him ten million."

"Dollars?" Chloe couldn't keep the amazement out of her voice.

"Which had already been deposited in a Swiss

bank account and needed only a divorce decree as a release. She liked to say, when she'd had one too many vodka and tonics, that she'd earned every penny.''

"Ouch.''

"Exactly. Maybe the old guy knew how she felt, or again maybe not. Who knows what goes through the mind of an old geezer like that, in the first stages of Alzheimer's and with more money than God?''

"And this oilman's wife invited you to...dance?''

"That's all it was,'' he said, raising his head and glaring at her as if he heard the doubt in her voice. "I don't sleep with other men's wives.''

"No, of course not.'' That didn't mean the woman hadn't asked, Chloe thought, or that she hadn't taken her disappointment elsewhere.

"Anyway, she was kidnapped, along with the vice consul, by Islamic terrorists. I was assigned to the find-and-rescue detail. We found her, all right, and op was set up with split-second timing. I went in, found her and the vice consul, almost had her out. Then something went wrong, the operation came apart and she...''

He stopped abruptly, as if his throat had closed. To fill the space, Chloe said, "She was killed. Her name was Sylvie.''

"Yeah. Was I yelling about it?''

"Among other things. You...seemed to believe someone other than the terrorists killed her.''

"Yeah. I think the old man hired those guys to take

her, then paid one of ours to make sure she died during the rescue. I was supposed to die, too, but I fooled them. Not that it made any difference. Nothing I said mattered, since nobody was going to investigate. It was an unfortunate affair that ended in tragedy. The grieving widower took the body home, and that was that. Only he killed himself a week later.''

''So her husband died and you had closure, of a sort.''

He shook his head. ''I should have saved her. I was close, so close. But I didn't see the danger. I forgot that the person most likely to kill a woman is a family member. Sylvie died because I didn't, couldn't, see that. And so did...''

''No!'' Chloe exclaimed as she saw the direction he was headed. She went on, the words tumbling headlong in her passionate need to make him understand. ''You weren't to blame for the greed and malice of the old man Sylvie chose to marry, nor are you to blame for Ahmad's fanatical judgment that condemned Treena. Other people deliberately caused both deaths. It isn't your fault.''

''I should have guessed what was going to happen. I should have stopped it.''

''Yes, and maybe you should stop the rest of the world from dying while you're at it. Maybe you should take responsibility for all the cruelty and ignorance and vicious, mindless fanaticism of belief that causes people to die every day? Fine, but it won't do any good. The only thing that will help is to make it stop.''

He was quiet while the fire crackled and the wind soughed through the dark green limbs that waved above them. Below them, they heard the sound of a truck coming from the direction of the pass. They watched its headlights from behind their screen of trees, fast-moving pinpoints in the darkness that grew brighter before sweeping past in a flash that left the night blacker around them.

''Is that what you've been trying to do,'' Wade asked finally, ''make up for the way your mother died by trying to stop the thing that killed her.''

It was so unexpected, his insight. She felt the tears rising, crowding against her throat so it ached. ''I couldn't stop the stoning,'' she said, her voice a thread of sound. ''I ran out to her, and when they finally let me go, it was too late.''

''You couldn't have stopped it anyway,'' he said. ''Mob mentality has nothing to do with reason.''

''Yes, I know, but...''

''But you still feel it, don't you? You still think you should have done something even when you know there was nothing possible. The rational mind sees one thing, but what you believe deep inside is different.''

His voice resonated in her mind, touching chords of recognition that she'd never quite dared examine. He could do it, she saw, because he knew the same pain, had the same doubts and regrets. She closed her

eyes, pressing her lips together as she tried not to
think and especially not to feel. "I'm doing something now," she said finally.

"You're fighting the Taliban that brought back the
old laws. And you're hiding behind your burqa because you're afraid of what will happen if you don't
keep it on."

"I remove it among family and friends," she said,
the words layered with protest. She refused to allow
herself to think that he might be right.

"But not in front of men."

"It's forbidden."

"Not here, it isn't, and not in front of me."

He sat perfectly still, watching her with a steady
regard that held no hint of command or threat, no
enticement, nothing at all to which she could take
exception.

"I'm not hiding," she insisted.

"No?"

"No!"

"Then I'll remind you, one more time, that we had
a bargain. My end of it was kept."

His voice was implacable. She thought he meant to
make her face the fact that she still wasn't free, even
though she had left the Taliban behind her. That
seemed to indicate a kind of pity, as if he thought that
she had no control over what she wore or why.

It was insupportable. With a quick gesture, she
caught the fullness of the cloth that covered her and
lifted it up, until she was lost in its folds, unable to

see, smothering in the clinging confinement. Then she wrenched the endless yards of cloth off over her head and whipped them aside. With a gesture of disdain, she let them fall to the ground.

She felt exposed. Felt cold. Felt an odd, senseless terror. She lifted a hand as if to catch the scarf that she'd borrowed to confine her hair and pull the end across her face. Having begun the gesture, it was impossible to stop it. To disguise that compulsion, she reached to unfasten the scarf and slide it off, baring her head, her neck, her ears, everything to his gaze. To lift her chin and look across the fire at him took every ounce of pride she possessed, and the last tiny shred of courage. She didn't know what she looked like, had barely seen herself in a mirror in years. She could feel the cool wind playing over her hair, filtering to cool her scalp, and the sensation was so acutely gratifying that the entire surface of her skin prickled into goose bumps. Panic gathered in her chest with suffocating pressure.

"Dear God," he said softly.

She swallowed, feeling the movement of her throat with the acute realization that it was perfectly visible. Only then did she allow her gaze to leave the point just past his shoulder that she'd chosen to focus on and actually meet his eyes. Reaching for anger because it was familiar and sustaining, she said, "All right, the burqa is gone. Are you happy now?"

"Ecstatic," he said as a slow smile curved his mouth. "Truly."

It was then, while they sat watching each other with the red and gold of the fire painting their faces and leaping in their eyes, that they heard a shrill cry, and the sound of a rock clattering downhill.

10

Before the sound had died away, Wade was on his feet, sliding his hand behind his back and drawing his weapon. He motioned for her to stay put then moved away from the fire. Seconds later, he vanished, his long dark form blending with the shadows under the trees. Chloe listened closely, but could hear nothing to mark his passage or tell which way he'd gone.

She felt far too visible in the campfire's glow. The need to get away from it, to melt into the darkness after Wade, was so strong that she could taste it. The only thing that kept her seated was the fear that he might mistake her for an assailant in the uncertain light.

A few minutes later, she heard the murmur of voices. Wade appeared at the edge of the small area they had cleared as they gathered sticks and dead branches for their fire. His weapon was no longer in his hand, though Chloe thought she saw its shadow under his shirt as he turned back toward someone behind him. Then he ushered forward a man and a woman trailed by two small children, a boy of about six and a girl a little younger.

They were Uzbek, from their style of dress, probably from the western border area. They had traveled far, and much of it on foot if their shoes were anything to go by. Their faces were gray with dust and fatigue. The woman hung back behind her husband, her head bowed and her children close against her. The man had a gaunt look but seemed strong enough otherwise. His face was long and narrow under his beard, and his dark-shadowed eyes were searching as he looked from Wade to her and back again.

"You are American," he said. "From the United States. Is it not so?"

"You have eyes to see, wise one," Chloe answered when Wade remained silent. "Come, please, and share our fire."

They edged forward a little into the light. The man's gaze rested the barest second on the tin can where they had boiled tea, but he answered politely. "We would not intrude."

Chloe looked again at Wade, since it was his duty to play host to these people he had brought into their camp. He was frowning, as if he couldn't quite follow what was being said, and perhaps he couldn't since the man's Pashtu was overlaid by an accent that made it difficult. He had brought these people into the camp, however, so she could only suppose his intention was to offer them hospitality.

"Permit me to give you tea," she said to their guests, and reached to tip water into the tin can and set it to heat on a flat rock at the edge of the glowing coals. She also added a piece or two of wood to the flames. Sparks swirled in the updraft of fresh heat and smoke, dancing into the cedar boughs above them.

The man licked his lips without taking his gaze from the water. "You are most kind, my lady."

She gestured toward a seat near the fire. "Sit, if you please. Would you and your family care to drink?" She wiped the edge of her cup with care, then filled it with water, and offered it with both hands.

The man took it, sipped as if from politeness, though she saw the reluctance with which he removed the plastic rim from his lips afterward. He turned to offer it to his wife. She barely wet her mouth before holding the water so her children could drink, first the boy, then the girl.

"Perhaps you'll tell me why you travel and where you are going?" Chloe asked as she took the cup when it was handed back, refilling it again with a casual air so that it could make another round.

The man had owned a farm near a tiny village, he said, where his family had lived since the time of Mohammed. But the opposition forces had stolen his sheep and goats, and the Taliban had burned his fields for the crime of not preventing this theft. They had burned his house as well, and he was lucky that they had not killed him. He had left the ruins of his life behind to save his children, and meant to go to a refugee camp. But they had spoken to other travelers this afternoon, after they had crossed the border, who told him there was no food in the camps, that it was promised and promised and did not come. They told him that the relief agencies arrived to take pictures of starving children and went away to show the films, but the money they took in donations went to line their pockets, and so people died. Now he did not know where to go.

Wade came to squat beside where she sat. Keeping his voice quiet, he asked, "What is he saying?"

Chloe told him, leaving out nothing. He listened, nodding now and then. Then he said, "It's a long way from the border to here for people on foot, especially with two kids to slow them down. Ask him how he came so far so quickly if they crossed only a few hours ago."

She did as he asked, then listened to the answer. "He says that they were given a ride by a leather merchant who works in Kashi, but whose Number Two wife is Pakistani and lives in a small village near here so he travels back and forth several times a week. He dropped them where he turned off the main road."

Wade nodded, but his gaze was on the youngest child, the little girl with hair down to her waist and eyes that seemed to take up half her face. She was staring at the small pile of nuts and dried fruit that Wade had left lying on the blanket. She inched toward it as if drawn, her small toes moving visibly in slippers made from pieces of old carpet.

Wade leaned forward, reaching his hand toward the food. The girl jumped back like a frightened rabbit, huddling against her mother. Wade stopped, then slowly picked up a nutmeat and held it out to the child.

"No," Chloe began, then indicated as Wade glanced her way that the father should be offered food first. Either he didn't understand the protocol or deliberately ignored it. He turned back to the child, still holding out the bit of food.

The little girl looked at her mother who had turned her face away. She looked at her father. She looked at Chloe. Then slowly, inch by careful inch, she crept closer to Wade. Reaching out with all the nervous delicacy of a frightened mouse, she put the tips of her fingers on the nutmeat. Then she snatched it and stuffed it into her mouth. Her small face bloomed in a smile like the opening of a morning glory to the sun. She put out her hand again in an imperious demand for more, and Wade carefully transferred the pile of food to her palm.

Chloe's own mouth curved in response. She glanced at Wade, then could not look away again. His strong features reflected such warmth, such rapt pleasure, that it made her heart ache. She had not known that a man could look like that merely from gaining a child's trust, that he could show something very like love for a small girl that he'd never met before and might never see again after this night. That he could give instead of take, willingly going hungry so a child he didn't know might not.

With a quick glance at the girl's father, Chloe said, "I am sorry. He is American, as you say, and doesn't understand our ways."

The Uzbek nodded gravely, his gaze on his daughter. "I am not offended. It was well-done."

From the corner of her eye, Chloe noticed the girl's brother, not much more than a year older than she was. He was not making a sound, but his distress and longing were in his face. Reaching behind her, Chloe

took the bag and poured out another handful of nuts
and dried fruit. With an encouraging smile, she held
it out to the boy. He was braver than his sister, or
else had learned from her experience. He took the
food that was offered at once, then stepped backward
until he could sit beside his father. He devoured his
treat to the last crumb before his sister was even half
done. But though he looked with longing at what she
had left, he made no move to take it.

Chloe gave him a nod of approval, and watched a
small, tired smile curve the boy's lips. Then remembering her manners, she extended the bag and the few
bits of food that were left inside to their ranking male
guest. She turned away at once, busying herself with
picking up her burqa and straightening its folds, to
give him the privacy to do what he would with it.

Something, some awareness that she felt as warmth
on the back of her neck, drew her gaze to where Wade
still knelt at the fire. The homage she saw in his eyes,
and the added heat behind it, made her flush to her
hairline even as she gave a rueful shake of her head
for the loss of their supper.

The Uzbek wife, who had come to squat near her
husband as she shared the last grains of trail mix,
reached to catch his sleeve and tug him closer while
she whispered in his ear. The man nodded with a
serious expression on his long face. Speaking to
Wade, though including Chloe in his glances as trans-
lator, he said, "My woman bids me tell you that she
believes we have come to your fire at the will of
Allah. You have extended your hospitality to us and
to our children, for which you will always have

praise. But there is a thing we may tell you in return for your kindness. Will you hear it?''

"Verily, and in gratitude, traveler,'' Chloe replied with a tight feeling in her chest. At Wade's inquiring look, she gave him the gist of what had been said.

"It happened in this manner. The leather merchant spoke to us while we rode. He said that he'd seen a great disturbance at the border when he crossed two days ago. Members of the Taliban were causing great delay as they searched for two people whom they had expected to attempt the crossing. With them was an officer in a great rage, because it seemed they had missed them. It happens that he had sworn a holy jihad against those he called bastard Americans for crimes pertaining to his honor. He intended to slit the throat of the woman, while the man he vowed to torture slowly and destroy utterly. He would wipe out the name of his tribe, even to the last and smallest child and if he had to travel to the ends of the earth to accomplish it. I believe, honored one, this Taliban referred to you and your lady, for there could not be many such as you here from your country.''

"And the name he would destroy?'' Chloe asked through dry lips.

"A difficult one,'' the man answered with regret. "I don't recall it.''

"Was it...Benedict?''

His wife tugged at his sleeve again, nodding as she watched Chloe. He didn't need her input, however, for he said at once, "Oh, aye, just so the merchant spoke. The name was Benedict.''

"Chloe?" Wade asked, his voice sharp with concern as he stared from her to their visitor.

She told him, and watched his face turn grim. The obvious implications took only seconds for him to assimilate.

"The only way he could destroy the entire Benedict clan is if he plans..."

"Yes," she agreed as he stopped. "If he intends to follow us back to the States. Our route would not be hard to guess, since he must realize that we'd have to cross into Pakistan by the nearest pass."

A frown drew Wade's brows together across his nose. "But would the Taliban spring for personal travel for Ahmad? Would they even allow it, much less make the special arrangements necessary for someone with his unsavory connections. It doesn't make sense."

"What are you saying?"

"I'm thinking he may have another purpose, that maybe he volunteered or was slated to go to the States already, and expects to combine his jihad with that mission. I need to make a few calls before I can work it out."

"I don't understand," she said.

The glance he gave her was brief. "Don't you? Did he never mentioned any assignment beyond his duty with the Taliban?"

"Not that I remember."

"Maybe not," he said with a dismissive gesture. "God, what I wouldn't give for the satellite cell phone I left back there."

"You'll be able to call from Peshawar. Or the airport."

"Yeah. Wonder how fast we can get there?"

"We'll find out in the morning."

His only answer was a distracted nod. It was plain to see that he'd forgotten her, forgotten everything except whatever problem was occupying his mind.

"Kemal may have had the right idea, after all."

That disgusted comment came from Wade after an hour and a half of trying to thumb a ride. Chloe sat on a rock beside the road with her elbow on her knee and her chin resting on the heel of her hand. She was tired and hungry, but most of all she was stifling under the burqa she'd donned again. She also felt extremely conspicuous sitting out in the open when Ahmad or someone who knew him could be in any of the trucks and cars that passed at lengthy intervals. It was possible that he was ahead of them, since he could not know that they had not left Ajzukabad immediately, but there was no guarantee of it.

She worried about Wade, too. He still looked indefinably American despite the turban bartered from their visitors of the night before in exchange for the pitiful gear that they'd rescued from the station wagon.

She cast a glance at that failed source of transport. It was completely intact, not that she was surprised. They should have slept in it. It would've been a lot more comfortable than a grimy blanket on rocky ground or huddling under the thin cover of her burqa to keep warm. Not that she'd have rested any better.

Her thoughts and fears had as much to do with keeping her awake as any discomfort.

Wade hadn't slept at all. His night had been spent prowling around the camp, watching from different vantage pints. The two kids had fallen asleep on the mat Chloe had laid out for him, and he'd refused to let them be moved. Offering to share hers had seemed necessary, in spite of their guests and an ingrained sense of the forbidden. Wade needed to conserve his strength, she thought. Going without both food and sleep was hardly a recommendation for recovery from a wound, and they still had a long journey in front of them. But he had cut her off, refusing before she had time for much more than a gesture.

As she lay staring up at the cold glitter of the stars above her solitary pallet, Chloe had wondered which of the several possible reasons for vetoing it had moved him, and if he realized she had shared his bed the night before. And she wasn't sure, then or now, whether she was glad or sorry that she had been left alone.

The blast of a horn brought her head around. She sprang to her feet as she saw Wade standing in the middle of the roadway with a panel truck bearing down on him at terrific speed. He held up one hand, palm turned out. As the truck swerved toward the other lane, he sidestepped. The truck began to brake, skidding with an ear-splitting squeal of tires.

"Come on!" Wade called.

Chloe glanced back over her shoulder toward where their guests were hidden among the cedars. The two children had still slept when she and Wade made their way down to the highway. The Uzbek father had been fashioning a snare for small game from a roll of nylon line he'd found in the tool bag, as if his need to feed his family was paramount.

"There's not enough room for everybody," Wade objected, as if reading her mind. "Let's go. Now."

She was already moving, running toward where the driver had reached across to shove open the door. A Sikh, he was complaining volubly about Wade's crazy methods, also of how he'd been instructed not to pick up refugees and only stopped because he could see that Wade was not such a person. He was still talking in high excitement long after Wade had boosted Chloe to the passenger seat and climbed up beside her and the truck was moving again. He didn't shut up, not until they'd reached the old caravan terminus of Peshawar and he set them down in the city center.

After that, it was almost ridiculously easy. A hired car to Rawalpindi, toiletries picked at a newsstand followed by a good wash and repairs in the rest room, and they were soon waiting in the gate for their flight to be called. This was the most trying time, as they scanned every face, every man who stood around them, expecting to see Ahmad. Finally the boarding process began. They found their seats, the plane doors were closed and they pulled back from the gate. Minutes later, they were airborne.

They had done it. They were leaving the Middle East. It was over. They were safe. They were free.

With her head pressed against the seat back as they climbed into the bright blue sky, Chloe turned her head to look at Wade. She met his eyes clearly, without obstruction, since she had discarded her burqa, once and for all, in the airport rest room. He held her gaze for long seconds, then he smiled and reached to cover her hand with his. His grasp was warm, firm. Feeling it, she realized how cold her own fingers were, how nervous and afraid she'd been until this moment. Turning her hand, she placed her palm against his and meshed their fingers, holding tight. Her gaze rested on that clasp with momentary amazement for how impossible it would have seemed only a few days ago, and how right it felt. At least for now.

A jumble of feelings crowded her chest, from disbelief to doubt about Ahmad's whereabouts and trepidation over what lay ahead. Sorting them out was too much however, when nothing could be done about any of it for the next twenty-four hours.

She looked up again at Wade, wondering what he was thinking, what he was planning for when they finally landed in New Orleans. His eyes were closed. He was asleep.

Her lips twisted in a wry smile. Then she let her own lashes drift down, soothing the graininess of exhaustion, shutting out the light. Sleep settled over her like a thick fog. But she did not release Wade's hand.

It was in Zurich that she had the first sense of dislocation. The airport was huge, incredibly clean and streamlined, and the echoing announcements in multiple Western languages fell strangely on her ears. Most unnerving, however, were the clothes people wore. They exposed amazing amounts of skin, and had what seemed a colorless and vapid chic that allowed the personality of the wearer to dominate. By contrast, her long-sleeved, high-necked blouse of aqua-blue and matching skirt bordered at the ankles in gold embroidery managed to appear both exotic and dowdy at the same time. She not only looked unusual, but was uncomfortably aware of having worn the same clothes for the best part of three days and nights, since changing at the RAWA safe house. She didn't blame people for the way they stared, still less for how they kept their distance. Their layover time in Switzerland allowed no time for leaving the airport to shop for replacements, however, even if she'd had the money. Her main consolation was that Wade had much the same problem.

By the time they reached Hartsfield International in Atlanta, the two of them were half-blind with fatigue, punch-drunk from jet lag and dehydrated from endless hours of flying. Their layover was more than three hours, however, allowing extra time for customs. Chloe was afraid that the passport provided by Wade, with its computer-aged and -enhanced photo of her, would be scrutinized more closely than in Europe, that she might even be pulled aside for questioning. The wait in the long line of passengers was excruciating, especially since Wade left her to hold their places while he used the phone. Her relief when she saw him returning was disturbing since it showed clearly how lost she felt, and how dependent she was becoming on him. Regardless, she was glad he was close as they were processed through customs.

"Your call was to your family?" she asked as they

sat in the departure gate, eating ice-cream cones and watching strangers with blank, distracted faces walk past in a steady stream.

He made a sound of agreement. "Getting an update on what they've been doing since my call from Rawalpindi. I also arranged a rental car."

"Where are we going, I mean from the airport?" It was odd that she hadn't asked sooner, she thought, but they'd been so exhausted that somehow it hadn't seemed to matter. The whole thing was only becoming real in her mind now that they were on American soil.

"Home. At least at first, until you can find your feet and decide what you want to do. Got any ideas?"

"Not...not really."

"Understandable."

His concentration was on his ice cream as he caught a drip with his tongue. Chloe watched the muscular agility of that movement while an odd sensation curled in the pit of her stomach. Finally she said, "I suppose I'll get an apartment. But first I'll need access to whatever money I'm supposed to have."

"No problem."

Her own ice cream was dissolving faster than she was eating it. She took care of the problem, relishing the cold, rich sweetness. A thought struck her and she swallowed with difficulty. "I'd also like to see...to see where my father's buried."

"Whenever you're ready."

She looked up as he spoke, but his gaze was on her lips. She licked them, reaching up to wipe one corner as she realized she still had a leftover bit of stickiness there. Wade blinked, returning his gaze to his cone. But not before she'd seen enough heat in his eyes to melt the ice cream in his hand.

Their flight was called then. A short time later, they were landing in New Orleans. Suddenly it seemed too soon, too abrupt a transition. She wasn't ready. She wasn't ready at all.

The people crowding around them were different from those in Europe. They smiled and laughed and talked nonstop with rich drawls that rose and fell in almost musical expression. Many of them seemed to know each other, or were part of family groups. Some business suits were in evidence, but the majority of those streaming back and forth wore T-shirts, jeans and running shoes, as if the combination constituted a kind of uniform. The women with their short hair and expertly applied makeup particularly caught Chloe's attention. They seemed unaware of the emphasis placed on their breasts and hips by their close-fitting clothing, and unselfconscious about the way men looked them over as they walked by. They were free in their movements and speech, so at ease with their natural sexuality that they were almost oblivious to it. They appeared so casually sophisticated, in fact, that they made Chloe feel out of place and incredibly repressed. And she wondered with mordant curiosity if there was a single virgin like her among them.

Chloe would have followed the stream of passengers headed toward baggage claim and public transportation, if Wade hadn't touched her arm. "This way," he said, indicating the main terminal. "We can get a taxi that's dropping off passengers without having to stand in line for it, then ride downtown to pick up the rental.''

"But the sign says there's a rental desk downstairs.''

"The lines will be miles long there, too. This will be faster.''

She was too tired to care one way or the other. Obediently she turned in the direction he indicated, not even bothering to pull away as he put a hand at the small of her back to guide her around an elderly woman in a wheelchair.

A man came at them from the side when they were less than three yards from the entrance doors. He moved fast and quiet, skimming between a pilot pulling a black case on wheels and a chubby guy with a sunburn and a straw hat that said St. Thomas, V.I.

Wade clamped an arm around her waist and spun Chloe behind him. Then he dropped into a fighter's crouch as he faced the threat.

"Damn, Wade!'' The would-be assailant skidded to a halt and threw up his hands. "If this is the way you greet kinfolk, what the hell do you do with enemies?''

"Shit, little brother. Don't do that to me.'' Wade sighed, and straightened. Then he took a long stride forward and folded the newcomer into a quick, back-pounding hug.

As they broke apart, Chloe looked from one to the other. Wade's brother was a fraction shorter, his hair a little darker, and his eyes vivid blue instead of green. Despite these obvious differences, they were more alike than not. Their features were the same, as was the proud set of their shoulders and their bearing that had such confidence it bordered on arrogance.

"Didn't mean to yank your chain," Wade's brother said. "I was afraid you were about to get away before I could reach you. I just got here myself, after dropping Adam off at Arrivals to watch for you."

"You didn't say you'd be meeting us."

"Didn't know it. Family decision, last minute, as usual." The younger Benedict tipped his head, trying to see around Wade. "So do I get an introduction to the lady, or you keeping her to yourself?"

"Guess I'll risk it, since I know that you've got your hands full with Janna. Chloe Madison, meet another Benedict, my brother Clay." Wade stepped aside as he spoke, and held out a hand to beckon her forward. As she moved to his side, she saw his brother's gaze widen. Then it traveled slowly from the top of her center-parted hair down to where it hung well below her waist. He inspected the soft leather sandals on her feet and, on the way back up to her face, the curves of her hips, slim waist, and front of her blouse.

"Oh," he said in a blank, almost stunned, tone of voice. "Oh. My. God."

"Well put," Wade said with dry humor in his voice. "You can take that as a compliment, Chloe, since this guy isn't the impressionable type."

"You said when you left that you had to go rescue a kid," Clay objected, though without looking at his brother. "I wasn't expecting a goddess."

"Ditto," Wade answered. "I only found out after the unveiling."

Clay's brows shot up toward his hairline. "You'll have to explain that."

"Later. For now, we want a hot bath and a cool, clean bed, in that order."

"Right."

"Separate baths, separate beds," Wade added with cut-steel precision in his voice.

"Sorry."

That single word was repentant enough, but didn't quite match the gleam of conjecture in his brother's eyes. Chloe thought the younger Benedict had missed nothing of Wade's rigorously correct attitude. It was no great surprise that he didn't get it, of course. She didn't quite understand, either.

Even as these thoughts ran through her head, Clay turned with a broad gesture toward the door. "This way, ma'am, your chariot is waiting, and about to run over its five-minute parking limit."

The vehicle he was talking about was a dove-gray SUV with four doors, mud-grip tires, leather seats and far more luxury than anything she had seen in the past decade. Wade handed Chloe into the back seat, since the plan was to drive around to the lower level to pick up Wade's older brother waiting there. It took several minutes because of traffic and construction, but they finally pulled up near the line of waiting taxis outside the Arrivals area.

"There he is," Clay said, and bumped his horn.

A man turned from where he leaned on a concrete

support, watching the door. Obviously another Benedict, he lifted a hand and started toward them.

Abruptly a flat report smacked the air. For a second, Chloe thought one of the taxis had rear-ended the next in line. Then Wade reached for her, dragging her off the seat to the floorboard. At the same time, he gave a shout. "Down! Incoming fire!"

Clay ducked, crouching over the wheel. The front passenger door was wrenched open, then slammed shut again. Two shots punched the back glass and zinged past overhead. Glass shattered inward in sharp-edged bits like a rain of ice-cream salt.

"Drive! Drive!" The order came from the addition to their number, somewhere above and in front of Chloe. Outside could be heard yells, screams, car horns and the staccato reports of more firing.

They pealed away with a screech of tires. The SUV swerved into a wide turn that slung her against the seat back, then straightened again, gathering speed. Chloe could see nothing, do nothing except clutch Wade's shoulder for balance and try to control the rage that filled her.

She'd thought she was safe, at least for a little while. She'd thought that even if her stepbrother came after her and Wade, it would be days, even weeks before he found her.

She'd been wrong. He had not come after them at all.

Ahmad was already here.

11

"We definitely have company," Wade said, his voice grim as he looked back to see Ahmad and two buddies pile into a late-model green sedan and pull into traffic behind them. He couldn't help wondering what the trio would have done if he and Chloe had walked out of that airport exit alone. Shot them on sight? Surrounded them and put a knife to their ribs before driving somewhere for a slower end to it all?

It hadn't happened so there was no point thinking about it. The real question was, what now?

Clay spoke up then as if in cheerful answer to his mental query. "They picked the wrong folks to follow. Not to mention the wrong town for it." He accelerated in a smooth surge of power. Swinging around the curves of the airport exit lanes with easy control, he emerged on the highway.

"They're still back there," Adam said as he watched his side mirror.

"Not for long," Clay answered.

The comment was followed by a rapid change of lanes. Brief seconds later, or so it seemed, they were merging onto Interstate 10. The sedan kept pace, but only by cutting off two vehicles and passing another one on the right. With any luck, Wade thought, the police would pick up their tail. He just hoped they didn't flag the SUV, since it felt as if it might sprout wings at any second.

As he glanced ahead again, he suddenly realized they were eastbound. "What gives? Why aren't we heading for Turn-Coupe?"

"Mom gave instructions to bring you back to her place." Clay checked his mirrors, then cut across two lanes of traffic to avoid rear-ending a pickup towing a bass boat.

"We can't do that," Wade said instantly. "If that crew back there can track airline schedules, they can figure out where she lives."

"In that case, we have to go see about her," Adam said in hard response.

"You're right," Wade said, wiping a hand over his face. The strain of the past few days must have clouded his brain more than he realized. His mother might not be a Benedict anymore, since she'd resumed her maiden name, but would still be a prime target. They'd be hamstrung, all of them, if she was taken hostage.

He glanced at Chloe. Her face was white. It wasn't surprising, since she knew better than any just what her stepbrother was capable of doing in his dedication to his fanatic ideas of right and wrong. However misguided the guy's beliefs and principles, Wade had to appreciate how he stuck to them. Reminded him of the Benedicts in a peculiar sort of way.

The beep of a horn brought his head around again. Clay was traversing traffic lanes again, asking for and getting concession from a fast-moving taxi before making a dive for a long, straight exit lane. As Wade craned to check the rear window again, he saw the rental car almost cut off by a big tanker truck, though the driver whipped around it to make the exit. Two cars following the truck slammed on their brakes with the sound of squealing tires and blasting horns.

Now the chase was really on, not that Wade doubted how it would end. Clay might be a backwoods boy who spent more time snapping art photos of alligators than prowling around New Orleans, but he didn't neglect visiting their mom or taking Janna and Lainey to town on medical visits and pleasure trips. He knew the city. It was a good thing, too, because it wasn't an easy place to navigate. The old French Quarter with its narrow streets was its heart, lying in the half-moon-shaped bend in the Mississippi River that gave it the name, the Crescent City. More modern thoroughfares either followed the great curve to avoid the Quarter, stopped just before they reached it, ran at odd angles to intersect with it, or bypassed it with a tangle of overpasses and underpasses. Then there were the many parks and big cemeteries to be circumvented. The result was a maze, streets that might run only a few blocks before vanishing altogether, alternate between one-way and two-way traf-

fic, or change their names three times between Downtown, the French Quarter, and Uptown. It took a
native or someone used to following obscure boat
channels through uncharted swamps to make sense of
it. Clay belonged to the latter category.

They lost their tail between City Park and Clai-
borne. A short time later, they pulled into the backyard of a French Quarter row house on Dumaine
Street where their mom and her visitors had parking
privileges. Keeping a sharp eye out for company, they
walked the three blocks to her apartment that was
located above a bar and grill where the odor of stale
beer vied with the knock-you-down smell of boiling
shrimp.

They rang the bell at the tall side door, identified
themselves, and waited for the buzz of the lock's release. Entering a dim hallway, they climbed a spiral
staircase with a wide mahogany railing and treads
worn a half inch deep. Their mom waited at the top
with a wide smile, hair hanging over her shoulder in
a silver-threaded brown braid, and arms that were
held wide and appeared wider due to the expanse of
a blue cotton caftan that she'd picked up in Morocco
years ago. The closer they came to the apartment
door, the more blatantly obvious it grew that she was
responsible for that aroma of hot shrimp that was
anathema to many but ambrosia to a true son of Louisiana. She was cooking. Of course.

"Honey," she said, folding Wade into the soft,

scented, bone-crushing hug that was her specialty. "Thank God."

"Yeah, yeah, I missed you, too," he said, his voice a little husky, and not only from the pain of having his slashed side thoroughly squeezed.

Everybody else got a hug as well, including Chloe. It was just the way his mother was, a hugger, a toucher, a feeder of hungry souls. Sometimes he wondered if that wasn't what she tried to do with her art as well.

"Get dressed, Mom," he began as Chloe emerged, dazed, from that enveloping embrace. "We have to go."

"But you just got here. Sit down a minute. Have something to eat."

"We don't have time. I mean we have to get out of here, all of us, and right now."

"Wait a minute," she said, breaking across what he was saying. "Come here again."

"Mom..." he began as she caught him close with one arm and lifted a hand to his face.

"You have fever, and I think I felt something here. She poked his side. "Right, a bandage. What have you done to yourself?"

"Nothing. Listen to me..."

"He has a what?" Adam scowled at him over his shoulder as he closed and locked the door.

Chloe spoke up then. "It's a knife wound, and probably needs attention and antibiotics."

"Figures," his mother said in exasperation.

"Later," he said with an accusing glance in Chloe's direction. "I'm telling you we have to get a move on."

"What's the hurry?"

Just then, a timer went off in the kitchen. His mother released him and moved away in that direction without waiting for an answer to her question. He followed her, talking with all the persuasion he could muster while watching her take a huge pot of broth swimming with shrimp, potatoes and corn on the cob from the gas range and pour it directly into the sink to drain. Steam redolent of pepper and spice rose to sting their eyes as they all crowded into the small room. His mother paused to stare at him over her shoulder as he reached the most salient part of his story, the arrival of Chloe's stepbrother with murder on his mind. Then she pulled a large plastic container from under the cabinet and began to scoop shrimp and vegetables into it.

"Didn't you hear me?" he demanded.

"If you think I'm leaving my good food here for a bunch of killers, you've got another think coming."

"There's no time," he insisted in exasperation. He looked at his brothers for support.

"We have to eat," she returned unanswerably. "Especially you, since you need your strength. We'll take this with us." She glanced at Adam. "Dump the ice from the fridge into that little ice chest behind you, will you, honey?"

"Mom!"

"You may as well stop arguing and help her," Clay said. Glancing around, he picked up two loaves of French bread in their white bakery wrappers and tucked them under one arm.

"I know just the place to go," his mother said with a smile of approval for her younger son. "That old place on the River Road where I stayed back in the spring, painting *en plein* air. Nottoway, it's called. They were wonderful to me."

"We can't involve other people."

"It isn't other people, it's a hotel. Well, sort of. Besides, it's closer to Turn-Coupe."

"A hotel is definitely out. We can't risk having anything show up in a credit card database. These guys may be medieval in their thinking, but they have computer capability."

"No problem. I know the manager. Besides, you were thinking maybe of Grand Point?"

Wade swiped his fingers back through his hair. "I don't know. It doesn't seem right to involve the family."

"We're already involved," Clay pointed out. Reaching over his mother's shoulder, he snagged one of the jumbo pink shrimps just before she closed the lid on her plastic container. Blowing on it to cool it, he peeled it with two quick moves and popped the morsel into his mouth.

Wade's saliva glands kicked into overdrive. It had been ages since he'd tasted really fresh seafood. Even as he recognized his weakening resolve, he was aware of Adam's almost casual drift to a point where he could see out the kitchen window to the street below. With a narrow glance from one brother to the other, he asked, "Meaning?"

"I called Roan," Clay answered. "Adam got in touch with Luke and Kane, too, since there's no telling how many limbs these jihadis mean to lop off the family tree. We all agreed that choosing a single point to defend was best. Grand Point is being turned into a fortress as we speak."

That had a good sound to it. Roan was the sheriff of Tunica Parish where the old home place, Grand Point, was located. He could bring in some heavy law enforcement artillery if necessary. Luke and Kane had a comprehensive knowledge of the lake and the swamp that backed up to the house, and also the consummate skill with weapons of men who had hunted since they were kids.

"Fine, but Wade needs a doctor first," his mother said. "Who knows what kind of infection he may have picked up over there?"

"She's right," Chloe agreed. "My friends and I did the best we could, but it wasn't a lot."

"I'm sure you did fine," his mother said hastily.

"Doc Watkins could come to the house," Clay suggested.

The look his mother gave him was unimpressed. "I doubt that old man has so much as picked up a medical journal since he retired a decade ago. Besides, these two are dead on their feet." She swung on Chloe. "When was the last time you really slept, either of you? Or had a decent meal, for that matter?"

"A while," Chloe answered.

"That's what I thought. So it's settled." She turned to the refrigerator and took out what appeared to be a bowl of potato salad and a large bread pudding. Handing one to Adam and the other to Clay, she lifted a brow. "There now, we're ready. So why are we still standing around here?"

Nottoway, located at the town of White Castle some thirty minutes or so from Baton Rouge, had once been a plantation house in the grand manner, the center of several thousand acres devoted to sugar cultivation. A huge pile in shining white, it had columns that soared three stories tall, miles of verandas, and at least a couple of hundred windows. According to the brochure Wade picked up in the reception area while his mom went in search of the manager, it was the largest antebellum home ever constructed in the South, with sixty-four rooms that included a bowling alley and a ballroom. The main house was open daily for guided tours, while the overseer's cottage and the *garçonnière,* where younger sons and visitors had once been housed, were fitted out as guest rooms. Set back in the center of a walled enclosure, reached only by entrance through a separate building that housed the gift shop, it had a secluded air and surprising degree of natural security.

"Now isn't this perfect?" his mother asked as she

led them to a back room on the second floor of the overseer's cottage and threw open the door.

Wade allowed Chloe to go first, then followed her inside. The place was actually a minisuite, with a table for two placed between a pair of windows, desk in one corner, fireplace with the bed opposite, a second, smaller bedroom that had an armoire and single bed, and the requisite bathroom. The furnishings, including the white-painted iron bedstead, looked like authentic antiques instead of reproductions. Though not particularly posh as hotel rooms went, it was comfortable. For him, brought up at Grand Point, it felt like home.

"Seems all right," he said in half grudging acceptance.

"I love it," Chloe said, gazing around with a serious expression on her face.

"There, that's the kind of answer I like," his mother said with approval. "Now, let's eat. The manager was kind enough to call the doctor from her cell phone so there'll be nothing to connect it to any of us. He'll be here in half an hour."

The accommodations were a little cramped for feeding a group, but the five of them managed. Wade wolfed down his share with more dispatch than finesse, and was happy to see Chloe doing the same. When he'd caught up with his appetite, he peeled a few extra shrimp for her, since she seemed to be having trouble. The smile she gave him as she accepted them was a better reward than any medal.

"So what about Janna and Lara?" he asked as he reached for the bread pudding. He spooned a serving into one of the plastic bowls they'd picked up when they'd run by a discount store for a couple of changes of clothes and other things to make life more comfortable. "They're at Grand Point?"

"Lara was out of the condo, out of New Orleans and on her way to Grand Point five minutes after you called," Adam answered with a shake of his head. "She's been telling me for three or four days that she had a bad feeling about you, and thought we ought to be there because you were coming home."

"Janna's at the house, too, with Lainey," Clay added. "School started this week, but we decided to keep her out. No use in taking chances."

The protective concern in the faces of his two brothers got to Wade, somehow. He must be more tired than he realized. Clearing his throat a little, he asked, "Tory? Regina?"

"At Grand Point, since that's where Roan and Kane are at the moment," Adam said, since Clay now had his mouth full. "April was off on some book tour, but cut it short. Luke should be picking her up at the Monroe airport about now."

That accounted for his close cousins and their wives. There were more, since the woods around Turn-Coupe were full of Benedicts, but these five, with their families, were the most likely targets after Chloe and himself. They were peace-loving men, slow to anger but formidable when roused. Ahmad didn't know what he'd done by threatening them.

The doctor arrived as they were finishing the last of the wine that had been brought as a welcoming gift by the tall black majordomo who seemed to run the place. Wade was led into the smaller bedroom for a thorough and somewhat painful inspection of his wound. The doctor announced that it was healing well except for a small pocket of infection around one stitch, something Wade could have told him if asked. But at least the medic was reasonable enough to allow him a hot shower before he scrubbed the area with peroxide, steeped it in Betadine, then applied a considerably less bulky bandage. There followed a quick injection of antibiotics before Wade was permitted to pull on a new pair of jeans and T-shirt. The doctor then left a handful of antibiotic samples to be taken later by mouth, accepted his fee with an awkwardness that suggested handling payment in cash was a rare occurrence, then left as quickly as he had come.

Not long afterward, Adam and Clay began to talk of everything that was being done at Grand Point or that needed to be done. It was a fair indication of their thoughts and a prelude to departure. Their mother gathered paper plates and cups and packed away what was left of the food. Hugs, handshakes and back slaps were exchanged all around. Clay offered to stay and stand guard in the small parlor outside the room, though it was plain to see that he was torn between that and a strong urge to check on his family. Adam mentioned a friend of his on the New Orleans police force who wouldn't mind a little off-duty security work. Their mother informed them both that the hotel had its own security, on top of which, the idea was to avoid attracting attention. They were still arguing as they went down the outside stairs.

Finally they were gone. Wade closed and locked the door. He stood staring at the mechanism that was as antique as the rest of the place, thinking that it probably wouldn't stop a six-year-old determined to get inside. Then he turned to face Chloe.

She was watching him with her arms clasped around her and her eyes dark blue with distress and exhaustion. "You have a nice family," she said, her voice so soft he could barely hear her. "I'm sorry they had to be dragged into this."

"Nothing to be sorry about. You didn't do it." He prowled to the back window where he stood to one side, staring out through the lace curtain.

"It wouldn't have happened if my father hadn't sent you after me."

"And he wouldn't have sent me if you weren't in trouble. Does that make it your fault? Some things can't be avoided. You have to make the best of them." As she made no reply, he glanced back but didn't know what to make of her odd half smile. "I mean it."

"I know you do. I was just thinking that for someone who seems so intense on the surface, you're very comfortable to be around."

Comfortable. He could feel one corner of his mouth turn down. "Thanks. I think."

Her smile flashed a bare second then was gone again. "It's a bad situation that your family is facing. I hope they understand how terrible it can be."

"They have a fair idea."

"Ahmad blames us for Treena's death, I'm sure, and not himself. His regret over it will add to his fervor. He needs to hurt somebody, hurt us so we understand and share his pain, then wipe out the images in his mind by erasing all trace of proof that we lived. He will remove the Benedict clan from the face of the earth, if he can."

"It won't be easy, I promise."

"He'll stop at nothing, not even his own death."

The fatalistic sound of her voice made the hair rise on the back of Wade's neck, though he refused to acknowledge it. "That can be arranged."

"The question is just how many of your brothers and cousins, their wives and children, he will eliminate first."

The thought wasn't pleasant. To head off this disaster by fighting shoulder to shoulder with those of his blood and heritage was an ancient yet immediate instinct. He could feel it pouring through his bloodstream, coalescing around his heart. It went against the grain to remain here, even when he knew he'd be more useful after he'd had a chance to rest and recover. "I don't know a lot about how fanatic Ahmad and those he has with him can be, but I'll tell you this much,'' he said in hard tones. ''If he harms a hair on any Benedict, particularly any Benedict woman or child, his life won't be worth Jack shit.''

Chloe gave a small shake of her head. ''That won't bring anyone back or make the pain of loss any less. I can't stand to think about it. And I can't imagine how it will end.''

Wade, deep in thought, made no answer. He was aware of the moment when she turned away, however, knew that she picked up the bags holding her new clothing and toiletries and moved in the direction of the bathroom. He heard the door close and, after a moment, the sound of running water.

He stood still a minute or two, staring at nothing. Then, driven by restlessness and a strong sense of unease, sick of being penned up, he swung abruptly and scooped the key from the desktop. He let himself out of the room, locking the door carefully behind him.

To his left was the cottage's front parlor, to his right a pair of double doors at the end of the hall that led onto a back veranda. He turned toward the rear exit, then crossed to run lightly down the wide stairs to the ground. Directly in front of him was a small lagoonlike pool with a statue on a mound in the center. He moved off in that direction.

The air was warm and incredibly humid against his skin. It felt right and natural, unlike the harsh, dry atmosphere of Hazaristan. He figured that people were formed and tempered by the climate of the place where they were born, that it entered their genes and their personalities in some fashion. Not that this accounted for the extreme attitudes and ideology of men like Ahmad. Parents, teachers and the sum of their experiences also helped create them. It wasn't often that Wade gave much thought to the kind of home he'd come from, other than its problems. But he had to admit that it had been safe, and its values solid and unchanging. He'd had the freedom to roam the woods, the lake and the swamp, to test himself against these things and against the elements. Though his parents couldn't manage to get along together, there had never been any real doubt about where he belonged or the fact that he was loved in spite of his faults. It made a difference.

Alert and on the lookout even in his reverie, Wade drifted around the perimeter of the pool and what had once been part of a carriage house without getting too far from the overseer's cottage. Seeing nothing unusual, he struck out at an angle that took him closer to the main house. He circled toward the front, reconnoitering and exploring at the same time, glancing up at the welcoming arms entrance stairs railed in wrought iron, the many windows that overlooked the landscaped lawn, passing the gift shop and the garden that fronted the restaurant. Following the walk, he prowled under huge banana trees and past other tropical flowers to where he could see the overseer's cottage once more. A tour group was just leaving after viewing the main house, the last few stragglers disappearing into the gift shop. Nothing else moved. Not even the majordomo or a custodian was in evidence, though a lawn mower sat near the walkway and an impulse sprinkler played water over the grass with a noise that was like a theme song for a late summer afternoon.

Intending to give Chloe plenty of time for her bath, he ambled between the cottage and the *garçonnière,* making toward the iron bench that he'd noticed in the shade of one of the great live oaks that dotted the rear lawn. He dropped down on it and leaned back.

The house that towered above him was a masterpiece of its kind, a majestic yet comfortable mingling of neoclassical, Georgian and Italianate elements. Its rounded balconies and deep porches behind square columns and voluptuously carved ironwork had been designed to make the climate more bearable before the invention of air-conditioning. The huge magnolia and oak trees that spread their branches around it had lent their cool shade through countless afternoons, and still provided a pleasant relief from the heat. Behind the latticed wall that fronted the house, Wade could hear an occasional car passing on the old river road that wound between it and the high embankment of the Mississippi River levee.

Grand Point was older than Nottoway, and not nearly as majestic, but the atmosphere was much the same. Birds called, and a pair of squirrels played chase along the railing of an upper balcony on the house. A breeze brought the mind-drugging scents of ginger lilies and newly mown grass.

Turning on the bench, Wade lay down with his neck resting on the arm and one leg trailing to the ground. It was so peaceful that he couldn't resist closing his eyes to savor the feeling.

He awoke to the soft shadows of dusk and the final glow of a red, chemical-tinted sunset slanting in low under the trees. Sitting up, he glanced around with narrowed eyes. Everything looked the same; nothing had changed except that he felt at least a hundred percent better. Even the cut in his side was less stiff and sore. Guilt and anxiety brought him up off the bench, however, and turned him in the direction of the cottage.

No light came from under the door. It took him several seconds longer than it should have to fit the key in the lock. Stepping inside, he stood listening while he allowed his eyes to adjust to the gloom.

Nothing moved. There was no sound. The front room with its big bed was empty.

Chloe was gone.

12

It was then that he heard a rustling sound in the connecting room, as if someone had shifted in sleep. He stepped to one side, until he could see the single bed where he'd sat while the doctor examined him. A svelte shape lay there outlined by the sheet and bedspread.

Wade breathed again, a winded rush that was loud in the stillness. Moving with care, he walked to the door between the two rooms and leaned on the frame. Chloe lay asleep with one arm angled above her head and her hair spread out in a silken flow that spilled across the pillow and halfway down to the floor. Its long strands had been brushed smooth, but still looked a little damp. Her lashes rested on her pale cheeks, and her breasts, unconfined under the soft cotton of the T-shirt she wore, rose and fell in a deep and steady rhythm.

Need hit him like a blindside tackle. The urge to climb into the bed and gather her close was so strong that suppressing it made cold sweat pop out across his forehead and upper lip. He wanted to feel her hair against his face, to breathe its fragrance, to smooth his hands over her and fill them with her yielding flesh, and to bury himself in her for an eon or two, or at least until morning. It was a primal urge, he knew, the body's natural response to passing danger and propinquity, and yet there was an ache to it that was like homesickness. To remain where he stood felt unnatural, as though he was being denied his rightful place.

He couldn't stand it. He had to get away before he did something really stupid.

The room key was still in his hand, held so tightly that it almost cut into his palm. He looked down at the key ring that was one of the pair they'd been given. Two keys were actually on it, the second for the back door of the main house. A major privilege of being a guest at Nottoway, so he'd been told, was private access when tours had ended for the day. That should have been an hour ago, at least.

It was a place to go, a way to remove himself from temptation.

The back door of the huge old mansion opened under his hand. To just walk into such a monument to pre-Civil War glory felt strange, but no one showed up to stop him. He was in a long entrance hall, with stairs rising above him from against the wall on his left. A reception desk stood at its end, but no one was behind it. He thought he could hear movement in the kitchen area that lay beyond, though he couldn't be sure. Special guest suites were somewhere upstairs, he knew, but they were apparently not in use just now, and the other guests were either out exploring the countryside still or having dinner. He seemed to be alone in this white castle.

Wade peered into the long room that was once the bowling alley, and used now for the breakfast room. After checking out an exhibit or two that lined it, he returned to the foyer area where he made his way up the mahogany stairs. With his footsteps alternately echoing on hardwood floors and deadened by rugs, he wandered through sitting and dining rooms, a smoking parlor where men had gathered long ago to enjoy their cigars and cards, and a music room where a harp sat as a ghostly reminder of past entertainment. He ran a hand over a marble surface here or a tabletop with glasslike polish there, since he had an appreciation for fine woods and antiques gained from years of living with them. Many of the furnishings here were particularly fine, the Sevres china, the ornate coal grates in the fireplaces, the hand-painted china doorknobs and silver call-bell handles. Still, they had a melancholy air somehow, as if they had outlived their usefulness.

The grand ballroom was something Grand Point was missing. He thought it must be over sixty feet long, with a multitude of tall windows that opened to a height near six feet for air and so dancers could move back and forth from the dance floor to the outside balcony. The marble fireplace mantel was white, as were the walls, the floor, and the ceiling with its ornate plaster cornice and medallions centered by sparkling chandeliers.

A piano sat to one side. It was a fine instrument with a great sound, as he discovered from touching a key or two. Since lessons had been a part of his life for a couple of years before his mother moved out, he sat down and played the few bars of a waltz that had been a practice piece.

Some slight sound or possibly a moving current of air jerked at his attention. He swung around on the piano bench.

"Don't stop," Chloe said as she moved from where she stood in the rear doorway. "It suits the house."

"I was just...fooling around." He could feel a guilty flush across the back of his neck, like a kid caught meddling in other people's closets and dresser drawers.

"I'd never have guessed that you'd enjoy this sort of thing." She walked toward him, brushing his shoulder lightly as she passed, then running her fingers over the top of the piano. "It's fascinating, isn't it?"

"Wait until you see Grand Point. It has even more history than this pile." She seemed to go with the house, he thought, his appraising gaze on white peasant blouse that she'd put on in place of the T-shirt she'd worn earlier, and the ankle-length, broomstick-pleated skirt in some lightweight pastel fabric paired with it.

"Really?"

With an effort he looked away from the sway of her hips and the silky swing of her hair, which trailed down her back in a long ponytail held by an equally long ribbon. "I used to pretend sometimes, on rainy afternoons, that I lived back in the old days."

"As what?" She turned to face him as he stood and moved after her. "A pirate? Or maybe a soldier going off to fight in some war?"

"Or holding what my brothers and I called a fort, though it was actually an old Indian mound with a root cellar dug into its side. But I also thought it would have been great to be a gentleman of leisure, nothing to do except eat, drink, ride horses and court the ladies. I was about sixteen, maybe seventeen by that time." He took her hand and swept her a bow, then placed her fingers on his shoulder and drew her into a classical dance position since the location seemed to call for it.

She gazed up at him with an odd, almost bemused expression on her face. "You liked the idea of that last part?"

"It had its appeal. Of course I saw myself as Joe Cool, super smooth, with all the right moves." He eased gently into the first steps of a waltz.

"Bowing, paying pretty compliments?"

"Instead of being tongue-tied and awkward as in real life," he agreed with a wry smile.

She gave a low laugh. "I can't believe you were ever that."

"Believe it. That was a long time ago, of course." He swung her into a turn, drawing her closer at the same time. The feel of her brushing against him, her skirt around his feet, her hair against his hand at her waist, her body against his, was so tantalizing that he knew he was in serious danger of making a fool of himself. He didn't intend to stop, however, at least not yet.

"I can't dance," she said abruptly.

"You're doing fine so far."

"I never learned how, not really, though my mother used to show me some of the steps in secret."

"I could teach you if you really want to learn." It was an excuse if he'd ever heard one, a reason to stay around her.

"You know something besides the waltz?" she asked.

"Whatever you want." Acting as an extra man at embassy parties had made good duty cover during high-alert occasions. Dancing had been a prerequisite for the job.

"Slow dancing?"

"Definitely."

"Latin dances?"

He was a little shakier there. "Within reason."

"Western swing?"

"Texas two-step, anyway."

"Rock and roll?"

He lifted a shoulder. "Maybe a couple of moves so you can fake it like everybody else. Also the Cajun

waltz, a different thing entirely from what we're doing now."

"Amazing."

"I aim to please." He gave her a reckless grin as
he whirled her into another turn.

"Could you teach me how to make love?"

He stumbled to a jarring halt. His heart kicked him
in the throat, so he nearly choked as he demanded,
"What did you say?"

"I said I would like for you to teach..."

"Yes, all right, I've got you. But you don't actually
mean it, not the way it sounds?" It was too conve-
nient for acceptance, far too much like having his
fevered daydreams come true.

"I do," she said, her gaze unnerving in its clarity,
though color rode high on her cheekbones. "I've
thought about it a lot in the past two days."

She'd thought about it. Wade wasn't quite sure
how that made him feel, knowing that when she'd sat
quietly next to him on the long flight home, she'd
been considering making love to him. Shock took all
finesse from him, leaving only a single blunt question
in his mind. "Why?"

"It's seems best."

"Best for what?"

"To fit in here, to be accepted." She tilted her
head, watching him expectantly.

"I don't get it."

"I've been isolated, almost imprisoned, for well
over a decade. You're the first man I've been near

who wasn't a family member of one kind or another. I'm too old to be a virgin, and I feel like a freak. I want to be like other women my age."

Wade cleared his throat. "I don't think," he said with firm emphasis, "that inviting men to make love to you is going to do that for you."

"Not men in the plural. Just you."

"Why me? I didn't think you liked me more than about half. In fact, I thought you laid most of your problems at my door." He must be crazy, arguing against something that the very idea of made his heart swell like a bullfrog about to croak. It was just that he had to be absolutely straight about what was going on.

"You're an attractive man who has seen something of the world, so you probably have a certain amount of experience."

"Not with virgins," he said with exactness.

"Maybe not, but I trust you to understand the difference."

It was an accolade he wasn't sure he deserved. Or wanted. "Look," he began.

"Please, Wade. I need to be accepted as a free American woman trying to help my sisters in Hazaristan, not seen as some kind of extremist who doesn't like men or an oddity with an ax to grind. Anyone can tell that I'm different. It's in the way I move, the way I look, or maybe don't look, at men. It's a thousand things, but each one important."

"Clothes," he said, grasping at straws. "Clothes

and makeup can go a long way toward making you look like everybody else. Though I think it would be a shame to take it too far.''

"You're saying you'd rather I didn't change?''

"Not exactly.''

"Maybe you would prefer that I be subservient and obedient, and never go out in public?''

It was a fantasy entertained by most men from time to time, he thought, a woman totally dependent and available to them alone. He wasn't crazy enough to admit that, however, and knew beyond a doubt that the reality would soon bore him senseless. "The idea never crossed my mind.''

A frown appeared between her eyes. "You don't want me then?''

"It not that,'' he said in harassed tones, since he was uncomfortably aware of his body's rampant response to the mere idea. "It's just that it isn't as simple as it may sound.''

"You aren't HIV positive?''

"God, no.''

"Or have some other sexual disease?''

"No! Though I can't believe you're asking. I thought you'd just come from a country where women never talked to men, much less got so personal.''

"I thought American women discussed these things up-front?''

"Some do, some don't but should. They just aren't so brassy about it.''

"Oh. What should I have said?"

"Never mind." The idea of her boning up on how to ask sexual questions gave him cold chills. "The point is that there could be other problems. Like pregnancy, for instance. I'm not exactly equipped for this situation, and I'll be really surprised if you are."

"No." Her expression was not happy.

"It's not a possibility I take lightly. If it happens, there will be consequences for both of us. I'm not sure you want to risk having to marry me after barely escaping it with Ahmad."

A frown pleated the space between her brows. "You'd really do that. You'd marry me."

"In a heartbeat. Benedicts don't run out on their own."

"I see. We wouldn't have to go that far then, if you'd rather not. Far enough for pregnancy, I mean. It would be your choice."

"Chloe..."

He stopped, at a loss for words. One part of him clamored for surrender, immediate and unconditional, while the other insisted that there was something fundamentally wrong with taking her innocence simply because she offered it.

"There's also Ahmad. He's controlled everything I do for so long, has seen to it that I have no possible contact with any man. If he has his way I'll either die a virgin or be taken by force to show his control. I don't...I can't stand..."

"I get it."

"Do you?" She gave him a doubtful look. "It's not just to spite him, and it isn't really about making love because we could both die."

"I know. You think that being with another man will make you unfit in his eyes, that he won't touch you afterward because it would be a pollution for him."

Relief bloomed across her face. "You do understand."

"I think he's fanatic enough that it would give him one more reason to kill you. For the sake of his precious family honor." The last words had a savage edge, even in his own ears.

She lifted her chin. "I'd as soon not have him defile me first."

"Given his code," Wade said distinctly, "he probably feels that you've already done more than enough to be beyond his touch."

"It's better to make sure of it."

"And what of mine?"

"Your touch?" She met his gaze, her eyes darkly blue in the soft light of the ballroom. "What may be a defilement from one man can be a benediction from another."

Wade didn't answer. She had left him nothing to say, even if he could have found words.

As he remained silent, she withdrew a fraction. "If you'd really rather not, it's all right. I can find someone else."

"No." The response was hoarse, but definite. The

very thought made him feel almost as sick as the idea of Ahmad having her, though he refused to even consider why.

She stood waiting, her gaze clear. "Well?"

"That's it, then? A cold-blooded decision, lots of reasons but no real emotion?"

"I didn't say that. You're the only man I've ever met that I could face this with."

"You haven't met that many."

"Sometimes one will do."

Her smile was tremulous but real, and carried a light in its depths that kicked his overworked heart into an even higher gear. The accolade behind her words affected him as nothing else she'd said had or could.

"Fine. I'm your man." His voice was taut as he gave in to the inevitable. And he couldn't help wondering if the words he'd chosen were truer than he knew.

Her smile rose slowly to warm her eyes. "You don't have to look so unhappy about it."

"I'm not. I promise." He stepped back, letting his fingers trail down her arm until he could catch her hand. "So when do you want to start these...lessons?"

"Now?"

The anticipation in her voice did things to his libido that should be against the law. If he followed his more base instincts, he'd simply lay her down in the middle of that white ballroom in the full glare of crystal chandeliers, pier mirrors and floor-to-ceiling windows, and make love to her for the next century. It wasn't a viable option. She wasn't ready, for one thing, but he also had a feeling that any kind of rushed operation wasn't going to do a lot for the craving that mounted inside him. On the other hand, he might well explode if he didn't do something about the expectancy in her face.

"Lesson one," he said, drawing her slowly into his arms and putting a finger under her chin to tilt her face to him. "Kisses come in all forms and flavors, but they usually begin something like this." He pressed his lips to her forehead and the delicate skin of her eyelids in slow succession, exquisitely aware of the sensations against his mouth. Her cheekbones were incredibly soft as he moved from one to the other, while the hollows underneath were as cool and fine-textured as silk.

"And lesson two?" she asked, her voice little more than a whisper.

"Delayed gratification increases pleasure." Wry amusement colored his voice before he kissed the point of her chin. "But flesh and blood can only stand so much, and giving in to temptation is an enjoyment all its own."

"I expect so."

"Believe it," he said, and brushed her lips with his. That light contact sent an electric jolt all the way down to his toes. Ignoring that response was an exercise in ultimate self-control as he carefully in-

creased the pressure, matching surface to tender surface. His reward was the lift of her breasts against his
chest as she took a swift, deep breath. To ease away
from that softness as he raised his head was one of
the hardest things he'd ever done in his life.

She opened her eyes, her gaze candid and perhaps
a little disappointed. "I tried that kind of kiss when
I was thirteen years old, with a lifeguard who was
seventeen. There has to be something more."

He laughed with a winded sound that just missed
being a groan. "If you have to ask, it must be a long
time since you saw a movie."

"An eternity. Not that I was paying much attention
then. Anyway, watching isn't the same thing."

"You've got me there."

"So?"

He smiled at the unconscious provocation in that
single word, even as the muscles across his back
clenched involuntarily against the need to give in to
more urgent impulses. "So lesson three?"

For an answer, she lifted her face again and closed
her eyes. Refusing that mute invitation was beyond
him, though he was fast coming to doubt the wisdom
of this demonstration. With a small prayer for
strength, he pulled her closer, until the soft yet resilient surface of her abdomen was against him. Taking
her lips again, he brushed them with delicate friction,
then used the edge of his tongue to trace the sensitive
line where they met. He tasted the pulse that throbbed
just beneath the smooth lower surface, followed the

finely molded edge, and dipped into one tucked corner.

Her breath feathered his cheek, a sensation so enticing that he drew her closer still without thinking. She came willingly, lifting her arms to slide her open palms along his upper arms to his shoulders as if absorbed in the gathered sensations. As he felt her fingers trailing along his neck and into his hair, he shuddered involuntarily. So great was his distraction that he almost missed the moment when her lips parted to permit, or even encourage, access to her mouth.

He was drowning in the race of his own blood and the rampaging need carried by its hot flow. It had been a long time since he'd held a woman, too long for this kind of torture. The urge to take her in a fast explosion of passion burgeoned in a red haze at the back of his mind.

It couldn't be done. She deserved better, and so did he. In the desperate resolve to hold on to his senses, he opted for the next best thing by invading her mouth in unavoidable parody.

She was so sweet and fresh. He felt half-drunk on the unique flavor of her, knew that he could spend a lifetime getting to know her every taste, scent and satin texture. His breath was trapped inside the walls of his chest. The pressure in his lower body was excruciating. The hesitant touch and retreat of her tongue against his caught at his heart, making him wild with the need to earn greater trust, more of her exploration.

Overwhelming tenderness came at him from out of nowhere. It crowded his brain, paralyzing thought, twining with aching gentleness around his heart. Amazement stilled his movements, and purest shock made him step back away from her.

"What?" she asked, blinking as if awaking from near sleep. "Did I do something wrong?"

He swallowed before he could find voice enough to answer. "No way. I just...it just seemed like a good idea, all at once, to take this somewhere more private."

"Yes." She studied his face a second before glancing around at the tall windows and door. "I suppose."

He wondered what she was thinking, but knew with passing despair that he was unlikely to find out. With a brief touch on her arm, he gestured toward the dim hallway beyond the room. Silent, but obedient, she moved ahead of him in the direction he indicated.

They descended the stairs, their footsteps loud in the quiet. Wade wasn't fanciful, had never seen a ghost at home or felt the presence of his ancestors there. Still he had the distinct feeling that if he turned his head and looked back quickly, he might see a flitting shadow or catch the echoes of parties and celebrations long past. It was rattled nerves, he thought, and that was entirely the fault of the woman who walked beside him.

Wade opened the back door but put a hand on Chloe's arm before she could move out into the night. He allowed his eyes to adjust to the gloom, then studied the shadows that lay in the narrow courtyard formed by an L-shaped house wing and the protrusion of the *garçonnière*. Nothing moved there or under the rustling banana trees that arched above the walk. The only sign of activity was the opening and closing of a door at the restaurant across the way, and the enticing smell of food from that direction.

Holding the door wider, he waited until she had moved ahead of him then let it close and lock behind them. As he joined her with a swift stride, he asked, "Hungry?"

"Not really. Are you?"

"We can eat later, if you prefer."

"Fine. That would be fine."

The exchange was stilted, ultrapolite. He was hard put to say whether it came from actual discomfort with each other now or was just the awkward manners of near strangers. Either way, he didn't like it. Slouching in the direction of the overseer's cottage, he almost wished that he had let caution go hang and taken whatever Chloe might have allowed him back there in that graceful old white-painted ballroom.

The man was sitting on the railing of the cottage's upper veranda. Wade saw him at the same moment that Chloe stopped, blocking his way. Almost at once, she stepped aside, putting her back to the house wall to let him pass.

Their visitor got to his feet, stepping forward so his coffee-brown features seemed to float from out of the shadows. The khaki and brown uniform he wore was surprising, but not the weapon at his waist.

Wade recognized the man before his face came into good focus. And he knew exactly why he was there.

13

"Damn it all, Nat, you scared ten years off my life."

"Well hell, old buddy, who'd have guessed I'd catch you flat-footed. Though I do have to say, I see the reason."

Chloe stared at the newcomer. He was the friend Wade had mentioned, the one who had recruited him for the DSS, as well as providing backup for her rescue. Her relief was so great that she slumped against the wall behind her while her hammering pulse slowly returned to normal.

Wade took the last few steps up to the veranda. "You might have told me you were coming."

"Didn't want to disturb your beauty rest or do anything that might remotely point a finger. I sort of like you, you know? And I purely hate funerals."

"I should have guessed you wouldn't be happy until you'd taken a hand. But what's with the uniform?"

"Special arrangement with hotel security. I'm supposed to look like staff if anybody happens to notice me hanging around—or be on watch."

"God forbid," Wade said, then turned toward

Chloe. "Come meet Nathaniel Hedley, top dog of the hostage rescue outfit I told you about. Nat, the lady we're all protecting."

Wade's friend lifted a finger to his forehead in a small salute. "Ma'am."

"Mr. Hedley." Emboldened by meeting the other Benedicts, she held out her hand as she came forward, and even managed a smile.

The man's grasp was brief and completely impersonal though his smile was warm. "Nat, please. Any friend of Wade's, and all that."

"Let's get inside, shall we?" Wade suggested with a quick glance around from their second-floor vantage point.

"Can't stay long, since it might not look right, but you can bring me up to speed since we spoke on the phone," Nat agreed. "You didn't give out with many details on this part of the op."

"That's because there aren't many."

Wade held the door while they all moved into the small upstairs parlor. Chloe didn't pause as the two men headed toward a pair of chairs, but continued down the hallway toward their room.

"Chloe?"

She turned back, surprised that he'd noticed her leaving or interrupted his discussion with his friend to call out to her.

"You don't have to go. This concerns you, too."

She could feel the smile that curved her mouth, was far too aware of her pleasure in being included as well as his thoughtfulness in making sure she knew it. She could become dependent on such consideration. That was dangerous, as dangerous as the lessons she'd set in motion earlier, but she really didn't care. The problem, she feared, was that she'd learned too well to accept risk and the spice that it gave to being alive.

Returning to the parlor, she perched on the edge of the sofa while the two men took the chairs pulled up in front of it. She listened to their jargon about perimeters, observation points and other things designated only by unknown acronyms, but her attention was only half-engaged. She couldn't help contrasting the man who now sat discussing military tactics and deadly maneuvers with the one who had, just a short time ago, danced to unheard music and made quietly assured jokes about lessons in love.

Delayed gratification increases pleasure.

That wasn't what she'd expected of him. What she'd thought he might do instead, she wasn't really sure. Take her there in that big house where anyone might have walked in on them? Take her standing up, as they'd pretended in Ajzukabad? Take her back to their room and to bed without question or preparation? Any of these had seemed possible, even probable. Sex was merely another appetite in the world where she'd lived so long. Kings and princes might have time for the unlikely postures and endurance of the Kama Sutra, but common people coupled and were done with it.

She wasn't sure she liked his inventive preliminaries. Or perhaps that was wrong. She liked them too much, could easily become addicted to them. But it wasn't what she wanted or needed. Any dependence on a man was unacceptable. And yet, she couldn't wait to see what he would do when they were alone again.

Delayed gratification increases pleasure.

More than anything else, she wondered how Wade felt about her request, if he accepted what she offered as he might a handful of figs when hungry, or took the same enjoyment in the caresses that he'd given her.

He'd called a halt so suddenly. What if he was sorry that he'd agreed to her request? What if he was searching for a way to avoid the lessons that remained?

He'd been so relieved to see his old friend. She'd thought that it was because he would now have someone to back him up, someone outside the threat of Ahmad's jihad. Suppose, instead, it was for the distraction the visit provided.

These things weren't what she'd expected to be concerned with while their lives hung in the balance.

Chloe stared down at her clasped hands as her thoughts chased each other in her mind, only half attending to the exchange between the two men. That was until Wade's voice took on a graver note.

"You ran a trace?"

"Took a while, but we got him," Nat answered. "This Ahmad likes to travel, though he's never made it to the States until now. He showed up in Yemen a couple of years ago, in Africa a few months before that, and also in Iran. Money seems to follow him around, the movement of large sums in a network of Middle Eastern firms with zero reliance on electronic transfer, so no magnetic trail.''

''Al Qaeda.'' There was little surprise in Wade's voice.

''You've got it. That he's entrusted with funds for the organization means he's rabidly loyal. Or maybe just rabid.''

''Tell me about it,'' Wade said with irony. ''The trace didn't happen to pinpoint his current location?''

''New Orleans still, best we can tell, along with one or two of his pals.''

''How the hell did he get into the country, with security the way it is now?''

''Same way everybody else does—a rigidly correct passport and visa along with a plane ticket. Can't do a two-week security check on every person who touches down here, can't keep out everybody who wears a turban.''

Wade swore under his breath.

''Exactly,'' Nat said. ''But it's a free country, and who wants it any other way? But I have to tell you, letting him in may have been deliberate.''

''You're joking, right?''

''Wouldn't do that. Seems one of the guys with Ahmad is ours.''

''Meaning an infiltrator, someone who has been

feeding info on movement within terrorist cells?'' The glance Wade sent Chloe suggested that the amplification was primarily for her sake.

''Yeah. So now the Feds are watching to see what else these guys have in mind beside wiping out Benedicts.''

''The plant is reliable?''

''Somebody seems to think so. He was recruited years ago. Hazara, of course, but loyal to the old regime, partly from conviction, partly because the Taliban destroyed the luxury good trade, jewelry, gold, silver and so on, that was his family's livelihood. Became our man because we're the best bet for getting rid of the extremists, not because he's pro-American. Word is that he's as devoutly Islamic in his way as Ahmad himself. All of which means that whether he's reliable may depend on what we want from him.''

''That would be mainly information about their objectives, I suppose,'' Wade said with a thoughtful frown.

''Yeah. New Orleans has a trade center, too, you know.''

''Don't even think about it. So has this operative made contact?''

''Not yet. We're waiting.''

Wade swore under his breath. After a short pause when neither man spoke, he asked, ''Have you had dinner? We could all walk over to the restaurant. My mom says the food was good when she was here before.''

"I'd take her word for just about anything," Nat answered, "but I ate on the way out of town. Besides, it wouldn't look right for security to be fraternizing with guests."

"You're sure?"

Nat touched his waistline. "I don't make a habit of missing meals, believe me. You and Chloe go right ahead."

"We may do that," Wade agreed with a quick glance in her direction. "An early night couldn't hurt. Jet lag, and all that."

His friend got to his feet. "Don't let me hold you up. I got things to do anyway."

Wade rose as well. Feeling dwarfed by the two men towering over her, Chloe did the same. Nat Hedley turned to her, again touching a finger to his forehead in salute. "Ma'am, it's been a pleasure."

"For me, as well," she said formally. "And may I say that I appreciate your coming all this way, though I know it wasn't for my sake."

Nat gave her a rueful smile. "A wasted trip, I expect. Wade here can probably handle whatever happens just fine. But I'm a great believer in overkill. Besides, I was the one who advised him on how to go in after you. I take it to heart that he got hurt."

"The blame is really mine," she answered, her gaze straight.

Wade made a sound of disgust. "It was my own fault, thank you both very much. I underestimated the enemy."

Chloe didn't intend to argue with him, not because he was right but because she'd learned to avoid confrontations she couldn't win. To Nat, she said, "Anyway, I'm sure he and I both will sleep better for knowing you're around."

"Now that's the idea. And if you don't mind me saying so, I understand why he was so all-fired set on getting you out of that mess over there. It's no place for an American, and especially for a woman like you."

She still wasn't used to compliments, either overt or implied. The heat of a flush burned across her cheekbones, and she glanced unconsciously at Wade for help.

"Get used to it," he said easily. "You'll be hearing that sort of thing often from now on. All you have to do is tell him thank you and good-night."

As she complied, Nat gave Wade a look that was both penetrating and amused. Wade shrugged, then stepped to clap a hand on his friend's shoulder and turn with him toward the door.

"I'll check with you later for a status report," he said. "In the meantime, watch your back. We're about as secluded here as it's possible to get short of heading into the swamps, but you never know."

"Same to you," Nat replied. Then he stepped out the door and closed it quietly behind him.

An uneasy silence descended in which Chloe could hear plainly the sound of Nat's footsteps on the outside stairs. Then Wade raked his fingers through his hair with an abrupt gesture. "Sorry about that. One reason for coming here was so you could have a little time to get used to being in this part of the world before meeting a lot of new people."

"It doesn't matter. Some things take precedence, though it's a shame you and Nat won't be working together."

"That wasn't in the plan," he answered, his gaze steady.

"No, but still." She hesitated a moment, then asked, "Did you really want to go to dinner, or were you being polite?"

"Polite, mainly. Though we can eat if you're hungry."

"I'm not really," she said without quite looking at him. "We had a late lunch and my stomach is still on Hazaristan time anyway. But I was just thinking..."

"About Nat? Or maybe about what happened in the ballroom."

"Both, in a way."

"You're thinking maybe you made a mistake, and having three at dinner would allow more time to think about it?"

"You could say that," she answered, the words constricted in the tightness of her throat.

"You don't have to go through with it. Say the word, the whole thing is forgotten."

"That isn't it. I mean, I don't want to forget it,"

she said, her gaze steady on his face. "I just...
wondered if you were having second thoughts."

He folded his arms over his chest, his face inscru-
table. "You were afraid I'd decided I didn't want to
be your teacher, after all, and was using dinner as an
excuse to get out of it?"

"Something like that," she agreed in relief for his
understanding.

"You thought, just possibly, that I couldn't drum
up any interest in making love to a beautiful and willing woman, or that it was just too much trouble?"

The combination of amusement and incredulity in
his voice made her acutely uncomfortable. "Not exactly."

"I guess it occurred to you that I could be insulted
at being treated like a sex object? That being wanted
for my body and so-called expertise hurt my feelings?"

"I didn't mean to make it sound that way," she
protested.

"Only like a one-night stand, right? No ties, no
obligations, no tomorrows?"

"Okay," she said in fatalistic acceptance. "You
really have changed your mind then."

"Never in a million years."

She met his gaze again. "But you said..."

"A lot of stuff, trying to find out what you wanted.
I have my own misgivings, you know. I'm afraid that
I'm taking advantage of you. I'm scared that you'll
recover in a day or so from whatever combination of

jet lag, culture shock and self-doubt that has you in its grip, and wonder what possessed you to ask me what you did. I'm almost certain that one day soon you'll regret the whole idea.''

A slow smile tilted her mouth, though she felt hot all over as she repeated, ''Never in a million years.''

The overseer's cottage was quiet around them, so quiet it seemed that they must have it to themselves. Beyond the dim hallway, with its high ceiling and indefinable smells of cypress wood and ancient dust, could be heard the calls of crickets and night insects, and the faint sigh of a breeze through the great, over-hanging oaks. They barely noticed as they watched each other in the soft gold-tinted light. Then Wade caught her hand, holding it as they strolled the few feet to their room. She glanced at him, smiling a little because she couldn't help it.

At the door, Wade used his key, then flipped on the light and stepped inside for a quick reconnais-sance. As he gave the all clear, she crossed the thresh-old and closed the door firmly behind her. Her hand was still on the knob as she turned to face him.

''Now then,'' he said as he tossed the key ring on the table and sauntered toward her, reaching to pull her into his arms. ''Where were we when class was interrupted?''

The low timbre of his voice seemed to vibrate through her. His grasp was sure, his body inviting in its heat. She moved closer with an inarticulate mur-mur. The feel of his arms closing around her, drawing her against him, set off a flare of need inside her that was almost frightening in its intensity. It flowed through her like a drug, altering her senses so she moved in a dreamlike languor, molding her body to his body, her mouth to his mouth, as he kissed her.

He was just a man, yet seemed more. His strength surrounded her; his internal power attracted her with magnetic force. A part of her deplored such a primitive reaction, though a more basic portion reveled in it.

He tasted of magic, a combination of sweetness and passion so potent that she slid her hands over his upper chest and shoulders and around to clasp the back of his neck. Drawing his head down, she increased the pressure of his lips.

He resisted, trailing a line of kisses from the corner of her mouth and over the curve of her cheek to her jawline. "I don't want to rush you or to hurt you," he said against her hair. "There's a time for wild, passionate sex, but also a time for something more tame."

"I don't feel tame," she whispered.

His breath fanned her ear as it left him in a quiet rush. "If we get wild right now, I promise it won't last long, and I'll get a lot more out of it than you will. The idea isn't to end this awesome torture but for both of us to enjoy it."

"You mean for both of us to come?"

"Now where did you hear that?"

"Teenagers talk, not to mention women, with or without a veil. So is this lesson number four?"

"I don't know. I've lost count."

"I haven't."

He loosened his hold enough to turn his neck and rest his forehead against hers. "Chloe, Chloe," he said, a sound near a groan in his voice. "You're going to be the death of me."

"But not yet," she said with a private smile. "At least I hope not."

An answering grin tilted his mouth. She watched it form even as she moved closer to stop it with her lips. His chest lifted with his quick-drawn breath, then his arms closed more tightly around her.

Sensations crowded in on her like small blows, the scents of warm cotton, lingering bath soap and virile male, the faint prickliness of his shaved skin, the abrasion of the minutely beaded surface of his tongue. Her eyelids drifted shut as she savored the impressions, taking them inside her and allowing them to merge with the warm current of desire that ran in her veins.

Was how she felt the sum of what he was doing and what he was, or was it produced by her own mind? She wasn't sure, nor could she think it mattered. They were here together, the two of them. The time was right.

He slid his hand from her waist, upward over her rib cage to a spot just under her breast. Pausing there, he pressed his palm flat, as if feeling the rapid beat of her heart. The warmth of his touch penetrated her blouse, increased the heat of her skin. An odd, waiting suspense gripped her so she caught her breath. Then gently, carefully he cupped her breast.

It felt inevitable. The stroke of his thumb across her nipple sent a slow, sweet thrill dancing along her nerve endings and whirling into the lower part of her body. So exquisite was it that she relaxed against him with an almost primitive need to seek his support, to give in to the delicious malaise that flowed through her.

Glancing behind him to locate the armchair at the desk, Wade stepped back, drawing her down onto his lap as he seated himself. The muscled firmness of his thighs under her, the enclosing power of his arms around her, were so perfect that she clung to him, wanting, needing more. She touched his face, tracing the hollow of his cheek, the square line of his jaw, the indentation in his chin. As he claimed her breast once more, she gave a soft gasp. "Would...would this be foreplay?" she asked as a distraction from her small, involuntary sound of pleasure.

"It would, or at least a small part of it. Do you want me to stop?"

"No." The word was a single breath of sound.

"Did you know that you have approximately four times as many nerve endings in your nipples as I do, or any man does?"

She shook her head, a jerky motion.

He brushed gently back and forth with his thumb.

"Of course you'd feel this even more without all the cloth in the way."

Abruptly there was nothing she wanted so much as to have his touch on her bare skin. Lifting her hands to the buttons of her blouse, she began to slip them from their holes. Her movements were not exactly nimble. He seemed not to mind, but followed them with close attention, leaning to press his lips to the soft, blue-veined curves as they were exposed. Then the last button was undone and her blouse fell open.

She'd bought underwear, but decided against wearing it because it felt too confining after years of going without. She didn't need it in any case. Her breasts were high and firm from years of manual labor in house and garden. That Wade suspected the lack of panties along with no bra was almost certain from the way his movements stilled, becoming rigid.

"Is something wrong?" she asked, even as she shrugged from her blouse and dropped it to the floor.

"No way," he answered hoarsely. "It's right, almost too right for comfort—or maybe for sanity."

That he seemed to be as affected by her as she was by him was good to know, since it made her feel less at the mercy of his whims. It gave her the courage to go on. "Now what?"

The only answer was a distracted sound as he bent his head and traced the tip of his tongue around one gentle peak before delving into the valley between it and the other. Scaling the second mound with slow concentration, he captured the nipple with delicate suction.

She was melting, flowing against him in boneless accommodation, pliant under his hands. Her will seemed to have vanished. She had no purpose except this. To consider that she might have lived without being held like this, by this man, was insupportable. That Ahmad or some other might have kissed her, touched and caressed her, was such a horror in her mind that she shivered. Pressing closer still, she threaded her fingers through Wade's hair then held him to her, rocking a little in the disturbance of her mind.

His grasp tightened, then he swept his hand along her thigh and hip, testing, kneading the resilient flesh. As his questing palm brushed the hem of her skirt, he slipped his fingers beneath it to follow the smooth curve of her leg to her knee. He made small circles along her outer thigh in sensuous exploration, the movements spreading ever wider until he reached the silken inner surface.

A muscle in her leg jerked as he trailed his fingertips over that sensitive area, nearing the apex of her thighs then retreating over and over in a slow sequence that reached ever higher. She drew breath then forgot to let it out. She wanted to close her legs, yet at the same time to open them wider. Suspended between warring impulses, she was perfectly still.

"Did you learn in school that skin is an organ of the body?" he asked in distracted softness. "It responds to any touch, which is one reason a massage feels so good. But extra nerve endings surround every opening, the mouth, of course, ears, everything, though none are quite as sensitive as...this one.''

She shivered as if with fever as he barely touched the small mound above that opening. "I...know."

He lifted his hand, began to move it away. With an inarticulate murmur, she closed her fingers on his wrist to hold him in place.

"You're sure?"

"I'm sure."

For long seconds, neither of them moved. Then she released him and reached to tug his T-shirt from the waistband of his jeans. She skimmed her hand underneath, avoiding his bandage, and spread her fingers over his chest.

He was so hot, also amazingly firm where she was soft, with ridges of muscle where she had next to none. At the flat plane of his waist was a line of softly curling hair that she followed upward to where it widened into a diamond shape at the hollow of his throat. His nipples were half buried in the soft thatch. They seemed almost as sensitive as hers were, though smaller and flatter. To tease them into tight nubs was fascinating. In that pursuit she was able to pretend, at least, that she didn't notice as he returned to his exacting exploration, questing ever higher and deeper.

But Chloe did notice, could not ignore that more intimate caress. Her cheeks felt on fire, her pulse throbbed with the tumbling race of the blood in her veins. Her senses expanded until she was exquisitely aware of the man who held her, the firmness and strength of his long form, the thick crispness of the hair that feathered back from his temples, the hard thudding of his heart against her.

That he was so affected brought the rise of an odd tenderness inside her. She had thought him armored by his competence and bound word, his military training and family ties, so that he needed no one, had no weakness of the flesh or otherwise. She'd been wrong. There was perilous affinity in the notion that here in this secluded room they were each at the mercy of their doubts, needs and fears.

Lifting her mouth for his kiss once more, she probed the smooth lining of his mouth with delicate curiosity, tasting it, running her tongue over the glassy edges of his teeth. Venturing deeper, she touched his tongue, retreated, advanced again until he joined her in sinuous play and then set a rhythm that tantalized with promises of something more. Enthralled by the incredible intimacy, she reveled in it, accepting yet barely registering his gentle, probing encroachment.

The sensory pleasure of it spiraled suddenly to a peak, rippling through her in a shock wave. In its wake, she was adrift in wanton desire, accepting, unable to think or do anything other than allow whatever he might choose to try next.

He didn't stop there, didn't stop at all, but fed the ardor growing between them with patience and consummate refinement. Chloe abandoned pretense of any kind, allowing him unimpeded access to her body, helping him as he pushed the sandals from her feet, skimmed her skirt down over her hips. She flattened her hand against the board hardness of his belly as he kicked out of his boots, rid himself of jeans and shirt. Rising then, she let him lift her to the soft contours of the mattress that topped the antique bed.

The night was warm and dark around them, and they had no reason to hurry. With warm lips, careful hands and fierce restraint, they sought the curves, hollows, springing hardness and liquid softness of their male and female bodies. They spoke in whispers, with sighs and half-moaned pleas as they learned the shaping under the bones, the texture of hair and skin, the hidden sites of most vivid response, and the outermost limits of endurance. Instinct moved them, and also watchful attention to signals, generosity of spirit and the ultimate grace of caring. With these responses, they refined the moment until it shimmered with unbearable tension, allowing the rise of something so near to devotion that it seemed an acceptable counterfeit.

Shivering and desperate, then, they moved together as one accord. He hovered above her with iron-hard muscles, silently asking entry. She guided him, fitted his strutted heat to her softness, and was still in careful accommodation as he pressed inside. She felt a single burning sting, but the way had been well prepared and the momentary pang was banished by fullness, pressure, and such beatific completion that she felt intoxicated with it.

Still, it seemed there should be something more. She stirred, rising a little to encompass more of him, press more against him. He answered that movement, easing into a slow, pulsating tempo that ebbed and flowed, steadily increasing. She met it, matched it, felt in its cadence the joyous music that animated the dance of life.

It took them, transfigured them. She accepted his strong surges against her, felt them dissolving the anxiety inside her, used them to remold some essential part of her being into a woman with the courage to accept her own needs and impulses. She wanted him deeper, could not bear to be denied.

As she opened herself wider in heated demand, he met it in unstinting effort and endless power, taking her higher, further still from the person she had once been, nearer to something that might well be divine. And in the quiet night, despite the threat of death that waited, they found the way to true paradise, or to the only one that this mad and puny earth allows.

14

The glow of daylight behind the drapes woke Chloe. Though she opened her eyes, she lay without moving while she examined the sense of well-being that hovered inside her. A part of it was the soft mattress on which she lay, the fresh sheets and the coolness that circulated in the room. The main thing, however, was the man who lay close against her.

She should be used to waking beside Wade, one way or another, after several days of it. This was definitely different. His long body was nestled against hers from waist to ankles, and his arm rested across the curve of her hip in a near possessive embrace. It felt natural and comfortable, as if they'd slept that way for years, even decades.

Impressions from the night before flickered through her mind. Heat moved over her, even as a small smile curved her mouth. It had been quite an initiation. Though she was aware of a little soreness here and there, she felt free and whole in a way she hadn't been in a long time. Whatever inhibitions she'd had were gone.

Wade seemed to be asleep still. That was hardly a surprise. He deserved all the rest he could get.

She eased from the bed and stumbled, yawning hugely, into the bathroom. It was odd to see herself in such a large mirror, at almost full figure. The woman who stared back at her seemed like a stranger. Her hair was tousled, her lips swollen, her cheeks pink from beard chafing, and her eyes marked by dark shadows. Though her gaze was bright, a species of apprehension lingered in its depths. She looked replete, well loved, but not really content.

It was a trick of the lighting, nothing more. Or else the grief and worry of the past few days. She'd cried in her sleep during the night before, while dreaming of Treena. It wasn't the first occasion, though she'd had little time to come to grips with that painful loss. Wade had held her, offering consolation, expecting nothing in return. Then there was the uncertain future. She hated the idea that others were in danger because of her. Someone, possibly some of the Benedicts, might die before this thing was done. Certainly, any misgivings she felt had nothing to do with a future to be lived without Wade Benedict.

Frowning a little, Chloe rinsed her face, then picked up a hairbrush and dragged it through the unruly mass of her hair that seemed, unexpectedly, to be trying to curl into ringlets in the Louisiana humidity. Feeling unsettled, and confined by events and personalities as well as the walls around her, she dragged on the caftan that Wade's mother had left her as a robe and crossed back through the front room where Wade lay sprawled in sleep. Easing open the door, she went through and pulled it closed behind her.

Sunlight lay in a golden dazzle beyond the front parlor windows. She turned in the opposite direction, emerging onto the back veranda. It was protected from the morning sun by the bulk of the house, so reasonably cool once her body adjusted to the change from the frigid air-conditioning of the bedroom.

The long, railed space of the veranda was set with white rocking chairs that were flanked by small tables. It was empty of other guests at this hour. Settling into one of the rockers, she set it in motion while gazing out over the expanse of lawn and the small lagoon that lay beyond. Birds called, and a squirrel scampered from branch to branch in the great live oak that stood near the lattice fence. From somewhere in one of the other buildings, she could hear the whine of a vacuum cleaner. It was comforting to know that other people were up and stirring somewhere, even if she did seem to be alone for the moment.

It was then that she heard the whistling. She thought it came from the front of the cottage, made perhaps by another guest or custodian. Still, the melody was disturbing since it was in a minor key with an odd, foreboding flavor.

Chloe got to her feet and walked to the end of the porch. Bracing her hands on the railing, she leaned over to look around the end of the building. A man was approaching along the sidewalk. In his hands was a tray that he balanced carefully as he walked. He didn't look up until he'd rounded the two-story building and paused at the foot of the stairs.

"Good morning, Nat," she said, her voice dry.

"Morning, ma'am," he said with a smile. "Could I interest you in coffee and sweet potato biscuits?"

The coffee smelled heavenly, but she shook her head. "I wouldn't want to deprive you of your breakfast."

"I've had mine with the manager. Since I was heading this way anyhow, I brought the wake-up tray that comes with the room, a fine old Southern tradition."

"Wade is still asleep, I'm afraid."

"But you're not," he returned as he mounted toward her. "Have a seat, will you, so I can tell where to put this thing down?"

Chloe moved back to the rocker where she'd been sitting earlier. Nat put the tray on the table next to it then took the chair on the other side. Chloe lifted a corner of the rose-colored napkin that covered the silver tray. Beneath it was a plate of golden orange biscuits along with butter and jam, also a carafe of coffee with three cups.

She set a cup on the table at Nat's elbow, then lifted the carafe. Since he didn't object, she poured the coffee for him. "What was that you were whistling just now?"

"Little ditty called 'House of the Rising Sun.' Guess being this close to the Big Easy brought it to mind.'' He paused, then added as she only stared at him. ''New Orleans, home of jazz and all that?''

''Oh, yes.'' Jazz hadn't been high on her list of favorite music as a teen, though she might have to look into it now. ''You're not from this area then?''

''Born in North Carolina but from everywhere, you might say, since my daddy was military. Virginia is my home base these days.''

It was a reminder of how far from home she was, and why. ''No trouble during the night?''

''Not a peep.''

''I know Wade slept easier for knowing you were out there.''

A flush darkened the face of the man across from her to the color of espresso. ''Wade would do the same for me. Besides, he saved my bacon one night, snatched me out of a truck about two seconds before a shell hit it. I owe him.''

''He called in a favor.''

''Doesn't work that way. Guy like him doesn't ask for help, it just goes against the grain. He said he had a little problem, so here I am. That easy.''

''You must have worked together a long time.'' She reached to take a biscuit almost without thinking, breaking off a corner and nibbling on it. It was delicious, an odd mixture of cake and bread that was better than either.

''We were together in the DSS for a while. Best damn agent I ever saw, had what you might call a sixth sense about trouble. I tried to get him to come to work for me after I set up my operation, but it wasn't really for him. Never did care for the undercover stuff, you know, likes things clear and out in the open. And he'd just as soon not be responsible for other people's lives.''

She frowned. ''Yet he came for me. Why would he do that if it goes so against the grain?''

''The Benedicts stand by their friends, and your dad was a good one. More than that, Wade's an idealist. Good is good and bad is bad, as far as he's concerned. He's for one and purely against the other.''

''No shades of gray?''

''Don't know that I'd put it that way. He's more than capable of looking at all sides of a situation. It's just that he has no use for the kind of sophistry that says it's okay to bend laws in the name of the greater good, or write off human beings, human pain for the sake of an idea. Way I understand it, the Benedicts have this code. They do what's right to the best of their ability, no exceptions and no excuses, and expect everyone else to do likewise. That's all there is to it.''

She reached for cream and poured it into her coffee, then took a sip. ''Seems like a good way to live.''

''It is, if you've got the guts for it. Of course it means giving up what you might want a lot of the time for the sake of what somebody else needs.''

''Or putting what you value in danger?'' The coffee, so ambrosial just seconds before, tasted suddenly bitter. She set it back on the tray.

"You mean Wade's family, I guess."

"He wouldn't have to worry about them if it weren't for me."

"That doesn't make it your fault. Some things just can't be helped."

Her smile was wan. "Thanks for the thought, but it doesn't do a lot to make me feel better."

Nat returned her smile. "I do have to say that I'm surprised Wade is still here. I figured he'd head for Turn-Coupe and that old home place of his by daybreak at the latest."

"He's been through a lot these past few days," she said, and was disturbed by that instant impulse to defend him.

"Been through a lot, period." Nat studied the liquid in his cup for a second. "Don't suppose he could have mentioned that business in Saudi?"

"The oilman's wife?"

He nodded. "She did a number on him, not that she meant to, I guess. It's that damn code I was telling you about, makes a man responsible for just about anything that goes wrong. Doesn't allow a lot of room for failure, you know?"

"Or forgiveness?"

"You got it, if you mean he can't forgive himself."

He watched her with steady intent, though Chloe couldn't decide exactly what might be in his mind. It could have been anything, from uncertainty over how much she really understood on such short acquaintance with Wade, to doubt about the wisdom of discussing him with her at all. "He can hardly be blamed for not realizing the man intended to kill his wife."

"That's just it. Wade thinks he should have seen it, that the signs were there if he'd just read them. Problem was, he was brought up in a family where hurting people you were supposed to love was unthinkable, much less killing them. Hell, lying was a crime in their code. It never occurred to him that a guy with all the money and lawyers in the world would rather whack an unfaithful wife than divorce her."

"You're suggesting he was naive?"

"*Was* is the operative word. He grew up fast. But the standards are still there and still apply, especially when it comes to women."

"I could be wrong, but from things Wade said while in a high fever, this business seems mixed up somehow with what happened between his father and mother."

"Well, now, yes and no. Divorce doesn't happen that often among the Benedicts, apparently. When it does, it's a big deal. Wade's old man was pretty broken up when his wife left—so were Wade and his brothers, come to that. Best I can tell, Wade sided with his mother and hard words passed between him and the old man about why she'd left. Family like that where few words are spoken in anger, such things aren't forgotten or forgiven."

"By his father, you mean?"

"Either one of them. Stubborn as they come, that whole clan, when they think they're right."

"I can see that," she said, her voice dry. It didn't take a lot to extrapolate Wade's attitudes about what she should and shouldn't do in small matters into something more serious over large ones.

"Of course, his old man seems to have had all the worst traits of your everyday redneck, pigheaded, arrogant, strong ideas on work and women, positive that God put him on this green earth to tell other folks what to do. Wonder is more of that didn't rub off on Wade and his brothers. His mom deserves the credit there, I think. She seems to have gone overboard with the tolerance bit, so things more or less balanced out."

"Yet Wade loved his father, or I suppose he must have since he regrets so much that he wasn't there when he died."

Nat's gaze was keen. "He told you that?"

"Not really. I just assumed it from a few things he said."

"Yeah. I think guilt's the problem. Seems they had words over a lot of things, including whether Wade should stay in Louisiana like most of the clan, or see something of the world. There was a long spell in there when Wade didn't speak to his dad, didn't see his brothers for years. Wade didn't go home right off when he heard his dad had cancer. Then he got shot up in the deal with the oilman's wife and couldn't go. His dad died without them ever having a chance to talk, straighten things out. Could be that's the tie. Wade thinks, somewhere in that hard head of his, that he could, and should, have been able to save them both.''

It made sense in an odd sort of way. It also fed into Wade's determination to get her away from Ahmad and out of Hazaristan. He needed to rescue her to live up to his expectations for himself and remedy past failures. What did that say about his feelings for her? Was watching over her, and even his half-reluctant agreement to make love to her, something he accepted in order to meet his own standard?

''Of course, if Wade ever mentions the subject, I never said a word. Fact is, I've probably talked too much as it is.''

''You got at least one thing right, old friend.'' That comment, deep-voiced and edged with anger, came from behind them.

Nat shot out of his rocker as if it had caught fire.

''Jesus H., man, don't do that! You nearly made me dump my cup in my lap.''

''Watch your back as well as what you're saying next time,'' Wade said without noticeable remorse. He glanced at Chloe. ''Any coffee left?''

She filled the third cup and passed it to him with only the briefest of glances. His gaze was cool, giving nothing away. Taking it by the rim, he moved to stand with his back to the railing, half sitting, half leaning against it. He crossed one arm over his chest before he sipped the strong brew.

Nat sent Chloe a quick, almost helpless look, though he spoke to Wade. "Didn't mean to get into your business. We were just talking."

"Pick another subject next time."

"May not be a next time. Unless I tag along when you two set out for Grand Point?"

"Suit yourself."

Wade's voice was hard and he appeared more intimidating than Chloe had seen him to this point. He was also devastatingly attractive in a rumpled pair of jeans with no shoes or shirt, and the morning light molding the musculature of his shoulders in light and shadow and gleaming white on the bandage that padded his side. His beard stubble was more pronounced than the night before, and his hair lay in dark windrows, as if he'd raked his a hand through it instead of combing it.

"Think I'll do that, since you've so kindly invited me, and since I'm damn sure you can use all the help you can get. Problem is, nobody can say when these guys might show up."

Wade didn't look up from his coffee cup. "Don't change your schedule or our account."

"Schedule, be damned. But I expect Maggie might be a little harder to put off. She kind of likes to keep tabs on me, you know." Nat sent Chloe a quick look. "That's my wife, Maggie."

"I thought it might be," she said with a slight smile that faded as she looked at Wade. "Don't blame, Nat, please. He was only answering my questions.''

''If you think he doesn't know how to avoid that, then you don't know him, particularly not well enough for early-morning chats.''

The look he gave her was a potent reminder that she was naked under the caftan. It was something he must know very well, too, since her discarded clothes were probably strewn over the floor of their room. She was trying to decide exactly what that meant when Nat spoke again.

''He's jealous, you know,'' he said, his manner confiding, as if Wade wasn't standing less than four feet away. ''Not that I blame him.''

''Thank you,'' Wade said. ''I'm sure she needed your opinion.''

''Hell, Wade, don't be so all-fired stiff-necked,'' Nat said, frowning as he turned back to him. ''You Benedicts may think you're off-limits as subjects of discussion, but the rest of the world isn't quite so nice in its ideas. It's no crime for a person to be concerned about you.''

''No compliment, either.''

''Didn't know you needed one, buddy.''

''I don't.''

''Fine. Great. Now if you'd just quit acting like a ten-year-old with a new bag of marbles, or an idiot with a fishing pole up the wahzoo, we might get somewhere.''

The look Wade turned on his friend might have

annihilated a lesser man. Nat only returned it with steady regard.

Abruptly Wade's mouth twitched. He looked away, rubbing a hand over his face as if to erase a grin. Finally he turned back again. "So what's on your mind?"

"Couple of things, like when you intend to light a shuck out of here. And how you want to go?"

"Now," Wade said with an intent glance in Chloe's direction. "We're leaving immediately, or as soon as we can get ready. And you can drive us, since you have a rental and seem determined to transfer to Grand Point."

"Good. I'll call Maggie while you're packing."

"Tell her I've got my eye on you," Wade said, his gaze steady.

Nat gave a nod before his mouth curved in a rich grin. "I'll do that," he said. "Yes, indeed. She'll get a real hoot out of it."

15

Chloe would have willingly undergone torture before she admitted any interest in Wade's home. She tried to act unconcerned and a little tired as they turned off onto the winding drive that led through woodland fronted by dense undergrowth. The last thing she wanted was to give him reason to think she might have hopes of any kind of permanent relationship.

She had not expected Wade Benedict to be a part of her life once she reached the States. She'd thought to contact other Islamic women's groups, become a member of their network and continue with her efforts to help their cause. There had been no place in her plans for a man, still wasn't. Why, then, did the idea of saying goodbye to him seem so terrible?

He was the only American she really knew, other than her mother's parents who hardly counted, the only person who really knew what she'd left behind so the only connection she had between that life and an uncertain future. That was probably the reason she had such an impulse to cling to him now.

She couldn't do it. He owed her nothing, regardless

of the transports of the night before. That had been the agreement, and she would stick to it. He would as well, she had no doubt. He might have agreed to rescue her, could feel some responsibility for seeing that she was safe, but he had not signed on to take care of her the rest of her life.

She'd forgotten the fecundity of the landscape, the sheer mass of the vegetation of all shapes and sizes that filled the ditches, skirted the tree trunks and dangled from their branches in long vines. She wished she knew the plant names, particularly for the wildflowers in pink, lavender and multiple shades of yellow that sprawled among the waving grass.

She'd had plenty of time to notice such things. It had been a quiet trip with desultory comment between the two men, mostly about local politics, sports, or national events over the past few weeks. Since she knew nothing about the first two and little about the third, she spent most of the time staring out the window and trying not to think.

The car rounded a curve. Ahead of them, a man stepped into the road, squarely in their path. Dressed in jeans and a camouflage shirt and with a camouflage cap pulled down over his eyes, he held a rifle like a natural extension of his hand.

"Whoa," Nat said as he braked to a crawl. "Looks like we've got us a sentry."

"My cousin Luke," Wade said. "You remember me mentioning him."

"Looks like he knows what he's doing."

He did indeed, Chloe thought. The tall dark-haired man could as easily have been Wade's brother, however. The resemblance was that striking.

As they pulled to a stop, Nat lowered the driver's side window. Wade leaned over from where he sat in the passenger seat. "Hey there, cuz," he called. "How come you got stuck with guard duty?"

"Just lucky, I guess. Could be nailing up windows and carting in groceries." Luke relaxed his rigid stance and sauntered forward. Nodding a greeting to Nat, he leaned to peer into the car in a fast, comprehensive inspection. "Ma'am," he said, touching the brim of his cap as he caught sight of Chloe in the back seat.

"Everybody here?" Wade asked.

"The clan has gathered, man, woman and child."

"Kane?"

"Taking care of logistics. He and Regina are in charge of food, water, ammo, baby diapers. The important stuff."

"Roan?"

"Lining up law enforcement all over the state to keep a lookout for the creeps."

"Clay and Adam did make it?"

"And your mom. Clay's in charge of water transport and escape routes, and has enough boats gathered down at the dock to move an army. Adam is watching the lake access to the house. Your mom is cooking. Thank goodness."

Luke's voice carried cheerful unconcern, but Chloe

wasn't fooled. He might appear nonchalant, but he was also deadly serious.

"The rest?" Wade asked.

"Taking orders like good little soldiers while waiting for the captain to put in an appearance at last. That would be you, cuz."

Luke winked at Chloe as she caught his eye. His grin was so contagious that she couldn't help smiling back at him. Wade, catching that brief exchange, did not appear amused.

"Sure it is," he said with irony.

"Your house. And you're the one with the commando training."

"DSS."

"Same thing."

Wade didn't argue, but said instead, "You didn't mention April. She got back from her book tour okay?"

"Yesterday, thank you God," Luke answered with a hint of fervor in his voice. "She's on deadline, though, so holed up in one of the upstairs bedrooms and doing her damnedest to write a love scene in the middle of bedlam. I do my humble best to provide inspiration now and then, but it ain't easy with fifty or sixty people milling around."

"I'm sure you manage."

Luke raised a brow at Wade's sardonic tone. "You need lessons, sonny boy, you know where to come."

"That'll be the day."

"What I thought."

"Surely there's not really fifty or sixty people at the house?"

"Minimum, came out of the woodwork when they heard somebody tried to cut out your liver."

"It's not that bad," Wade protested.

"Glad to hear it. But the clan is madder than hell that some nutcase wants to wipe us out."

"Besides which, they can't stand to miss a fight."

"That too."

The glib words were a cover for more deeply felt emotions, Chloe thought. They were there anyway, in the warm camaraderie between the two men and the look in their eyes.

"Right." Luke straightened and stepped back with a mock salute. "Carry on. I'll see you all later up at the house."

"Take care," Wade said. "I mean it."

"You got it. Don't eat all the bread pudding, especially the one with the rum raisins and whiskey sauce."

Wade lifted a hand. Nat put the car into gear and drove on. When Chloe looked back, there was no sign of Luke. He'd faded back into the woods as silently and completely as if he'd never been there.

Seconds later, they rounded a curve, and the house appeared in front of them. It was big, though not as large as Nottoway. Rambling, with odd angles and decorations, including a widow's walk, and a conglomeration of styles from French West Indies to neoclassical, it made up in character what it lacked in grandeur. It couldn't be looking its best, since its windows were boarded up with plywood and the small entry court was barricaded with sandbags. The front lawn had been turned into a parking lot for every kind of truck and SUV ever manufactured, as well as a couple of truck campers and even a motor home— and every one, it seemed, flew the Stars and Stripes. Sentries were posted behind the entablature of the roof, and guards could be glimpsed in a line around the perimeter of the woods that encroached from all sides, and also along the lakeshore. Wade's home was, for all intents and purposes, an armed camp.

Yet children were playing ball in a clear area toward the rear, next to a peculiar mound of earth that might have been Wade's old fort. Nearby, a group of women peeled potatoes around a picnic table set up next to a pair of gas burners on metal stands. A couple of older men watched over the enormous cook pots on the stands, while others played dominoes on a card table that was kept level by a brick under one leg. Clothes flapped on a makeshift line stretched between two trees, fanning the pack of hunting dogs that lolled beneath them. If there was fear and panic anywhere among the group, it was well hidden.

As Nat rolled to a halt at the side of the house, the dogs rose with a great baying and began to lope toward the car. A teenager playing pitch with a younger girl turned and yelled at the dogs, calling them off. They dropped their tails and ruffs, but came on, circling the car.

"Don't worry about the hounds," Wade said as he got out, then opened the door for Chloe. "They belong to Roan, and are harmless mutts unless he gives the order to hunt."

"I'm not worried." She rubbed the silky-feeling heads of the half dozen or so that pushed and shoved around her the instant she put feet on the ground. It was easier to concentrate on the dogs than face the curious stares of the other Benedicts who turned in their direction.

Wade glanced at her with a measuring look, then motioned the boy and his teammate forward. "Chloe, Nat, meet Jake. He's Roan's son. And this gorgeous shortstop with him is Lainey, Janna's daughter. Janna is married to Clay, has been since this time last year."

Chloe smiled at the pair, wondering at the same time if Wade actually realized that starting with the younger members made it easier or if that was an accident. The boy showed every sign of being a true Benedict when he grew up, which was to say, handsome, confident, and with a habit of looking people in the eye. The girl seemed shyer, but was pretty in a fragile way and had a sunny, uncomplicated smile. This was the child who had received a kidney transplant, Chloe thought. She appeared to be adjusting well.

"Pop Benedict," Wade said with a wave in the direction of an older man who ambled up to the car, "Roan's dad, so Jake's granddad, of course."

She offered her hand while mentally cataloging

names. At least the surnames were the same, for the moment anyway.

"Welcome, Chloe, glad to have you. I remember you as a kid, in the pictures your dad used to show. We used to fish together, he and I." The older man glanced at Wade. "You want Roan, he's in the house, checking with his office and Lord knows who all, seems to have a phone permanently attached to his ear and his son and heir glued to his shoulder. Clay's around somewhere. I know because I caught him and Janna in the pantry when I looked in for a broom a little while ago. Said they were checking on bread-and-butter pickles for the fish fry, but that's a likely story."

"Mama's chopping onions for gumbo now, Uncle Wade," Lainey piped up. "But she's not crying."

Pop cleared his throat. "Yeah. Guess maybe Regina and Tory are with her. As for the rest of the crew, who knows?"

"Fish fry, huh? Sounds good." Wade ruffled Lainey's hair in an affectionate gesture. "Go easy on Jake, little bit. He's not used to playing with pros like you." The glance he sent Jake over the girl's head carried a message.

That the boy understood was plain from the serious expression that descended over his face and his quick nod. "We'll both go easy," he said. "I'm starving from just smelling all the good things to eat, without working up more of an appetite."

Wade's smile held approval before he turned to-

ward the back door of the house. Chloe, moving with
him, considered the scene she'd just witnessed. Lainey's tender ego had been stoked and her pride spared
while insuring that Jake remembered her limitations.
Jake had been reminded of his responsibility to take
care of those younger and weaker than he was, and
also rewarded for his ready acceptance of the task and
approved for his tact. It was how consideration for
others was taught, she thought, no lectures, no de-
mands, just example and oblique instruction that was
a lesson in itself. That it worked was obvious from
Wade's level of manners. That it could be learned
from etiquette books was doubtful.

The question was, just how far did such consideration go? Would Wade make love to a woman in
whom he had little interest simply because he was too
much of a gentleman to refuse? And if he did so at
her invitation, did that make anything that happened
afterward her own fault?

They entered the house by way of a living room
that combined English country house comfort with
antique parlor furnishings. It was empty, however,
and the murmur of voices indicated that everyone was
gathered in a room to the left. This turned out to be
the kitchen, an open area with windows tall enough
to flood it with light when they were not boarded up,
and done in blue and white with a collection of flow-
blue porcelain arranged in the space between the wall
cabinets and ceiling. Fixtures were of stainless steel
and sized for a restaurant, including the walk-in re-

frigerator. Counter space was generous, more than enough to accommodate the five women who worked there.

Conversation that had been so animated died away to nothing as the women turned from what they were doing. They appeared like a team, facing Chloe as a solid front. Each one exceptionally attractive in her own way, they had a gloss of natural, effortless sophistication that was more than a little intimidating.

These women, his brothers' and cousins' wives, were the standard to which Wade must compare any woman who came into his life. There was no way on earth that she could ever measure up. Not that she wanted or needed to do that, of course, but it didn't make her feel good, all the same.

Then Wade's mother turned from where she stirred something in a huge pot on the monster of a range, waving her wooden spatula in greeting. Her smile and recognition seemed twice as warm, twice as welcome. The rich, homey smells of chopped onion that hung in the moist air along with those of diced celery and green peppers, browning flour and caramelizing sugar seemed to belong to her alone.

One of the wives, tall and with a long, braided rope of blond hair hanging over her shoulder and the rounded shape of midterm pregnancy, reached to wipe her hands on a kitchen towel before moving toward them. Wade opened his arms and enclosed her in a quick hug. Then holding her casually in the circle of one arm, he introduced her as his brother Clay's wife, Janna.

Her greeting was pleasant enough but a degree of reserve lingered in her eyes. She didn't release Wade, but gingerly brushed her fingertips over the bandage he still wore under his shirt. "You sure you're okay? Clay said the gash you picked up over there was a nasty one."

"Not that bad. I'll live, promise." Affection made his eyes a darker green as he gazed down at her a second. "How's Clay junior doing?"

"He's great," Janna said with a wry grimace, "and I will be, too, in about three and a half months. So is this Chloe?"

"And Nat Hedley that you may have heard me mention," Wade agreed, then looked up to point out the others along with a bit of information to place them.

Chloe dutifully noted that the rather fey beauty with her hair like a cloud around her shoulders was Adam's psychic bride, the redhead with softly freckled skin next to her was Regina, married to Kane, and that Tory of the shining brown hair and patina of moneyed perfection should be paired with the sheriff. All of them spoke, all of them smiled, and yet it was plain that they weren't precisely happy to meet her. It wasn't surprising, perhaps, considering the turmoil she'd brought into their lives, but Chloe felt the sting of it.

An awkward pause settled over them all. Wade's

mother opened her mouth to speak. Then Clay appeared in the doorway that opened off the kitchen into a long hall.

"Unhand my wife, sir," he said in mock anger as he strolled toward where Wade stood with Janna, "or suffer the consequences." Then his frown disappeared, replaced by a grin. "Never mind, I'll just hug Chloe as a substitute."

He did just that, sweeping her into a quick, brotherly embrace that was over before she had a chance to be flustered.

"You're the one who'll suffer," Janna told him as she disengaged herself from Wade and went to her husband. "I may have to maim you severely."

"You're welcome to try," Clay said, catching his wife in a close yet careful embrace. "I do love an aggressive woman."

"You'll think aggressive after this kid makes his appearance." Rich color spread across Janna's cheekbones and she avoided looking at anyone else, reserving her gaze for her husband.

"Promises, promises."

Embarrassment at such a public display of affection warred with fascination inside Chloe. No one else seemed surprised, much less shocked. Tory and Regina rolled their eyes at each other while Wade's mother looked on with indulgent humor.

Wade shook his head at his brother with a wry grin, then sobered as he asked of no one in particular, "So whose idea was it to turn this into a family reunion?"

"Mine," his mother answered. "You have a problem with it?"

"Everybody's scattered all over, so hard to protect. It will take time to get them to safety if something goes down."

"That's why Luke and the others are on guard duty. At least we're all together, and the kids won't have to be scared out of their wits by extreme safeguards unless it's necessary."

"There's a plan," Clay said. "Even if you weren't here to direct it."

Janna spoke up, perhaps to smooth over what might have sounded like a reproach. "Everybody knows the drill for taking emergency cover. The kids think it's a game."

Wade gave a slow nod, though he didn't look convinced.

"When you've settled in, then come take a look at my new pickup, a dually club cab that I traded for in place of my shot-up SUV," Clay said. "I'll clue you in while you drool."

"Nat, here, has a couple of new developments to explain at the same time."

Chloe, hearing the grim note in Wade's rejoinder, suspected he was talking about the fact that Ahmad had been allowed into the country and brought someone with him who might, eventually, supply information on his movements. How that would be greeted, she didn't even want to think.

"In the meantime, we have people to feed,"

Wade's mother said as she returned to her pot on the stove. "Why don't you show Chloe to her room, son. And Clay, honey, that batch of fish over there is mealed and ready, and the grease ought to be hot enough by now. You can take the pan out to whoever is doing the cooking."

"Pop's in charge there."

"Good. At least he won't be cuddling in corners."

"Not unless he can get you alone," her younger son returned with a wicked glint in his eyes.

"That'll be the day."

"Or night."

"Out," his mother said dangerously, waving her spoon toward the door.

"This way," Wade told Chloe, steering her back in the direction they had come, "before we get caught in the cross fire."

Traversing the living room again, they left what seemed to be the oldest section of the house and entered the right-hand wing that had a late Victorian appearance. More polished wood paneling and less plaster were in evidence here, and the furniture had the dark, Gothic influence and antimacassars of that era. The staircase that twisted its way upward from one side of a different living area was of aged golden oak, with a stained-glass window over the landing and a heavy railing polished by generations of use. The muted glow of a converted gaslight fixture with milky globes lighted their way, reflecting also in the stained glass that was dark from the plywood behind it.

"Do you and your brothers all live here together?" Chloe asked as Wade waved her upward then mounted the runner-covered treads behind her.

"Only Clay and Janna are here permanently. They claim the antebellum section on the far side of the kitchen. Adam and Lara have a place of their own in New Orleans, and I'm in and out, mostly out. The place is like three houses in one because families used to be a lot bigger and additions were made as they expanded. We inherited the old pile jointly and no one wants to sell. Adam has dibs on the center part of the house, then, being the oldest, and this wing is supposed to be mine."

"Do you think you'll ever live here full-time?"

"Who knows?"

It wasn't much of an answer, though Chloe wasn't sure what she'd expected. Or even why she'd asked.

They reached the top of the stairs. A long upper hall stretched before them, carpeted in burgundy wool with a design of gold scrolls and cabbage roses. Wade opened the door of a bedroom on the left and flicked on the light to reveal a large, high-ceilinged room done in chintz and organdy, and with a heavy oak bed and matching marble-topped washstand set with a pitcher and bowl.

"Bathroom's through there, and more modern than it looks," he said, indicating a white-painted door. "I'll bring up your things from the car in a few minutes. My room is just down the hall. Feel free to take whatever you might need from the closet. Come back down when you're ready, or not at all if you'd rather rest.''

"Yes. Thank you.'' His voice was so neutral and polite that it seemed best to follow suit. He was telling her, she thought, that she was a guest, not family. Also that he didn't expect her to share his room or his bed. "I understand.''

He watched her a long moment, as if debating whether to say more. Then he gave a short nod and turned to go.

"Wade?''

He stopped with his hand on the door, looking back over his shoulder. Wariness sat on his features as he waited for her to go on.

"I really am sorry...for all the trouble, the danger and everything. I didn't quite realize how big your family is or how it would seem to them, until I saw them. I shouldn't have come here. I wish...''

"We've already been over this,'' he said, his voice even.

"Yes, but none of this would be happening if it wasn't for me.''

"None of it would be happening if people were reasonable, if they could manage to live without look-ing for someone to blame for where and how they were born or needing someone to hate in order to feel better about themselves. You've harmed no one, threatened no one. Let me say it again. You are not to blame.''

"If I could talk to Ahmad, offer him the money from my father..."

"No." The negative was implacable, leaving no room for argument. "The time for that is long past. He'll kill you now. He has to and you know it."

"What if he kills your kin? How could I live with that?"

"To get to them, he'll have to go through me and every other male Benedict alive."

"Is that supposed to make me feel better."

"Just stating a fact. Anyway, if it happens then..."

"Then Ahmad will get to me, too, and it won't matter."

"Exactly."

She turned away from him. "But it does matter. I can't stand it. I should never have spoken to you, never have listened to what you had to say, never have gone away with you, and certainly never have asked...what I did last night. I'm sorry for all of it, so sorry."

He made no answer for long moments. Then he spoke with perfect distinction. "I'm not."

She swung around, but the door was closing. He had gone.

She didn't move, but stared blindly at the wall in front of her that was papered with ribbons and sprigged roses. Did he have any real idea of what he faced in the hard warrior spirit and ferocity of men like Ahmad? Did any of the Benedicts? She wished she could be sure.

Their courage, she feared, was grounded in endless decades of utter security. Instead of secluding the women and children and turning the woods around Grand Point into an armed camp, they arranged a family reunion. How could they hope to prevail against men who considered killing a natural and holy act and death a promise of paradise?

The scene in the yard outside and in the kitchen played itself in her mind, again, and yet again. Something was missing, but she couldn't quite grasp what it might be.

Then she had it. Terror, that was what was missing, particularly among the women. The wives of the Benedict men were worried, yes, but unafraid. Trust in the ability of their men to protect them was in their smiles and in their eyes.

That would change. She had brought terror with her. Soon Ahmad and the men with him would come with their guns and explosives, their fanatical ideas and disdain for women and for the lives of children. The reality of the threat he represented would alter forever the way they lived and the looks in their eyes, the way they thought and planned and dreamed.

She couldn't bear it. This thing had to be stopped. There had to be a way.

Ahmad was a fanatic, but he was also a realist. His personal honor might be sacred, but that didn't prevent him from seeing advantage to himself. Changing alliances, changing sides, changing plans were often seen as intelligent decisions among the Hazaris, actions based on altered circumstances or agile bending before the winds of fate. If she could show Ahmad that he would benefit materially from abandoning his personal jihad, he might go away. The chance was slim, but better than being the cause of the utter annihilation of all she'd seen this morning.

She didn't want to die. But neither could she live with the idea that others must die for her sake.

Chloe shut her eyes, squeezing them tight. Her voice barely above a whisper, she repeated, "I should not have come."

16

Wade and Adam met Lara as they were coming out of the woods. They had been scouting the east property line that ran along a dirt road giving access to the lake. A guard had been posted at that potential entry point, one of many that now staked out the perimeter. How Adam's wife had managed to find the two of them was no great mystery. She had a sixth sense about where her husband was at all times. Adam complained about her psychic ability and the fact that he had no secrets from her, but it had its advantages.

Wade expected Lara to have some message for her husband. She walked up to him, instead. He saw the pity in her eyes even before she spoke.

"Chloe's gone, Wade. At least an hour ago."

He felt his heart stop dead still for a full second before it kicked into a harder beat. "How? Why?"

"In the back of Johnnie Hopewell's pickup truck. I seem to see her under a tarp or cover of some kind...Johnnie had an emergency call, an obstetrical emergency at the hospital. As to why, you'd know that better than anyone."

"Luke didn't try to stop her?"

"He wasn't checking vehicles coming from here, since it's his job to keep people out instead of the other way around. Anyway, who'd have thought she might want to leave?"

"I should have," Wade said. And he would've if he had really listened to what she'd been trying to tell him earlier, instead of cutting it short because her regret about everything he'd done or been asked to do wasn't what he wanted to hear.

"Where would she go?" Adam asked, his gaze on Lara's face.

"In search of something, or someone," she answered.

"Her stepbrother. Though I can't imagine how she hopes to find him." Wade hoped that it wasn't possible, prayed that it wasn't.

A frown drew Adam's brows together. "You don't think she might be in with this stepbrother of hers? That she could have come to the house to check out the lay of the land, then left to report back to him?"

Anger hit Wade with hurricane force. "Where did you get an idea like that?"

"Hell, Wade, it's just a suggestion. She may be American, but she's been over there since she was a kid. People have been brainwashed before."

"Not Chloe. She blames herself for what's going on, and I think she's scared to death that every single Benedict here will be massacred."

"You understand her very well for someone who just met her," Lara said.

Wade twitched a shoulder. "We've been through a lot together."

"I see."

He thought she might have, at that. At any rate, he had no intention of asking what she'd found.

"What now?" Adam asked, putting his hands on his hipbones.

"I have to go after her."

"How? Where?"

He had one possibility, a single hope. "Let me borrow your cell phone?"

Adam unclipped it from his belt and passed it over without a word. Wade flipped open the cover and dialed a number.

"Yeah," Nat said in his ear. "What took you so long?"

"Otherwise occupied," Wade answered. "You got her?"

"Been following her for the past hour. Next time, make sure I have access to you before you set me up for a wild-goose chase."

"You might have come back for me."

"Afraid I'd lose her."

"Or kept her in one spot long enough to call the house."

"Did you say hold her prisoner? Did you even think about it?"

He hadn't and wouldn't have, not after what she'd

been through. The main idea had been to give her a bodyguard while he was otherwise occupied. He had to swallow an odd obstruction in his throat before he could go on. "Where is she? What's she doing?"

"Turn-Coupe is where she left her transport, in the hospital parking lot after the driver went inside. She walked back uptown from there. As to what she's doing, the answer is not much."

"She's not trying to find her stepbrother?"

"Nope," Nat said. "Just wandering around, mostly in and out of the stores opposite the courthouse. Seems to be shopping."

"She doesn't have that much money."

"Looking then. Or maybe she intends to let the stepbrother find her instead of the other way around."

Wade closed his eyes. The tactic had some chance of working if Ahmad was looking for him and his family in their hometown.

"What?" Adam asked, his voice sharp.

Wade ignored the question. "I'll be there in fifteen minutes," he said into the phone. "Stay with her. Don't let anything happen to her. Call this number if anything changes." He raised a brow at Adam who gave him the required digits. After repeating them into the phone, he slapped the cover shut.

"Sounds like you're going after her," his brother said. "Want company?"

Wade considered that for a tense moment. Then he shook his head. "You're needed here. Ahmad may know where we live already."

"And if he doesn't?"

"I'll handle it. But you could tell Roan. He must have a deputy or two left in town for reinforcements."

Lara spoke up then. "Chloe isn't doing this for herself, you know. It's for you and all the rest of us."

"But what if it doesn't work?" Wade asked. "Or what if it does, and Ahmad still wants her as well as her money?" What he didn't say, because he couldn't, was that any desire Ahmad might have would probably be temporary. Afterward, he would kill Chloe as easily as crushing a butterfly.

"She knew the risk."

Wade didn't answer. He couldn't. The obstruction in his throat, he realized, was fear.

The ten miles or so into town were covered in record time in Clay's new dually. He scoped out his cousin Betsy's motel and coffee shop on the way in, but saw nothing unusual, no sign of the green sedan Ahmad had been driving on the chase from the airport. Parking at the courthouse, he surveyed the main drag in a single glance, a mere four blocks of stores crowded together to accommodate nineteenth-century foot traffic. Nothing moved except a couple of elderly women just going into the beauty shop and the black cat grooming itself in the window of the Magnolia Gift Store and Tea Room. He'd glimpsed Nat's rental near the feed and seed store one street over, but his friend was nowhere in sight.

Chloe wasn't in the dress shop when he looked

inside, nor was she at the flower shop. Checking didn't take long, since they weren't big places. The clerk on duty at the dress shop said a woman answering her description had been in but left without buying anything. Emerging again, Wade paused on the sidewalk in front of the shoe shop, staring up and down. There was still no sign of her or Nat.

Wade took out the cell phone, but stood weighing it in his hand. He wasn't sure calling Nat again was such a good idea. Could be he was in a situation where a chirping phone might attract unneeded attention. If not, then he'd have made himself available.

Wade's side hurt and his stomach felt on fire. The need to do something pounded inside his skull. He couldn't stand this waiting, not knowing. When he got his hands on Chloe Madison, the two of them were going to come to an understanding. He was responsible for her. If he was to keep her safe, she had to cooperate. He couldn't do it alone.

The appalling death of Chloe's stepsister gnawed away at the back of his mind. For a woman to be killed was worse, somehow, than the death of a man. He thought that was the unspoken reason a lot of men hated the idea of women in combat operations. Something inside them held a female body with its power to produce life as sacred, inherently more valuable than that of a male. They couldn't stand the thought of everything tender and precious, everything they tried so hard to keep inviolate outside their military lives, annihilated in the stink of sweat and blood.

He knew he couldn't. Even less could he stand to think of Chloe deliberately putting herself in Ahmad's hands, no matter what the cause.

It was possible of course that they were wrong about why she had left. It could be because she didn't care for the whole situation. She hadn't bargained on being cooped up at Grand Point or put into a bedroom only a step down the hall from his own. She'd only wanted one night with him, after all.

He should never have agreed. The trust between them had been fragile, not up to the strain the night before had placed on it. He'd attempted to show her the pitfalls, but maybe he hadn't tried hard enough. Willpower was a fine thing, but only went so far.

He'd done what she'd asked to the best of his ability. There'd been no critique of the performance, and he was positively not the kind to ask if it had been good. He'd been enthralled, knew very well there was no such thing as having enough of her. She'd seemed lost in the moment, but women had been known to fake it before. Nothing said that she'd gotten a thing from the experience except an end to virginal inconvenience.

That was the last thing he wanted to explain to Adam or anybody else. Even if he could find the words, which he was fairly sure would be impossible.

Something moved at the periphery of his vision.

He snapped his head around in time to see Chloe step out of the hamburger joint a block down from the courthouse. She had a white paper bag in one hand and a drink cup in the other. After waiting for an elderly woman in an ancient Cadillac to pass, she crossed the street to the courthouse lawn and took a seat on an iron bench under one of the big oaks. Setting her drink beside her, she pulled her hamburger out of the bag. Even from where Wade stood, he could see the ceremony with which she peeled off the wrapping and the way she closed her eyes to savor the first bite.

A wry smile tugged one corner of his mouth. It must have been a very long time since she'd tasted anything so totally American. He wished he'd known it was what she'd wanted.

Hard on that thought came recognition of just what she was doing. Could there be a better place to see and be seen than the Courthouse Square? And what more logical reason could there be to sit there in plain sight than to eat her lunch?

He had to admire her initiative and her courage. He might even tell her so, after he gave her a piece of his mind.

At that instant, a sedan turned the corner. It cruised past the flower shop and restaurant, slowing as it neared the courthouse. It eased past where Chloe sat on her bench.

Instinct kicked in with a vengeance. Wade pulled his weapon from his waistband and broke into a hard, ground-eating run even before his mind registered the identity of the man behind the wheel.

He thought for a second that Ahmad had missed

seeing Chloe. Then the vehicle swerved toward the curb. Brakes squealed as it jarred to a halt. The doors swung open and four men scrambled out. They swarmed toward Chloe.

She had just picked up her drink. With it still in her hand, she wheeled to face the threat.

The sedan with its doors wide open sat between Wade and the others. He dropped into a crouch, using it for cover. Reaching it in a few swift steps, he braced his arms across the hood and drew down on his quarry.

"Halt!" he shouted. "Hold it right there."

The Hazaris flung him a fast glance, then scattered like a flock of chickens, rolling, scrambling for cover. A shot exploded and the bullet zinged over the sedan. Wade ducked, but held his fire. He couldn't risk hitting Chloe.

Ahmad expected that or else didn't care. He sprang from the cover of the big oak, firing as he ran toward Chloe. She whirled away, but was caught from behind. Wade cringed, eyes strained for the flash of a knife. Instead Ahmad grabbed her wrist and jerked it up behind her back. Then he dragged her around in front of him as a shield while he backed across the street. Within seconds, they disappeared inside the gift shop.

At that instant, two men burst out of the doors of the courthouse and raced down the steps. A quick glance was enough to identify Nat and the uniformed deputy with him. The remaining jihadis broke and ran before this new threat. The deputy pounded after them, but Nat came on.

Wade rounded the sedan and sprinted headlong for the dress shop. Nat joined him, weapon in hand, just outside the door.

"Sorry I wasn't closer," he said, trying to catch his breath as they flanked the opening on either side, backs to the wall. "Deputy flagged me down. Had to call Roan for verification that I was really who I said."

"Figures." Wade clenched his teeth against the ache in his side, then risked a fast look around the door facing. Nothing moved in the interior, nobody shot at him. He nodded to Nat. "Go!"

They whipped inside, guns ready. The only person in the shop was a saleswoman behind the checkout counter, standing frozen with a ceramic turkey in one hand and a pricing gun in the other.

"Which way?" he demanded.

She pointed toward the back, her eyes as big as the ceramic pumpkins scattered around her.

A framed opening led into a storeroom. With Nat close behind him, Wade raced through dusty shelving and stacked boxes, and crunched over foam packing peanuts. A metal-clad door at the rear was just closing on its compressed air hinge. He hit it hard, then leaped down the rickety steps that led into a narrow access alley. Directly across the way was the rear loading dock for the feed and seed store that backed up to the alley. Ahmad and Chloe were just disappearing inside.

Nat headed for the steps, but Wade took the dock in a single, athletic leap. Seconds later, he was inside.

Cursing could be heard from the front of the store. The voice belonged to a crusty old reprobate named Zach Buchanan, longtime proprietor known for giving good deals in spring and summer bulbs to pretty gardeners and keeping a double-barreled shotgun under the counter by way of a security system. A shattering roar punctuated his profane comments. Then everything was quiet.

Wade's forward momentum carried him into the front room. A single, comprehensive glance showed Zach looking down the second barrel of his shotgun at Ahmad. Chloe's stepbrother held her in front of him like living body armor even as he pressed a knifepoint against the jugular that pulsed under the white skin of her throat.

A poisonous mix of rage, fear and déjà vu flooded Wade's mind at the sight of Ahmad's knifepoint denting Chloe's skin. He'd been here before, twice, and each time it ended in death. This time had to be different.

Ahmad swung Chloe around as Wade skidded to a halt. "Drop your weapon," he barked, "or I cut her throat like a pullet."

Zach belonged to a generation that had been brought up on cowboy movies and had a tendency to fall back on their jargon in tight situations. "Can't tell what he's saying, Wade,'' he drawled. "But I don't much like the looks of this hombre, and sure as hell don't like his attitude.''

"No shit,'' Nat said in heartfelt agreement as he edged through the door from the back.

"Dead right.'' Wade met Ahmad's hot eyes as he answered him in his best Pashtu. "Spill even a drop of her blood and I'll personally send you to hell.''

"You think I care?'' Ahmad demanded. "She has dishonored herself and defiled my family name.''

"Yeah, yeah, but she isn't your family, never was, never will be. What she does has nothing to do with you.''

"My father accepted her. I accepted her. She is ours.''

The claim raised hackles Wade didn't even know he had. Also a fierce possessive instinct he'd never felt before and had no right to express now. "Not on your life,'' he answered in tones of steel. "She belongs to herself and to this country. She's an American.''

"Looks like we got ourselves a Mexican standoff,'' Zach said.

Sunlight angled through the store's glass door to make a patch of yellow on the floor. Dust motes, glinting in the brightness, spun in lazy eddies around them. The smells of cottonseed meal, dog food, deer corn and pesticides were familiar beyond words, since Wade and his dad had visited the feed store a thousand times. Still, it wasn't where he wanted to make a life or death decision.

Chloe spoke then, her voice a little breathless but more reasonable than it had any right to be. "Wait. There's no need for this. I'll...I'll go away with you, Ahmad. You can have the money from my father if you will relinquish your jihad against this man."

"No!" That instant rejection seemed to have jagged edges as it tore from Wade's throat. He'd guessed she had something like this on her mind, but hearing it was something else again.

"My righteous jihad?" Ahmad pressed his knife tip deeper so a trace of red stained the tip.

Chloe winced, shifting a little to keep her balance as she strained away. "Yes, you are right, my brother, to be angry at the...the interference. But Wade was forced to come for me. It was a vow made to my father as he lay dying. You must understand that."

"He does not agree." Ahmad was listening, though belligerence was still strong in his voice.

"He will accept my decision for the sake of his family. But if you attack them, it will be too late."

She was speaking to Ahmad, but Wade knew that her message was also for him. He was to back off, let Ahmad go and her with him. He appreciated her need to avoid endangering those he held dear, but there was no way it was going to happen. If worse came to worst, he had the perfect way to prevent it, one she had given him herself.

"We may have this money now, today?" Ahmad

asked. "You can take it from a bank and give it to me in American dollars?"

She swallowed with a hard movement that was perfectly visible in the craned angle of her throat. Holding Wade's gaze, she answered, "Not today, maybe, but soon."

Wade, his voice softly lethal, said, "It can be done. But what of afterward?"

She knew what he was asking for her eyes turned dark blue before they flickered away from his. The blankness that smoothed over her features told him that she had already considered and accepted the fact that she would die and refused to let it matter.

It mattered to Wade. The pain in his chest was so great that he could barely draw breath, the rage to destroy so savage that he understood without question every crime of passion ever committed. If Ahmad harmed a hair on Chloe's head, someone was going to have to pick up what was left of the jihadi with a shovel.

But before Wade would let her risk being alone and unprotected when Ahmad found out that she was no longer untouched, he'd tell him, here, now. He'd make damn sure it didn't happen when he wasn't there, when there was not a prayer in hell of being able to save her.

At that moment, the three missing Hazaris slid into the store from the front door. Dividing their gazes between Zach's shotgun and the weapons he and Nat still held, they silently ranged themselves on either side of Ahmad.

Chloe glanced at the one to her right, then her gaze widened. "Ismael!"

"Even so."

Wade eased forward a step. Something in the face of the man who had been married to Ahmad's sister ratcheted his nerves a shade tighter. Or maybe it was something that was missing. The Hazari's eyes were dark and fixed, as if he was drugged or else looked inward on some desperate mission.

"But why?" Chloe cried.

"Because I care," Ismael said with echoing desolation in the gentle cadences of his voice. "Because of my wife whom I loved as I loved my life. And because I have my own personal jihad."

Wade felt the hair rise on the back of his neck. His muscles tensed as he got ready to make a move. A quick glance at Zach showed him squinting along the barrel of his shotgun, though the weapon would make a hole the size of a basketball in any target he hit at that range.

"You blame me?"

The twist of anguish was in Ismael's smile. "You were the instrument, as I am now. It is enough."

Wade didn't know what the guy was getting at, but it seemed that Chloe might. Or maybe she'd figured out that if Ismael could blame her for what had happened, it was useless to hope that an extremist like Ahmad would ever relent. Regardless of the cause, her features hardened and she took a deep breath, as if some decision had been made, or possibly made for her.

Then beyond the glass entrance door, a shadow appeared on the sidewalk. It eased forward, the image of a man wearing a Stetson. The missing deputy, Wade thought. He must have seen the Hazaris enter the store, and it looked as if he was getting ready to rush the place.

Wade glanced at Ahmad to see if he'd noticed. Ahmad was scowling at Ismael. Chloe had caught that stealthy movement, however. She looked away almost immediately, as though afraid of directing attention toward it.

The shadow slid forward an inch, and then another. Wade thought he could make out the silhouette of a weapon held in the man's fist.

The door slammed inward, and the deputy catapulted inside. Chloe lifted her knee and stamped her heel down hard on Ahmad's instep. He stumbled back with disbelief stamped on his features at the attack from a female. In the same instant, Wade sprang to grab his knife hand.

The next seconds were mass confusion. Nat jumped Ismael. One of the other jihadis lifted a weapon but couldn't get a clear shot in the melee. Zach cursed and danced from side to side with the same problem.

Abruptly Ismael rammed his shoulder into Chloe, knocking her off her feet. Wade grunted as she fell against him with her elbow digging into his side. Pain rose in a red haze in front of his eyes. His grip began to loosen and he felt Ahmad jerk free. With desperate effort, he caught Chloe, twisting, dragging her with him and away from the flash of the knife as he went down. As they hit the floor, he rolled, covering her with his body.

Zach's shotgun boomed out. Nat yelled. The deputy shouted an order that was lost in the uproar of another shot. Footsteps thudded, vibrating the floor under Wade, and the glass door was flung open to crash against the wall. Then everything was quiet.

"You okay?" Nat demanded as he knelt beside him.

Blood was creeping in a warm path along Wade's waistline and his side felt on fire, but he didn't bother to answer. Levering his weight off Chloe, he turned her to him. Her face was pale, but her throat was barely scratched. As he hovered over her, she opened her eyes and gave him a watery smile. Suddenly he could breathe again.

"Casualty report?" he said.

It was the deputy who answered, coming toward him as he holstered his weapon. "Zach's hit. He got one of the bastards, though."

It was easy to tell that the feed storeowner's wound was nonfatal, since his curses turned the air a royal shade of blue. "Damn idiot stepped in front of that Ahmad," he said on a grunt, "or I'd a had the sumabitch."

Wade climbed to his feet, wincing a little as he

reached down to help Chloe to stand. With a glance at the deputy, he asked, "You all right? You can get an ambulance here pronto for Zach?"

"I got it."

Nat looked him over critically, his gaze resting on the red stain blooming on his shirt. "What about you?"

"I'll live. Let's just get the hell out of here and back to Grand Point. Before they beat us home."

17

Chloe felt like a prisoner as Wade marched her into the house at Grand Point. The clasp of his hand on her upper arm wasn't hurtful, but neither was it gentle. He didn't stop for the many queries about where he'd gone so fast or what he'd been doing, appeared not to hear the exclamations over the blood on his shirt. Face grim, he led her up the stairs and down the hall to his room. When they were inside, he shut the door and turned to face her.

"Talk," he said. "I want to know exactly what you were doing by sneaking off without a word?"

"I had to see Ahmad..." she began.

"You thought you could give him what he wanted from you, and in return he'd decide to play nice and leave us alone? How could you even imagine that he'd agree? And if he had, how was that supposed to make us feel, knowing you preferred whatever punishment he might inflict to being safe here with us?"

"I didn't," she said with a helpless gesture. "But there are women and children here. They don't deserve to die because of me."

"You think we're like sitting ducks, is that it? No

match whatever for battle-hardened veterans like Ahmad and his men?''

That was cutting perilously close to her true views. ''You and the others have no idea how cruel and vicious they can be.'' She moved away from him, into the connecting bath where she found the first-aid supplies.

''We don't have to be either one in order to know how to fight,'' he answered as he followed her to the door. ''This is our turf. We know every creek, every hill and low spot, fence line or crossroad. It's terrain that we've walked over, hunted over and camped on for generations. It's a part of us, something we can use for cover or for ambush that the creeps out to get us can never understand, much less duplicate. We can't be cornered here, and we won't be defeated.''

''All right, I was wrong,'' she said, bowing her head as she moved toward him with the things in her hands. ''I didn't mean to cause so much trouble.''

He was silent for long seconds. When he spoke, his voice was tight with scorn. ''Don't give me that drooping, lowly female stuff. Ahmad may be stupid enough to be taken in by it, but I know better. You aren't servile at all. You're proud and you're cagey, and you've learned to pretend in order to fit in, but that's all. You have a brain in your head, and you know how to use it. What I want is for you to do just that. Think, before you go doing things that can get you killed.''

''I did!''

"Oh, right. You thought you'd give yourself up and that would make everything just fine? Female sacrifice may be a big deal where you've been the last few years, but we don't have much use for it around here."

Anger surged along her veins at his summary dismissal of what she had thought was an unselfish gesture. She pushed past him, giving him a hard stare. "I was trying to save your family. If that bothers you, I'm sorry."

"It bothers the hell out of me, lady. They don't need saving. Get that through your head once and for all. And stop saying you're sorry!"

She would not apologize to him ever again, not if it killed her. "You think posting a guard on the road and boarding up a few windows will take care of everything? You really believe that throwing a family party is the best way to prepare for the worst?"

"There's more to our defense system than lookouts and a few boards, thank you very much, and every adult on the place knows exactly when and how to yank the kids into a safe haven without traumatizing them for life by shutting them up in the dark for days. We could have sent them away, and the women with them, but we prefer to know every minute that they're safe. We could all have hightailed it for the hills, but Benedicts don't run. We could have shut ourselves up here and yelled for the police, but Benedicts don't expect others to do our dirty work. We take care of our own."

It was possible that she had misjudged the situation, and things weren't quite as they appeared on the surface. That didn't change her part in it. "While you're busy taking care of things, you want me to do nothing? I'm supposed to let you and your family risk everything while I have a nice little vacation?" She tossed the items she held onto the foot of the bed, then walked up to him and caught the edges of his shirt placket in her hands. The rage that burned inside her supercharged her strength, so she nearly tore the buttons from their holes as she yanked it open.

He blinked at her violence, but made no effort to stop it. "You were tired, you'd been through a lot and needed the rest. But no, this is a mutual effort. You're supposed to help when the time comes."

"Your family doesn't want me here." She lifted one end of the tape that held the blood-soaked compresses and ripped it free.

"Damn, woman," he said with a growl in his voice as he grabbed her arm.

"Let me go."

He hesitated a moment, watching her face, then he complied. "Anyway, you don't know what my family wants. You've had no time to find out."

"I saw how they looked at me."

"You're a stranger. What did you expect?"

"Nothing. Nothing at all." She kept her gaze on what she was doing. His gash had stopped bleeding, but looked bruised and painful again. Tossing the old bandage to one side, she applied antibiotic ointment to a long rectangle of gauze, then pressed it to the semihealed line of stitches and began to tape them in place.

"You have to make an effort. They can't do it all."

"I'm not needed here," she said without looking at him. "Nor am I wanted."

"I want you."

The words, steely in their precision, echoed with truth in the enclosed room. She looked up, her eyes wide. The planes of his face were still flat and tight with anger and his mouth was set in grim lines, but in his eyes was a hot and consuming need. Something inside her rose to meet it, moving through her in urgent flood. They stood immobile for long seconds while their chests rose and fell with their hard breathing. Then his face changed and he reached for her.

She flung herself against him in that same instant. She wanted, needed to feel his hard chest against her breasts, the strength of his arms around her. His mouth came down on hers, devouring, demanding. She opened to him, clashing her tongue with his, desperate for the taste and feel and thrust that let her know that he was alive, and so was she.

He shoved his hand under the T-shirt she wore, cupping her bare breast, kneading the nipple between thumb and forefinger like a tender grape. She felt his fingers slip under her waistband at the small of her back as well, gliding lower until he cupped the firm curves he found there. Feverish with internal heat, yet shivering with the mix of anger and excitement in her veins, she rubbed her palms over the muscles of his back, reveling in their ripple and slide and the power they promised even as she pushed his shirt from him.

They shed the rest of their clothes on the way down to the floor. The prickly wool of the floral carpet scratched her back, but she didn't care. She didn't mind the crisp hair on his thighs that abraded the insides of her legs, welcomed his weight upon her. She was on fire. Moist, hot and welcoming, she rose against him. He opened her, dipped inside, eased into her tightness. Then with a hard twist of his hips, he plunged deep.

Her very being coalesced around him. She arched toward him, burying her face in his shoulder, tasting, nipping his skin. She could feel his hot breath against her hair, feel him stretching her, filling her, throbbing hot and hard so deep inside her that he seemed a part of her. And she wanted him there, wanted him deeper, wanted to take him and hold him in raging, half-mad possession, making him hers inescapably.

Wade seemed to sense her need. Holding her close against him, he rolled with her so she was on top with her hair tangling around them, binding them together. Free of his confinement, she could control the depth of penetration, the speed and fervor of it.

She did, too, riding, striving in mind-bending exultation, until her body was covered in fine perspiration, the air rasped in her lungs and her muscles felt on fire. And still the final triumph escaped her.

A touch, a whisper, and he turned with her again, and this time he was so deep that they were one being, the completion so infinite that tears rimmed her lashes in wet heat and spilled into her hair.

But with them came a hot deluge of purest and most transcendent pleasure. She moved with him then, with sobbing breaths and shuddering effort, with mindless acceptance that banished anger, soothed tension. And somewhere in the dim corners of her mind was an infinite gratitude that he could not see, did not know that with her every answering surge she abandoned pretense and gave to him her love.

Seconds later, he stiffened with a low, guttural cry. Muscles rigid, he held her while brushing the tender skin of her neck with his lips, burying his face in the waves of hair that trailed across her neck.

For long moments, they were still. Then he sighed, and eased to one side, resting his weight on his elbow though keeping their lower bodies entwined. He brushed the fine strands of hair away from her face, letting his thumb trail over her lips. "You're okay? I didn't hurt you?"

"I'm fine. Though I'm not so sure about you." There was a smear of blood across her rib cage, and she couldn't tell whether it was from before or if he'd opened the wound yet again.

"I'll live."

The humor in his voice, and lack of anger, were like a balm. She let it wash over her while her heartbeat slowed and the rise and fall of her chest returned to normal.

A niggling thought touched her, then remained long enough to become a worry. Lifting a fingertip to trail it through his chest hair, she said, "I wonder what your family thinks is going on up here."

"I expect they can guess." A wry grin curved his mouth.

The word that slipped from her in Pashtu was expressive if inelegant.

"Not to worry. The guys will think it's perfectly natural, what they'd be doing in my place, and their women will probably wonder if it's anything like what goes on between them and their men."

"No."

"No?" He tipped his head as he considered her.

"It isn't. Clay hugged me, remember, and it was nothing at all like...that is, well, you know."

He gathered her close, so their bodies were intimately connected once more. "Nothing like this?"

"Not in any way." She wished fervently that she'd kept her mouth shut.

A smile twitched his lips. He pressed them together, but it did no good. The amusement spread until laugh lines cut deep into his cheeks. "Well," he drawled, "that's nice to know."

Heat rose to her cheekbones. She suddenly felt exposed, both physically and mentally. Putting her fingertips to his shoulder, she applied pressure. It was enough. He shifted, giving her the room to slide from under him, though his gaze was watchful. Refusing to meet it, she gathered up her clothes and padded into the bathroom.

She turned on the tap, letting the cool water run over her hands and wrists for several seconds before splashing her hot face. Then she stood with her hands braced on the basin's edge and her eyes closed, letting the water drip down her chin and neck onto her breasts.

She was a fool.

What she had just done could trap her, prevent her from doing the one thing that could give her life meaning. If unprotected sex left her pregnant, that baby would become a hostage binding her to this place and these people. She would have all the duties and obligations that left no time for other things. She could not work to save the women she'd left behind in the ignorance and near slavery of life behind the veil.

She was also foolish because she'd come so close to forgetting that she had that mission. She had allowed herself to be seduced by the ancient and visceral appreciation of women for masculine strength. She had seen in Wade the opposite side of male power from that shown by the Islamic fundamentalists of the country from which she had come, the use of it to protect rather than to subjugate.

Listening to him just now, as he spoke of himself and his family, she had heard his deep commitment to taking care of his own. She had seen the closeness between the men of his family and their women, the care and concern and easy, unrestrained affection between them. She had heard and she had seen, and the yearning to be a part of it, to belong naturally and completely to something or someone had crept in upon her so quietly that she'd not known it was there until she'd seen, abruptly, that she could never have it.

The Benedicts didn't want her here. She'd brought trouble and fear into their safe, easy lives, and for that she could never be forgiven. If a single man or woman was lost, a hair hurt on the head of even one child, then she would be hated forever.

"You sure you're all right?"

She lifted her head. She could see him in the mirror as he stood behind her, leaning with one shoulder on the door facing. His hair was tousled and the sleepy look of spent passion lingered in his eyes. He'd stepped into his jeans, but that was all. As she said nothing, he lifted a brow and tipped his toward the water tap that was still running.

"Sorry," she said, forcing a smile as she reached to turn it off. "I'm fine. Really."

"Good. Marry me?"

"What?"

He moved away from the door and sauntered up behind her, wrapping his arms around her and spreading his fingers across her bare abdomen. "You heard me."

"I can't."

"Sure you can."

"We hardly know each other." The lazy circle he was making with his hand, barely brushing the small triangle of hair at the base of her belly, made it hard to think.

"I know enough. And it would give me the right to take care of you, always."

His words said one thing, but his caress another. It didn't matter. Wade had made no secret of the fact that he wanted her. What he meant, she thought, was that he desired her. It was only a physical craving, sex without permanence or meaning beyond the pleasure of the moment, Mother Nature's great trick on humanity. That was all right. She didn't want more from him, didn't want love or promises or all the other things that made a prisoner of a woman.

"I don't want you to take care of me," she said, not quite meeting his gaze in the mirror. "I have other things to do with my life. The women I left behind are my family, just as you have yours. I can't run out on them any more than you could desert those you care about."

His movements stilled and his hold loosened. "You don't want a family of your own."

"I'd be trapped in it as surely as I was ever trapped in Ahmad's house."

"You see marriage as a threat."

"Is that so hard to understand? I thought most men looked at it that way."

"Not Benedict men. So you don't want me?"

She did want him. What she didn't want was to love him. She didn't want to, but she did, heaven help her.

That was something he must never guess. The longer she was near him, the more he touched her, the worse it would get. The more time she spent here, the harder it would be to ever go. She needed to get away, but there was no one she could turn to, no place to run as long as death and danger waited beyond these walls.

She could see only one way out.

"No," she said, and met his eyes, finally, with hard-held purpose. "No, I don't want you, don't want to marry you now or ever."

He opened his arms. His face was bleak as he stepped away, then backed slowly from the bathroom. "Forget I asked," he said.

"I intend to," she answered, giving the words the low intensity of a vow.

"Fine. I'll do the same."

He turned then. Seconds later, the bedroom door closed behind him. The quiet click of the latch was unmistakably final.

18

The smell of wonderful things to eat met Chloe in the upper hall and drew her down to the kitchen. She hadn't left her room all day, hadn't felt hungry and still didn't, but the food spread out on the countertops was almost enough to make her reconsider. Platters of sliced meats, bowls of vegetables and salads of all kinds jostled huge casserole dishes holding what looked like dressing and dumplings and jambalaya. Tall pots were filled to their brims with soup and gumbo and fluffy white and brown rice. Then there were the desserts, an endless array of layer cakes and pound cakes, puddings and cobblers, meringue-topped pies, crusted pies, and pies coated with coconut and pecans. Plastic plates, glasses and utensils were stacked in one place, and crushed ice filled two large coolers. Everything sat ready, waiting for people to gather for the evening meal.

As Chloe hesitated in the doorway, a woman with her long golden-brown hair in a knot on top of her head and a pen behind her ear turned from where she stood at the stove. She took one look at Chloe's face and gave a low laugh before she continued ladling gumbo over rice. "I know, culinary overkill. But when the Benedict guys go hunting, Benedict women cook. It helps the stress level, for one thing, but it also feeds the horde on their return. This time, it's also meant to keep us from starving in case of a siege."

"It should work," Chloe said stiffly.

"Help yourself. That's what it's for—though I say it who cooked not the first dish."

"I don't think so, not just now."

"Whenever you're ready. No need to wait until dinner. I'm certainly not going to, since I missed the fish fry, only had cheese and an apple at my desk for lunch." The woman stepped forward and offered her free hand with friendly warmth in her gray eyes. "You're Chloe, aren't you? I'm April Benedict."

"The writer?"

"Afraid so. I'd have been here to welcome you earlier, but deadlines go on, regardless."

"You had to cancel your tour, too, I think. I'd say I'm sorry, but Wade seems to think I've done that enough."

April gave a light shrug. "I can't imagine you actually wanted to be followed back to the States. So what was the trouble in town this morning?"

"He didn't tell you?" Chloe moved to a platter of smoked ham and took a slice, then peeled off a sliver. It had been years since she'd tasted such a thing. The hickory and honey flavors that met her tongue were laden with childhood memories of Sunday breakfasts and picnics.

"It was discussed, though I wasn't there at the time. Luke gave me the capsule version before he went back on watch, but you know how that goes."

"Not much detail?"

"Exactly. Besides, I'd like to hear yours."

Chloe told her, also answering the quick and penetrating questions that April put in at intervals. When she was done, she was afraid she'd said more than she should, certainly more than she'd intended.

"So Wade was upset, was he?" the writer asked. Her gaze was veiled as she dipped into her gumbo with appetite and precision.

"You could say that."

"I thought he looked like a thundercloud for some reason."

Chloe made a noncommittal sound as she reached for another piece of ham. To change the subject, she asked, "Where is everyone?"

"Here and there." April watched her for a moment. "Are you sure you don't want a plate?"

"Maybe I will." Chloe picked up one from the stack nearby, and put a slice of roast on it that would be big enough to feed a family in Hazaristan. After a moment, she asked, "Wade ate earlier, I suppose?"

"Probably." April tipped her head as she watched her. "Would it bother you if he hadn't?"

The bite of roast she'd taken suddenly tasted like

ashes, but Chloe swallowed it anyway. "Why should it?"

"I thought you might be concerned about him."

"He can take care of himself."

"Of course he can." April's voice was dry.

A silence fell in which the only sounds were the dull scrape of plastic against plastic and the distant noise of children playing outside in the gathering twilight. An idea occurred to Chloe as she sat beside the writer. Since she wasn't sure how much time she might have before someone interrupted, she spoke at once. "Are you famous?"

"I don't know that I'd say that."

"But you were on tour, which must mean that you have radio or television interviews? You know people in the media?"

"A few." Caution was strong in April's voice.

"So if I had a videotape of atrocities against Hazaristan women, you'd have an idea of someone who might make use of it?"

April watched her an instant, then moved her chair a little closer as she said, "Tell me more."

Chloe was glad to comply. Short minutes later, she knew a great deal about the news media across the country, and had April's pledge to see that the RAWA tape was aired to the best advantage. The relief she felt at fulfilling that obligation was an indication of how much it had been weighing on her.

The writer's wide-ranging knowledge and ready compliance made Chloe curious about her, however.

With a glance at the pen behind her ear and the ink stains on her fingers, she asked, "You don't type your books?"

"Honey, I use whatever it takes. Sometimes it's a keyboard, sometimes voice recognition software or pen and ink. If one thing doesn't work, another may."

"And nobody interferes with you going off by yourself to create your books?"

"You mean does Luke interfere? Why should he? It's my job, what I do." She paused. "Now ask if he minds."

"Does he?" Chloe asked obligingly.

"He'd much rather I spent my time with him. I mean, he's a man, isn't he? But he understands that I have things I want to do, that I need something of my own."

"That's very...reasonable."

April smiled. "Benedict men are pretty considerate, if you lay it on the line for them in a logical way. Well, and if you let them know that what you're doing really isn't as important to you as they are."

"You believe your husband will always be this way?"

"Why not?"

"Some do change. When the vows have been spoken and the dowry counted, even the most tender of bridegrooms can become a tyrant." She'd numbered women among her friends who had learned that lesson the hard way.

"Luke would never do that."

"You must trust him very much to say so."

"I trust him, yes. I truly don't believe he has that kind of duplicity in him. But if he did, and allowed me to see it, then I'd have to realize he was never the man I thought him to be. In that case, I'd probably leave."

Chloe set her plate to one side. "It's easy for a woman to do that here, just leave a marriage. But don't you ever feel...confined?"

"If I do, I have only to remember that Luke and I are in this together, that we're both confined. And I'll tell you a secret to go along with that." She leaned closer, lowering her voice at the same time. "We like it that way."

"What about the other wives, Janna and Lara and..."

"Regina and Tory?" April supplied. "I guess you could say we all do our own thing. Regina buys and sells antique jewelry, Tory deals with land and property she inherited in Florida, Janna designs specialty fabrics for textile manufacturers, and Lara has a quilt shop in her grandmother's old house."

"And their husbands really don't mind?"

"If they do, they have the good sense not to mention it." April smiled. "No, really, we all contribute to the family bottom line. We're part of the team."

For the first time, Chloe allowed herself to question whether she might actually be able to do what she wanted and needed for her friends while remaining with Wade. She had assumed for so long that it was impossible for a married woman to carry on the work that the idea had become ingrained. But she wasn't in Hazaristan anymore, and Wade wasn't of that backward country. He was different, an American, a Benedict of Louisiana. Thinking back, she recognized that though he might have disagreed with her ideas and her aims, he had not challenged her right to have them, never failed to listen when she spoke of them.

"How do you do it?" she asked, the words barely above a whisper. "How do you find the trust it takes to marry a man knowing that it may not turn out as you hope?"

"It isn't easy," April answered with candor. "The basic requirement, I suppose, is courage."

"And where do you find this courage?"

"The same place women have always found it, and also the trust it takes to allow a man into their bodies and their lives, the faith to risk bringing children into the world. If you love a man, these things are just there, a part of life."

"Yes," Chloe said as she thought of the women she'd left behind and their consummate and unending bravery. "But how do you and the others make time for the things of your own? I mean, don't you feel as if you're shortchanging something or someone?"

"Women make time for the things they really want to do, and those who care about them do their best to help out. In an ideal relationship these days everybody adjusts, men as well as women. It's no good becoming a martyr to another person. You lose yourself in the process and, because of it, wind up hating the one you loved.''

"That's what I'm afraid of," Chloe murmured, almost to herself.

"Do you realize what you just said?" April spooned up the last bite of her gumbo then stepped over to put the bowl in the sink.

"Oh, but I didn't mean..."

"I think you did. I'm so glad. We were afraid, the other wives and I, that you didn't feel anything for Wade. We thought you might be a taker, or one of those needy, clinging types who would leave him flat the instant you felt safe.''

So that was the reason she'd been given such a lukewarm welcome. She had misjudged the Benedict women, or so it seemed. Their reaction to her had little to do with what or who she was but what she was doing to one of their own. Was it possible that she had also misjudged Wade? The idea made her feel sick inside, especially when she remembered his face in the instant before he had left her alone upstairs.

It was possible, however, that the Benedict women had not misjudged her. She moistened her lips before she spoke. "I don't know that I can stay."

"There's someone else somewhere waiting for you?"

"Not exactly."

April seemed to hesitate, then spoke anyway. "I don't like prying into other people's business, but it might be best not to make any major decisions until this is over. Wade obviously cares about you. Give him a chance.''

"Do you think so? That he cares, I mean?'' She looked away because she couldn't bear to see the pity that might lie in the eyes of the woman beside her.

"He could have done a lot of things, taken you a lot of places, to keep you safe. He chose to bring you home to Grand Point. That says something, believe me.''

Chloe hadn't thought of it that way. But even if it might be some kind of indicator, it was too late.

The pain of desolation and regret rose inside her, not only for what she'd done, but also for how Wade may have felt and what that meant. Wade wouldn't ask her again. He wasn't the kind of man who needed to be told anything twice.

The back door banged open from the direction of the living room. Chloe spun toward the sound with her nerves jangling. It was only the little girl called Lainey, however, giggling and looking back over her shoulder as she ran into the kitchen. Behind her was Jake, obviously chasing her though moving at a fast walk.

"No running in the house,'' April called out with the sound of an automatic warning.

"We're not,'' Lainey said, decreasing her speed at once but still making excellent progress.

"Hide-and-seek,'' Jake explained in an uneven rumble as he passed. "Uncle Clay said keep Lainey entertained, that it wasn't good for her to be upset.''

April rolled her eyes. "Carry on, then, since you're on a mission of mercy."

"A what?" The teenager lifted a brow in a gesture so like his older cousin's that Chloe felt a small ache in her heart.

"Never mind." April waved an airy dismissal. "Just don't damage the furniture, especially anything that looks old."

"You got it. Anyway, I really think Lainey wants to see if she can make out where Clay is right now."

"The windows are covered over, remember?"

"Always the roof."

"The what!" The pair had disappeared down the hall, forcing April to raise her voice.

"Widow's walk," Jake called back. "Don't worry, I'll keep an eye on her."

The footsteps faded, then could be heard on a set of stairs somewhere in that side wing. April looked at Chloe and shook her head in mock despair though indulgence warmed her smile. "I hope it's all right. Clay will murder me if anything happens to her."

"It's nice of Jake to look after her," Chloe said.

"He's a neat kid. Of course, he probably wants to check out the situation from up there himself. And it doesn't hurt that Lainey has a terrible crush on him amounting to hero worship."

"He likes that?"

"It makes him feel good about himself and also more considerate of her feelings, neither of which is a bad thing."

Chloe could only agree. "Should she be running and climbing stairs, though? I mean, if it's not good for her to be upset?"

"It's okay, at least according to her mom. Janna says she'll never be entirely out of the woods, but she's doing better than they had any reason to expect. Something about the happiness factor, if I remember. You've heard about Janna and Clay?"

"Wade told me."

"Did he? Interesting."

The back door opened again. From the increase in noise, it seemed as if the whole family reunion was moving inside. Women talked in a low hum, with the voices of men like a bass obbligato beneath the chatter. Children laughed and called. Mothers shouted. The door slammed, then opened again. Then it slammed shut and stayed that way. Chloe wondered about sleeping arrangements for everyone, but figured it was probably under control.

People trickled into the kitchen. They appeared a little disoriented, as if they didn't quite know what to do with themselves. Food offered an acceptable solution, and many began to mill around the kitchen, taking plates and peering at dishes and serving themselves a little of this, a little of that.

Janna, pushing her way through the crowd, began to dispense coffee. Tory appeared almost immediately afterward and picked up a knife to cut pies and cakes. Regina handed the sleeping toddler she carried to an elderly woman with hair as fine and silvery as a spider's web, then pitched in at the kitchen sink. Chloe watched them for a minute or two before moving in beside Kane's wife and beginning to dry the dishes as they were handed to her. The quick smile that passed between April and Regina, over and around her, held such approbation that it made her feel almost tearful.

"Is it getting dark outside already?" she asked when she had a chance. "Is that why everyone came inside?"

"Orders," Regina said, her face serious. "Roan gave them, but I think the guys got together and decided it was time."

Chloe's movements slowed as she wiped a plate. "Something is happening then."

"Or will soon."

She thought fleetingly of the children on the roof. "I wonder if this is such a good idea, everybody piling in here. An old house like this would go up like kindling if an incendiary shell were fired into it. I mean, it's a grand and solid old place, but with so much dried-out wood..."

"I know what you mean," Regina said unhappily. "I worried about the same thing at The Haven until poor Kane got tired of hearing it and installed a sprinkler system. The danger now is that little Courtney may drown in her bed if we have a fire."

"Maybe we should do something besides worry."

"Like what? Where would we go? What would we do? The guys wet down the walls and rooftops with water hoses this afternoon, but I really think they have other plans in mind. We'll just have to hope they know what they're doing."

Chloe didn't want to hope, but to know. She needed to be sure that Wade would live so she could talk to him. There were things she needed to say, things she must explain. She couldn't stand it that he was out there not knowing how much she cared or how wrong she had been. Even if he didn't love her, he should know that the hurtful words she'd spoken had been self-protection, because she'd been afraid to let him know what she felt, afraid he might take advantage of it.

Chloe glanced around, but there was no one to ask, no sign of Wade or Kane, Roan and Adam. In fact, the only one of the Benedict cousins that she could see was Luke, who had apparently just come in from his post on the driveway after being relieved. She watched a second as April went to greet him and was swept into a rib-crushing hold before being thoroughly kissed to the cheers and jeers of those closest to them. Then she looked away, scanning the crowd again and even backing up a few steps to see into the living room.

Most of the male Benedicts inside the house were either senior citizens or teens. The men of fighting age were nowhere in sight.

"Where are Wade and the others?" she asked as she stepped closer to Regina again. "Where did they go?"

"Out there," Regina said, tipping her head toward the area beyond the house walls. "Into the woods."

Chloe could feel her heart start to jar against the walls of her chest. "What do you mean? What good will that do?"

"If you're afraid we've been left unprotected, don't be. It's to take care of us that they're out there."

"But Ahmad and the others are experts in guerrilla tactics. They practically invented them. And they'll be armed, I'm sure, with sophisticated assault weapons, grenades, the kinds of things that aren't in your ordinary gun cabinet."

Regina gave her a serene look. "The Benedicts aren't exactly unarmed. Men who can bring down a deer at long range with a single shot from a high-powered rifle should have no problem bagging a different sort of game."

Regina, with her cloud of red hair, pale, freckled skin and soft voice might seem like a lightweight, but it would be a mistake, Chloe thought, to depend on it. She hadn't become a Benedict woman without reason.

"That's where you and Tory and the others were just now, wasn't it?" she asked in slow comprehension. "Saying goodbye to your men."

"I don't know that I'd call it a goodbye," Regina demurred.

"Sending them off, then."

"You never know." The red-haired woman looked down at her hands in the soapy water.

No, you never knew. Wade had gone with the rest of them, and she hadn't been there to say anything, to do anything to erase the last hurtful words between them. He'd taken up an unprotected position in the woods while thinking that she didn't appreciate what he'd done to keep her safe or that he was now forced to protect his family because of her. He was out there waiting for Ahmad and the others to show themselves, possibly in an explosive hell of flame and firepower, blood and death. Wade was gone, and it was too late.

He was out there, ready to fight and to die, because of her.

She couldn't breathe, could barely think. Her heart felt as if it were trying to beat its way out of her chest. With burning eyes, she stared at nothing while seeing images of death and destruction that made her feel faint.

The plate she was holding slipped a little in her hands. She caught it, then put it down carefully on the cabinet and dropped her drying cloth on top of it. Turning away, she moved almost blindly toward the living room, heading for the stairs that would lead to some place, anyplace, where she could be alone with this grinding pain.

It was then that the sound of gunfire crackled from far down the drive. Immediately afterward, they all heard the thin, high-pitched scream of a child.

19

Three evenly spaced shots crackled through the woods with a traveling echo. Wade shoved away from the tree he'd been propped against, instantly alert. It was the signal. Time to get this show on the road.

From two hundred yards away, Clay whistled with the melodious three-note call of a whippoorwill. Wade returned that signal to pinpoint his location. Then they closed the gap, heading at a ground-eating lope for the deadfall they'd spent all afternoon constructing in the sharp curve of the driveway just short of Grand Point.

Clay reached it first. By the time Wade made it, he could hear the roar of oncoming vehicles. Their fast-traveling headlights flickered among the trees, gaining speed. Then they rounded a bend and came into view as they hit the straightaway that led to that last curve.

Wade whipped his hunting knife from the sheath on his belt. Placing the blade against one of the guy ropes holding a sizable pine that had been sawn through at its base, he held it ready while applying pressure to the trunk with his other arm. He could feel the huge tree waver, unsteady on its stump.

Glancing across at Clay, he could just make out his brother in position at the opposite guy rope. They turned their heads to watch the end of the race.

Roan, driving Clay's pride and joy, the big, gleaming white one-ton turbocharged diesel truck, was giving it all he had. Dust flying, gravel grinding under the dual wheels, he bore down on them like the Nascar speedway champion he'd been a few years back. He was coming hard, closing the distance in high-speed chase like a hundred others he'd been in as the parish sheriff. Only there were a couple of differences this time. Roan was being pursued, and the car behind him was the green sedan they'd last seen in Turn-Coupe.

The waiting was over. Ahmad and his friends had finally arrived.

The dually thundered past where Wade and Clay stood. Immediately Roan slammed on the brakes and locked the wheels, throwing the heavy vehicle into a hard turn. The back end skidded in a tight half circle, flinging gravel among the trees like grapeshot and kicking up dust so thick the truck cab disappeared in the cloud. Under that cover, Roan bailed out and raced for the firewood piled in one ditch that, repeated on the other side, finished off the ends of the roadblock. Slapping a hand on top of the logs, he vaulted over behind their protection.

Wade didn't wait to see him land. The sedan was rounding the curve, barreling down on the barricade formed by the truck. Brakes squealed and tires squalled. The lightweight car fishtailed and slid sideways, plowing up grass and weeds along the shoulder like a road grader. It crashed into the back fender of the truck with a solid thud and the tinkling rain of safety glass.

Instantly Wade slashed the thick rope under his knife, then put his shoulder to the pine. Clay matched his movement on the other side.

The mighty tree began to topple. It gathered momentum, giving in to the inevitable pull of gravity. Wood creaked. The smell of resin filled the air. Branches thrashed with the sound of a great wind. Then the trunk crashed down on the back end of the sedan, jolted off, then slammed across the driveway behind it with a thunderous impact. It closed the trap, cutting off escape.

A hail of gunfire poured from the open windows of the half-destroyed car. It cut through the night, thudding into the trees. Wade dived for the cover of a big sweet gum, sucking in his gut and keeping his head and spine in alignment with the trunk. From the crash off to his right, he thought Clay had done much the same. Moving with care, he slid his rifle strap from his shoulder and waited for the volley to end.

It ceased as abruptly as it had begun. Wade heard the car doors open and the yells of what sounded like instructions in Pashtu. He ducked his head out from behind the sweet gum in time to see Ahmad and his cronies roll out of the vehicle and plunge into the woods on the far side of the road. Wade counted four of them. Ahmad had brought in reinforcements, it seemed.

Wade sighted on the moving shadows through his scope and squeezed the trigger. The shot spooked them like jumping deer in the middle of hunting season. A yell rang out as if he'd done some damage, though he couldn't tell how much. Still, their crashing progress through the woods had all the earmarks of panicked flight.

The strategy they'd worked out back at the house was on target. The jihadis were on foot and on the run. The home advantage belonged to the Benedicts since they knew every hill and hollow, every snake burrow and rabbit trail of this stand of woods. Armed with high-powered deer rifles accurate to five hundred feet—or as far as they could see in the dusk darkness—and shotguns loaded with buckshot, they were on the hunt.

Everything was fine, so far as it went, but it was still no cakewalk. The men they had to stop were trained soldiers armed with who knew what kind of weapons. Most dangerous of all was their state of mind. They meant to wipe out every Benedict that breathed, and didn't mind dying to make it happen.

Wade stepped from his cover and quartered the night with a narrow gaze until he spotted Clay. He gave a short wave as a signal to advance. Clay whistled his night bird call, and it was answered by Nat and the others up and down the road. Shadowy forms converged from all directions, forming a long line parallel to the driveway. At another signal, the Benedict band began to advance in this formation that could, if necessary, close on their prey like the jaws of a bear trap.

It was then that the sound of a screaming child came on the night breeze. Wade froze in place, listening.

"Lainey," Clay said from a short distance away, his voice grim.

He was right. The little girl was crying out for her daddy over and over. Someway or other, God alone knew how, she must have seen the dually as it came near crashing, heard the shots. She thought Clay was hurt. But the part that made the hair stand up on the back of Wade's neck was that her wails were traveling, coming toward them from the direction of the house. Then in nightmare horror, he caught the low rumble of Jake's cracked baritone, protesting, following.

Clay said something under his breath, a sound halfway between a curse and a prayer. Wade echoed it with the virulence of helpless dread. The two kids were running straight into danger. On top of that, their presence in the woods would hamstring the carefully constructed defense, interfering with the ability to fire by forcing identification of targets with absolute certainty. If they should be taken by the jihadis, then they were all dead since every single Benedict on this patch of ground would step straight into the mouth of hell before letting either youngster be harmed.

Then, when he thought the situation could not be worse, he heard a third voice. It was a woman calling to the two kids, moving after them. She spoke in tones of warning. It might have been for silence, since all sound ceased immediately.

Chloe. The woman's voice belonged to Chloe.

Wade's mind went dark. His chest felt as if it was being ripped open from the inside. Sweat broke out on him that had more to do with the images of the past than with the warmth of the night. He swore with soundless fluency and blackest dread.

Abruptly he was quiet. Going off the deep end wasn't going to help. Only one thing might, and that was to revert to the soldier-protector he'd been before. He took a deep, steadying breath and closed off all thought, all feeling and purpose other than the one thing that had to be done. He had to get those three out of there.

Clay was coming toward him, a gray ghost that made no more noise than a hunting night owl. As he neared, he spoke in tones that carried only a few feet. "I've got Lainey. Chloe is all yours. Roan is probably after Jake already, but if he can't get to him, then one of us looks out for the boy. Okay?"

Chloe is all yours.

"Got it." It was a promise, resolute and unbreakable. Without waiting or even looking back to see if Clay followed, Wade headed for the place where he'd last heard the woman who was at the heart of this mess and his sole, eternal responsibility.

He needed to reach her before Ahmad, had to remove her from the line of fire before more innocents died. He could not fail. This time, please God, everything had to come out right.

They moved along the line back toward the house, he and Clay, spreading the word of what they were doing as they went, passing the order to close ranks. Even as they made tracks, Wade could sense the clan slipping through the woods in search of the trespassers. He and Clay had scant minutes, maybe seconds, before all hell broke loose.

It felt like desertion to leave the line. They needed to be in two places at once, though it was plain which objective was most important at this second. Though the Benedicts paid lip service to him being in charge, they had no real need of a field general. They were used to going their own way, even preferred it. In any crisis calling for leadership, the first man on the scene could and would handle the job.

As if in answer to the thought, a fusillade of shots broke out back toward his left. They were closer to the house than Wade liked, but sounded as if somebody was alert. A man signaled. An answer came. Flashes sparked the night as more rounds were fired.

Under cover of the noise, Wade and Clay were able to move at a faster clip. They paralleled the driveway, keeping their eyes and ears open. Progress wasn't in a straight line, however, as they avoided the more open shoulders of the roadway. Instead they wound their way around trees and tangles of briers, and jumped a branch that was dry now but ran full during heavy rains.

The small, pale shape came at them out of the dark. It smacked into Clay at waist level and held tight. "Daddy, Daddy," Lainey said on a gulping sob. "I thought you were wrecked."

"I'm fine honey, really I am." Clay wrapped his arms around the shaking child, holding tight. "But what are you doing out here?"

"I was watching from upstairs. I saw the bad guys chasing you and forgot we weren't supposed to be outside. I had to see you, I just had to."

"It was Uncle Roan in the dually. He's okay, too. Where's your mother? Why didn't somebody stop you?" The strained note in Clay's voice was an indication of his fear that their quarry might have someone eluded them and penetrated the house.

"She's inside. I was running really fast. Jake came after me because he told April and Chloe that he'd watch me. But then, oh, but then..."

"I thought I heard Chloe just now," Wade said.

"She came after us because Mama can't run fast with the baby inside her. I heard her calling me but hadn't found you yet and didn't want to go back. Then Jake caught up, just before the bad man came." Her voice broke on a sob. "Oh, Daddy, it's all my fault!"

Clay went to one knee in front of her. "Take a deep breath, sweetheart. Then tell us exactly what happened."

"Jake," she said, the word jerked from her by a hiccuping attempt to follow his instructions. "These men were in the bushes, two of them. They caught us, but Jake fought them so they turned me loose. He told me to run, but I saw the big one hit him really hard. Jake fell down and they picked him up and carried him off. Then Chloe found me. I told her about Jake, and she said that she would see about him. She said I should go this way and find you as fast as I could."

"What did she do then?" The words were sharper than Wade intended, but he couldn't help it.

"I don't know. When I looked back, she wasn't there!"

"Take Lainey on back to the house, Clay," Roan said, his voice deadly quiet as he stepped from a dense tree shadow. "I'll go with Wade."

"I don't want to go back," Lainey cried. "I have to find Jake. He took care of me, and now I have to help him."

"You did your part. You found us, sweetheart," Clay said. "Now we have to go home."

He ended the argument by picking her up and carrying her. Wade and Roan moved with him for a short distance then peeled off, circling in the direction from which Lainey had come.

Wade moved in a rage so consuming that he lost all contact with notions of time or distance. Operating on finely honed instinct, he saw little except what was directly in front of him. He was aware of Roan beside him, knew his objective, but little more than that. He had become the machine that he'd once been trained to be, and was grateful for it.

He was grateful because the alternative was to recognize the fear that ran beneath his surface preoccupation. He was passionately afraid that he was going to be too late. To admit that was something he couldn't afford. Jake's life, and Chloe's, might depend on how well he was able to ignore it.

Abruptly they reached the woods' edge with the rear of the house looming in the darkness. Just in front of them lay the old Indian mound where he'd played knights and soldiers as a kid.

A man-made hill of earth worn down through the centuries to less than a tenth its original size, it was kept clear of trees and brush because of its supposed historical value. A root cellar and storm shelter had been dug into one side and fitted with a heavy door in the old days, when Native American sites were so plentiful that no one gave them a thought. The heavy door had been wedged open for years, had certainly been open earlier while Lainey and the other kids used it for a playhouse. Now it sagged on its hinges, almost shut.

He and Roan weren't alone in the tangled undergrowth of saw briers, wild myrtle and huckleberries. Wade was as certain of that as he was of the moon just rising into the sky. He was sure even before he caught sight of Chloe standing a short distance away. A slim figure in the moonlit darkness, she turned toward him and he saw the white mask of desperation that was her face.

"Ahmad is in there, isn't he?" he asked, the words so harsh he barely recognized them as coming from his own throat.

"I suppose it looked familiar."

She meant, he thought, that it resembled the caves of Hazaristan, the bunkers of choice during centuries of warfare. "And Jake?"

"He's there, too."

Roan stepped forward. "Alive?"

"They wouldn't have bothered with him otherwise."

She had a point, though it wasn't one Wade wanted to examine in detail. Jake's father, he was sure, would be even less willing.

Judging from the sounds in the woods behind them, the others were moving in their general direction. They must have cleared out the missing jihadis. The whole group would be on the scene in a few short minutes. Whether that would force Ahmad to act or prevent it was anybody's guess. Waiting to find out was not an option.

Wade looked at Roan. His cousin nodded. Then he swung toward the mound and raised a shout.

"Ahmad! We know you're in there. Come out now!"

No answer came for long seconds. Wade lined up the Pashtu phrases in his mind to repeat Roan's message. Then Ahmad spoke with a second voice trailing his words in translation, that of the man Chloe had called Ismael.

"Come out where you can kill us, infidel? We are not so stupid."

Roan hefted the 30-06 he carried. "It's the only way you might stay alive."

"Life or death is of no importance if we carry Benedicts with us," came the reply in a singsong rhythm like something learned by rote. "What matters is holy vengeance and family honor."

It was Wade who answered that. "Benedicts know a thing or two about honor, my friend, since we've done our share of breast-beating over it. It's a strange brand that needs the blood of women and children to satisfy it."

"You are an ignorant American who knows nothing and understands less. Our people were wearing silk and jewels and discussing the mathematical probabilities of the universe when yours were still worshiping trees and painting their faces blue."

"And what does that matter when you act the patsy for megalomaniacs who think history can be reversed and the worn-out glory of Islam returned? Your kind would rather destroy modern civilization than admit that you can't keep up with it. I may be an ignorant American, but I live in freedom while you think it's only a word. I know that you pervert the teachings of Mohammed to legitimize murder without understanding that you can't build future greatness in a graveyard."

"Enough!"

"The truth bother you?" Wade jeered. "Tough. It's time somebody pointed it out."

"Wade, please," Chloe said, her voice not quite even.

He was pushing it, he knew, but holding Ahmad's attention seemed better than letting it return to the boy who shared the dark cellar with that madman.

"I have no need to listen to you," Ahmad said through Ismael. "We have explosives, more than enough to blow a crater big enough to swallow you and everyone near this place. This pile of earth will become the graveyard of us all, Benedict."

"Ahmad, no," Chloe called, stepping from the shelter of the trees. "You don't have to do this."

Wade reached out and caught her arm, snatching her back to safety. Chloe flinched, stumbling, and he steadied her with a firm grasp on her upper arms. She stared up at him for a second with all the terror and fury inside her glittering in her eyes. Then she wrenched away from him.

Just behind them, men began to drift in from all directions, a quiet congregating in case of need. Wade glanced around, spotting Adam. "We have two holed up here," he said as he caught his attention. "You got the others?"

"One dead, one captured. Hopewell was tying the one still alive to a tree when I left."

Wade nodded. Hopewell was Johnnie's husband, the nurse who had inadvertently given Chloe a lift earlier. A good old boy of the first order, he could be trusted to make sure the jihadi stayed out of the action.

"Any of ours down?" he asked.

"One, a leg wound."

"Could be worse," Wade said. "And may get that way yet, since we have a situation here." He outlined the details, then invited suggestions.

"We could rush 'em," somebody said from the back. "It would be over before they know it."

"It'll be over all right, you danged idiot," came an irate answer. "Didn't you hear the part about them blowing us to kingdom come?"

Nat materialized out of the undergrowth just then. "No windows in that place, right? No exit except the one door?"

"Right," Wade answered, grateful that somebody appeared to be bending serious brainpower to the problem.

"No water source, I suppose, no food. We could starve them out if we knew we had the time."

"We don't."

"Right. About all I see is a flanking action, send a detail around to come up from behind, then storm the door at the same time."

Wade had already considered and discarded that option. "Too risky."

"For the boy, yeah," Nat agreed. "But you don't have much choice here. It's one life against a chance for the whole clan."

That same conclusion burned like a hot coal in Wade's mind. He couldn't seem to get a good breath. The urge to smash something or someone was so violent that it took most of his willpower to control it. He dragged air into his chest through flared nostrils, before he said, "I can't make that decision."

"Somebody has to."

"No," Chloe said in simple contradiction. "No, they don't."

Wade thought for a second that her objection was a purely emotional reaction. Then something in her voice snagged his attention. "What are you saying?"

"Ahmad might come out if you use the right bait."

"I don't think so." What he meant was that he refused to consider it since he had an idea what she was getting at.

"He did once."

"Yeah, and look what happened."

She shook her hair back as she faced him. "It's worth a try. He's here because of me."

"And me."

"You're secondary. I'm the one he blames for the stain on his family honor. I'm the one who corrupted his sister, or so he believes. He has promised a more personal revenge for me, so he may be enticed to send out Jake in exchange, or even leave himself open to your fire."

"No." It was all he could think of to say, all she had left him with her soul-chilling logic.

She watched him, her eyes dark and fathomless.

Her voice when she spoke was entirely too self-contained. "You have no choice, not really. Shall I speak to Ahmad? Or will you offer the substitution man to man, as if I have no value compared to one who shares your blood and your name?"

20

Chloe waited with a suspended feeling inside her chest for Wade's answer. No particular motive for her question had been in her mind, and yet more than her life seemed to depend on his answer. Her sense of who and what she was, her whole worth as a person and her reason for existence was wrapped up in it. Everything she had done and the reasons for it would be affirmed or denied with what he said to her now.

"I won't do that," he said in tones of iron. "I can't. If it has to be this way, then it's up to you."

It was the reply she needed. The gladness of it bloomed inside her, giving her strength and purpose. She had no idea if what she intended would succeed, but she had to try. And if she failed, it would still be worth it to know that for a few short minutes she had been valued as the equal of any male, or any Benedict man or woman.

Swinging toward the dark wedge that was the cellar doorway, she called out. "Ahmad, my brother? Attend to me. What shall I tell these Americans of you before we die? Is there nothing that you want them to know? Are there no last words you would say?"

"Do you imagine that I need such as you are to speak for me?"

The arrogance and prejudice she had expected were there in his words, and the contempt. That was good. "Someone must since you have no eloquence, no poetry at your command. Perhaps Ismael, who has both, will find words for you as well as translate them?"

"Ismael is nothing. He has fallen from grace and seeks only redemption."

"So you say," she returned, her voice reflective. "Yet he is a man. He has enjoyed a wife, fathered children. He has loved and been loved. His name will live on as yours will not."

"Silence, whore!"

Behind her, Chloe could hear whispering and muttering. The Benedicts might not understand the spoken words, but the threat in Ahmad's answers was plain enough. They feared she might anger her stepbrother so much that the world around them would disappear in a billow of fire and destruction. So she might, but it would happen without fail if she stopped.

Wade moved to stand beside her. His voice quiet, he said, "I hope you know what you're doing."

"So do I." She closed her eyes and swallowed hard, tasting suppressed tears. "Ahmad might not notice if you and the others leave one or two at a time."

"Leave?"

"Or at least get back out of the way as far as possible. Just in case."

"That won't help you."

She didn't answer because there was nothing to be said. Moving closer to the cellar door as a distraction for any retreat by the others, she lifted her voice again.

"All women are whores to you because of the teaching of the mullahs, Ahmad, or so Treena said before she died. Can it be you despise us so much because they forced you to become one of us? Did you kill Treena because she knew it."

"It was for honor!" he thundered in answer. "But you will die as she did, for the disease of sedition that you carry and because you have no respect for anything that is not of your benighted country."

"By your fine bloody knife, my stepbrother? Come and get me," she invited with all the mockery she could manage. "If you are man enough!" She could hear the stealthy departure of the Benedict defenders from the darkness behind her. However, neither Wade nor Roan made any move to go. She hated that.

Movement shifted in the shadows of the cellar opening. Chloe could just make out two dark forms, one large and one more slight, as if Ahmad had Jake in front of him as he'd used her as a shield in Turn-Coupe. Another shadow emerged after them that had to be Ismael.

"Such is a woman's bravery, to talk while hiding behind men with weapons," Ahmad sneered. "You would not dare without them."

"You think so? Perhaps it's not I they protect at all. Perhaps they will leave me to your revenge, if you release the boy? You would do it, would you not, if a mere woman was offered in exchange for a comrade?''

''Don't be a fool.''

''You are the one who suggested it with your talk of protection. But what can such a test hurt when we are all to die anyway?''

''Chloe,'' Wade began.

She stopped him with a sharp gesture, afraid that even a small protest might sway the issue. There was less rustling, less shifting of bodies behind her, as if the Benedicts had drifted back into the woods until only a few were left.

Ahmad gave a sour laugh. ''You would never dare come close enough.''

''What do I care?'' she asked as she moved forward again. ''To die one way is as good as another.''

''Come, then,'' he taunted her. ''Come taste my knife.''

She took another step, even as she heard Wade breathe a curse. On the periphery of her vision, she saw him raise his rifle as if waiting for any false move from the cellar.

''Release the boy,'' she said with a firm lift of her chin. ''Then I will close the distance.''

''Come close first. Then I will see.''

''Let Ismael bring him halfway, releasing him when I hold out my hand. That is fair.''

''That is stupid!''

''You let him go then, when Ismael has me. What

do you have to lose?'' She turned her gaze to Treena's husband. ''Ismael? You accept my suggestion?''

''This I will,'' he answered as he stepped fully into the light and inclined his body in a bow as he touched his forehead and then his heart. ''I swear it on the memory of my wife who loved you, Chloe Madison, as she would a sister of her blood.''

That gesture of respect was so much more than she expected that she stared at him in the dimness. Then she saw where his raised hand remained, saw what he was doing.

She knew then. She knew, with the bone-deep chill of terrible foreboding, exactly what was about to happen.

The night was deep and warm around them, the air damp and soft, as they stood in their frozen tableaux. Trees sighed, as if shifting in disturbed sleep. Water lapped, endlessly, at the edge of the lake not far away. Clouds drifted overhead, covering the face of the rising moon with dark splendor. Somewhere a mating frog called then fell silent. Life went on, uncaring. It was nature's way.

''Ismael,'' she began.

''It is fate,'' he said, ''and is right. As you Americans say so often, it is just. It is fair.''

I have my own personal jihad.

''I think I've changed my mind,'' she said abruptly.

Ahmad laughed, a harsh sound of irony and scorn. Ismael only smiled with tenderness spreading across his young, aquiline features. "No, sister of my heart, that will not suffice. Do not fear for me. Consider instead my young daughters who may share their mother's fate. Think of my family harmed years ago. Remember all you taught us about freedom, Chloe Madison, while you were with us. Think, now, of the many ways there are to be free, and the one that is the ultimate. Come. Now."

He held out his left hand. With his right that was still at his breast, he unclipped the grenade hanging from the belt that crisscrossed it.

"Don't!" Wade commanded from behind her.

Was he speaking to her or to Ismael? Did he realize Treena's husband must be the operative who had infiltrated the al Qaeda? How much did he see? He'd spent years in the Middle East, yet what did he understand of Ismael's long patience or his reasons that were steeped in ancient laws and traditions? Was it enough? Was it? If so, then he should recoil immediately, putting distance between himself and the cellar while there was still time.

Being Wade, he could not do that. Of course, he couldn't, not while Jake was still held prisoner. Nor could Roan who had moved to stand behind him. They had both eased from the shelter of the woods, she thought, though she couldn't turn her head to look, not now when every second counted. She had no answer for her doubts, none for anything as she took a steady stride toward Ismael's outstretched hand. It was not his right hand, the hand of respect, but what did that matter?

His grip was warm and dry, but not confining. Over his shoulder, he said to Ahmad, ''Now the boy?''

''It is fair,'' Chloe's stepbrother repeated in virulent ridicule. Then he pushed Roan's son away from him.

Jake's face was white and his bottom lip cut and swollen, but his shoulders were rigid with pride and he allowed no trace of fear to show in his eyes. He was all right. He could walk, even if he moved with a teenage swagger calculated to show how little he cared. Chloe willed him to look at her instead of his captor, prayed that he wouldn't be so humiliated by her rescue that he could not.

Then he met her gaze. His crooked smile of approbation was so like that of his cousin that her heart turned over in her chest. ''Run,'' she said. ''For God's sake, run. Now!''

It was the trigger.

Ahmad lifted his weapon. Ismael pulled the pin on the grenade, turned with it in his hand. In the single glimpse she was allowed, she saw him lunge at Ahmad, grasping him tightly in a parody of a lover's hold as he fell with him to the ground.

The hard thud of running footsteps sounded behind her. She was struck from behind, snatched away from Ismael even as she saw Roan hit Jake in a hard dive that carried him out of sight on the far side of the mound. Then she was falling, rolling, tumbling in the circle of Wade's hard arms while the world blasted apart with a thunderous roar. Deafened, blinded by the white, stabbing light, she felt the earth tremble. Dirt and grass clogged her mouth. Something heavy covered her, stopping her breath. And in her mind were horror and grief and an endless agony of gratitude for which there could never be any acknowledgment. Not in this life.

Then the night was quiet again.

"So you're leaving."

Chloe glanced up as Wade spoke from the doorway. He looked as tired as she felt, she thought. "It's time. I can't stay here forever."

"It's only been four days."

"It seems longer." She paused with her shower cap and a lipstick in her hands. Then she went back to filling the plastic bag that served as her luggage.

"Mom says you asked to go back to New Orleans when she goes with Adam and Lara." Wade turned and put his backbone against the door facing, shoving the tips of his fingers into the pockets of his jeans.

"A phone number for the RAWA group in California was with the video Freshta gave me. I'll stay in a New Orleans hotel until I can make contact and finish settling my father's estate."

"What then? You're going to go and live with people you don't know, in a faith that's not yours, and probably a household where you'll be expected to cover your hair and almost every inch of skin when you go out in public?''

"Something like that."

"Why?" Exasperation rasped in his voice. "You know what it will be like. You've seen the problems that can be created."

She refused to look at him. "The RAWA is helping to change attitudes, here as well as in the Middle East. I need to belong somewhere, to do something worthwhile."

He digested that for a moment. "You can stay here. I told you that before, and it still stands. Janna would love to have the company, and she could certainly use the help when the baby comes."

"I...don't think it would work," she said, keeping her voice steady with an effort.

"I won't be here, if that's what you're thinking."

That got her attention. With her hairbrush in her hands, she turned and sat on the mattress. "You're going back to the oil fields?"

"Nat's been after me to work with him for ages," he said with a careless shrug. "Rescuing people seems as good a job as any."

"It's dangerous!"

He studied her for a moment, his eyes narrowing until it was no longer possible to see their green tint. "I have to do something, and it's worthwhile."

"Don't." She looked down at her hands twisting the brush.

"What?"

"Don't mock what I want to do!" The glance she gave him was brief but hot.

"Not what you mean to do, just how and where you intend to do it."

If he couldn't understand, then explaining further was useless. "Anyway, you don't have to leave your home because I might be in it."

"You think that's why I'm going?"

"What else? Unless, of course, you just prefer leaving everything here behind you."

It was his turn to look away. "Hardly."

"You left years ago because of your father. Now you're going because of me. It seems to be a pattern."

"Of running away from trouble?"

"I didn't say that. And I'm no trouble to you."

The look he gave her was incredulous. "Honey, you've been nothing but."

She twitched a shoulder. "At least it's over."

"Yeah." He didn't sound particularly happy.

"If I'm not going to see you again, I...suppose I should say thank you for what you did out there the other night, getting me away before..."

"Forget it."

The words were curt, dismissive, and hurtful because of it. "I don't think I can. Or will. Ever."

"It's done. You did what you could, but some things can't be changed. Let it go."

"That's easy for you to say."

"No it isn't," he corrected in strained intensity. He stopped, took a deep breath. "It isn't easy at all. I was so afraid I was going to have to watch you die. I couldn't have stood that.''

"There was no need. You didn't fail,'' she said in quiet answer to his pain. ''You saw it coming this time, and that made all the difference. If anyone needs to let it go, it's you.''

He closed his eyes with a small shake of his head. ''Maybe I will. One day.''

"I suppose we both will.'' It wouldn't be soon, however, and they knew it. The memory was too fresh, as was the raw earth bulldozed over the crater that had once been an Indian mound. The state authorities had come and taken charge of the artifacts that were uncovered. Federal authorities had arrived to conduct interrogations into Ahmad's al Qaeda activities and to take charge of the other injured Hazaris. Local authorities had helped clean up the rest of the mess and ship Ahmad's and Ismael's remains back to Hazaristan for burial. All that was left was the forgetting.

"I'm glad I didn't fail with you,'' he said quietly.

She thought for an instant that there might be more to that simple declaration than was on the surface. It was so unlikely that she didn't pursue it. Whatever was personal in their relationship, she had instigated and she had ended.

As silence stretched uncomfortably, she asked, ''Your side is okay? It wasn't reopened by the fall?''

"It's fine.''

"Jake seems to be all right, doesn't he? He was

laughing with Lainey while he was over yesterday.''
Chloe smiled a little. "I think she called him, actually.''

"They're young, both of them, and they have plenty of people to talk to or to hold them when they need it. They'll be okay.''

"No counseling?''

"Why would they need that when they have family?''

It was a good point. Realizing that she had twisted the hairbrush until she'd almost destroyed it, she shoved it into the bag. The crackling of the plastic seemed unnaturally loud in the strained quiet.

"Anyway, Roan and Tory are pathetically grateful for what you did for Jake,'' Wade went on. "The whole clan feels as if they owe you. Whatever you want or need, whatever you think you have to do, they'll help you.''

"I didn't do it to make anybody feel obligated. No one owes me anything.''

"Maybe I put that wrong. They don't feel that you need to be repaid. It's just that you're special to them. You always will be, no matter where you are or what you decide to do. You can always come back here, anytime, no questions asked. Always.''

Her throat ached with the sudden press of tears. To have a place where she belonged, where she would always be accepted, meant so much. That was what family really was in her mind, people who valued and wanted you regardless of what you did or didn't do, simply because you belonged.

With a small, helpless gesture, she said, "I can't possibly come back here if it means you have to go. This is your home, after all."

He gave a short laugh. "The only way I can stay around is if you take to wearing a burqa again. You might be safe then, but I don't guarantee it."

"You mean...you want me?"

"I thought I'd made that abundantly clear," he said with irony.

"Not lately."

"Not for four days. But who's counting?"

"Maybe I am?" she said tentatively.

"Meaning?"

She took a deep breath. "Meaning I'm sorry."

"Don't!"

The tears crowded behind her nose, threatened to fill her eyes so she had to hold her head high to prevent it. "All right."

"I told you not to say that. You've nothing to apologize for, not to me, not ever."

"Not even for refusing to marry you?"

He was quiet for so long that she thought he didn't mean to answer. When he did, his voice was uneven. "Well, okay, maybe for that."

"I've been thinking about it," she said, encouraged by her ability to throw him off balance. "April told me that Benedict women do pretty much what they want. Is that true?"

"I don't know that I'd go that far." His tone was doubtful, but the beginning of a smile tilted one corner of his mouth.

"What I'm trying to say is…"

"I know what you're trying to say," he interrupted as he moved toward her and reached to take her hand, drawing her to her feet and into his arms. "You want to know if I'll try to stop you from rescuing all the downtrodden females of the world. And the answer is that you can do whatever you want, so long as you don't bring them home with you."

"You really won't mind?"

"As long as you're happy, I'll be happy. But will that be enough?"

"I think it will," she said seriously. "I thought once that I had to be on the front lines, teaching, helping, healing those who had been hurt by barbaric laws and ideas. Then I was forced to stop, made to realize that it might be more useful to bring the deplorable conditions in Hazaristan and other Muslim nations to public notice as world events have done in Afghanistan. That's still a worthy goal and something to which I'll always want to contribute. But I've come to see in the last few days that what I truly want is to make the world a better place, one where all people can find the freedom and peace that exists here at Grand Point. It's too big a task to take on single-handedly, too enormous to know exactly where to tackle it. The best place, I think, may be in my own backyard. The best way to do it may be by bringing up children who have morals and manners, who love and respect each other and their parents and have concern for their fellow human beings. In other words, to bring up more Benedicts.''

His smile was warm and wide and his voice husky as he asked, ''Need any help?''

''Always.'' It was a lovely word, and she felt a tear track slowly down her cheek as she said it. She didn't care, didn't mind how many followed.

''I'm going to remember you said that,'' he warned, his voice not quite steady as he gathered her closer against him. ''I love you, you know, for all the things you want to do and all the things you are. For your bravery, which scares the hell out of me, and even for the streak of martyrdom that makes you do things that nearly kill me. And if you ever, ever, do anything that comes as close to giving me a heart attack the way you did the other night, I swear I'll shut you up in this house and never let you out for the rest of our natural lives.''

''Please do,'' she whispered. ''I think if there was ever a man who could make me like it, it would be you. You are the most steadfast and honorable man I've every known, and I've loved you since you knocked me down in the stadium at Kashi. You were ten feet tall and the hero of my dreams, and I would have followed you anywhere.''

''Then why in heaven's name was it so hard to get you out of there?''

''I was afraid, afraid that when you did it would

be over. And that all I'd ever have would be your pity.''

He shook his head. ''Very good for my ego, but I don't believe it.''

''Why else do you think I asked you to make love to me?''

''Because,'' he began, then stopped. ''Are you saying it wasn't a public service I was performing there?''

''You've got to be kidding.'' She waited to see how long it would take him to get the point.

''You wanted me,'' he said after a bare nanosecond.

''I did. I do. And yes, when I said I didn't, I lied through my teeth.''

''Thank God,'' he said, and kissed her with hunger and unrestrained passion and much, much promise.

It was some time later that she shifted on the much-rumpled bedspread, and settled closer against him. Freeing an arm and hand, she traced a finger over the bandage at his side, then upward to his chest where she made small circles in the silky hair on his chest. ''So,'' she said in musing tones, ''I'm not to bring veiled women into the house, am I? Does that mean you don't want a harem?''

''Heaven forbid. One veiled woman is about all I can manage.'' He captured her fingers, raised them to his lips, then replaced them where they had been.

She doubted that, but it was nice to hear anyway.

"Veiled, huh? You actually liked the burqa, didn't you? Admit it."

"Not on me, I didn't! But it has its points if a guy's the jealous type."

"Come on. It turned you on and you know it. It's the mystery. It stirs the male imagination. It stirs…"

"I know what it stirs, thank you. But I have to tell you that there's only one way that I'd want you waltzing around here undercover, so to speak."

"And that is?"

He leaned close to whisper against her ear.

"No," she said distinctly. "Not naked under it, not in a million years."

"Not ever?" he asked, his voice laden with disappointment.

"Never."

"Really never, or maybe never?"

"We'll see," she said, her smile bright as she gazed into his eyes.

Author Note

On the morning of September 11, 2001, the first half of *Wade*—with its setting of Afghanistan—was almost completed. I awakened at 3:00 a.m. as I often do and went downstairs to my office to finish writing the final pages of Chapter 10. In these, Chloe and Wade return to the United States from Taliban-held Afghanistan only to realize that her Islamic stepbrother, a militia officer with connections to Osama bin Laden and the al Qaeda network, has preceded them to Louisiana to carry out his declared jihad against the Benedict clan. Several hours later, with the chapter done, I hit Save on my computer then returned upstairs to have morning coffee while watching CNBC with my husband. I was just in time to catch the first report of a plane crashing into one of the twin towers of New York's World Trade Center. Standing in front of the TV, I reached to put my finger on a bright, moving dot flying near the towers, saying, "Look, isn't that a helicopter or another plane? What do they think they're doing?"

The answer to that question, with its proof of a

direct and horrific terrorist attack, came very close to spelling the end for *Wade.*

The plight of women in Afghanistan under the Taliban regime first came to my attention in the early fall of 2000. Sympathy over their treatment created within me a strong need to help bring the situation to public notice. Almost immediately, I began to mentally construct a story with an American heroine living behind the veil, one who is rescued by the last of my Benedict heroes, Wade. At the same time, I wanted to involve the entire Benedict clan in a grand finale for the Louisiana Gentlemen series. What greater threat could there be to the happiness and well-being of my fictional family than to put them in jeopardy of attack from Islamic extremists? How better to illustrate the heroic capacity of my Louisiana gentlemen than to have the heroes from the first five stories and their families come together with Wade and Chloe to meet this ultimate threat?

Background research for the book was begun in earnest in January 2001, and the proposal for *Wade* was written and shipped to my editor in March. She soon gave it her stamp of approval, and the actual writing began in April. A publication date was set at this time for September 2002.

Considerable space in the initial chapters was given to descriptions of the Afghan political situation, climate, topography, customs and particularly the restrictions imposed on women and harsh penalties for failing to abide by them. The idea, of course, was to establish immediacy and mood for an exotic locale little known to the average reader. Much of this background information suddenly became unnecessary in the first few days after the Attack on America. Suddenly the whole world knew exactly what Afghanistan looked like, the names of its cities, how people dressed and the conditions under which the female population lived. Watching details unfold in the media that I'd spent so much time studying and writing about during the previous months was surreal.

But now countless changes were required in my manuscript, plus the inexorable march of international events put *Wade*'s basic plot in danger of obsolescence. These were problems that had to be fixed before I could go on. That was if I could find the heart to continue at all with a story that had abruptly become too immediate for comfort.

My first move was to contact my editor at MIRA Books. Others at the publishing house were also brought into the discussion, along with my agent. A major concern for everyone was to avoid all appearance of attempting to profit from the disaster, especially since publication was already set for the one-year anniversary of the attack. In desperation over an increasing state of writer's block, I suggested abandoning the whole idea and starting over with a completely new story.

After the pros and cons were hashed out, however, a decision was made to continue with *Wade* but remove any reference to actual persons and relocate the setting to a fictional "mirror" country. These changes would allow for mental distance and relieve the need to align the plot with daily news reports from the Middle East. Accordingly, Hazaristan was created as a substitute for Afghanistan, and I was able to complete the book only two weeks behind schedule.

The version of *Wade* that you hold in your hands, then, is not the same story I started out to write. Regardless, the points I intended to make are still there, still valid. Severe restrictions continue to be imposed on women by Islamic fundamentalist governments other than that of Afghanistan. The need to fight to preserve our right to live without fear is even more imperative now than prior to September 11. The power of love to strengthen and to heal is just as certain, no matter where or how it begins. It's my hope that readers will take these grains of truth from the story, as well as some small insight into what it means to live as a woman in certain portions of the world.

I'd like to take this opportunity to thank my editor, Laura Shin, MIRA Books editorial director Dianne Moggy, and my agent Richard Curtis for their faith and support. Special thanks are also due Mehmooda, Web mistress of the Internet site of the Revolutionary Association of the Women of Afghanistan (rawa@rawa.org) for answers to pertinent research questions. The RAWA organization as a whole deserves the utmost praise for their courage in shining the bright light of public opinion on the atrocities committed against women by Islamic fundamentalists. Without them, this book would have been impossible, and might have been another story altogether.

Jennifer Blake
Chatham, LA
December, 2001

P.S. It would not be fitting to end the Louisiana Gentlemen's series without including a recipe. Here is the unusual bread pudding baked by Wade's mother in the story.

Pirate's Bread Pudding

1 loaf French bread
2 cups milk
2 cups half-and-half
4 eggs
2 cups sugar
$\frac{1}{2}$ tsp. salt
1 tsp. cinnamon
$\frac{1}{2}$ tsp. nutmeg
2 tbsp. vanilla
3 tbsp. butter, melted
1 cup chopped pineapple
1 cup pecans
1 cup raisins
1 jigger rum

Pour rum over raisins and set aside to soak. Break bread into bite-size pieces and place in large bowl.

Pour milk and half-and-half over bread and set aside for an hour. When well softened, stir until mixed. Whisk eggs, then add sugar, salt, spices and vanilla. Add to bread and milk and mix well. Fold in raisins. Melt butter in the bottom of a heavy 9x12 cake pan, then slowly pour pudding mixture into the pan. Top may be dotted with more butter if desired. Bake at 350 degrees for 45 to 50 minutes or until set.

Whiskey Sauce

1 stick butter
$^3/_4$ cup sugar
1 egg
1 jigger whiskey (usually bourbon)

Whisk egg, add sugar and beat thoroughly. Melt butter in a saucepan over low flame. Add egg and sugar mixture and stir constantly over low heat until steaming hot, but not boiling. Add whiskey and stir to a creamy smooth texture. Drizzle over warm bread pudding.